# The Genius

*A Novel*

By Jack Nebel

*Our mission is to efficiently provide the world's finest, most comprehensive
book publishing service, enabling every author to experience success.
To find out how to publish your book, your way, and have it available
worldwide, visit us online at www.trafford.com*

*Trafford rev. 4/12/10*

 www.trafford.com

**North America & international**
toll-free: 1 888 232 4444 (USA & Canada)
phone: 250 383 6864 ♦ fax: 812 355 4082

# CHAPTER 1

The pink lace bra, the one hanging at the far end on the last rafter, was new. There were maybe hundreds hanging from the open wood ceiling and rafter beams, but I had most of them memorized by now. I set the case of Budweiser down and wandered over to get a better look. Women of age that went the whole summer in Northern Minnesota without getting a bra hung on a nail from a rafter in Mulroney's Island Tap fell a little short on the possibilities. It had been that way for forty years running. It was a pretty easy sell. Girls walk in, see all the bras hanging from the ceiling, they figure, at first, who would be *that* crazy? Then, they have a few beers, catch an earful of the lore that goes with the evidence, next thing you know, one of them gets just the right song going on the juke box and reaches underneath that summer t-shirt. Snap, snap, maybe even snap-snap-snap-snap, a shoulder strap wiggle, then I hand them a Sharpie for the signing. Next, a hammer, a nail from a drawer behind the bar, and I find a spot among the hundreds, pushing cups and straps around like they are party decorations. With great ceremony, male patrons assist the girl up to stand on a bar stool and steady her as she hangs it just so, and assures herself a place in immortality that shouldn't show up on the internet. She spends the rest her evening thinking every man in Mulroney's is staring at her nipples, and she is probably right.

1

I was slogging through a bar restocking Monday morning in June, but I couldn't be fooled. What was the deal with that pink bra? I climbed up on a chair and began to read the black Sharpie scratchings on the transparent upper part of one of the cups- *Size C* cups for the record. The process of elimination had taken a leap forward.

I pulled at the material to get a closer look. "Maria?" I read slowly, trying to flatten it out. "*Maria...?*" I laughed, pulling it down and scratching at my chin stubble. Without much of a hesitation, I looked around, then walked back through the kitchen. Nobody around. I checked out the walk-in cooler. Nothing. I walked out the back door and around the side of the building to a little lean-to structure near the water's edge that customers used when they needed a smoke. Smoking inside of Mulroney's inner walls had gone the way of the world. This was nothing more than a corrugated roof on some wood beams that provided some protection from wind and rain, with an old two-bench spruce picnic table underneath. The thick scotch pines around it gave it a cave-like feel- or, when the name stuck- Smoker's Roost.

The only Maria I knew was the hottie who worked as a waitress in Mulroney's the summer before, a Mankato State college student- music major, I believe it was. She was untouchable as far as I was concerned, magazine cover face and body so tight and perfect it made men look away in shame for their thoughts. And so it was with an abrupt end to my search, I found Maria angled on her side across the picnic table in Smoker's Roost, her short, fringed blue jean skirt high and tight on her upper thighs and a creamed colored denim shirt unbuttoned, her finger toying with one of the eyelets.

"Thank God," Maria said, stretching. "You found my favorite bra. I was timing you. And, I had it about right, slow draw."

I smiled at c-cup breasts and then at her and put the bra over my head. And just when I was losing my faith in the need for Mondays.

"Maybe later you can help me find my panties, too." She reached out, apparently for me, and I began to stagger over to her, not knowing if this was real or someone was punking me. The only thing I knew for sure was my blue jeans were a mighty bit tight.

Not an hour before, I figured I was getting too old to be doing this summer gig work. It was an alter ego of my junior college American

History teaching job back in Chicago the rest of the year, but twenty-eight was old in this crowd, even if you were the bartender.

The thought of being punked was quickly a distant memory. Not much was said as I remember, but it was as if we were both ready and waiting for this to happen and it was overdue. Most of it was in fast forward, urgent grabbing, legs wedging, feet digging in, gravity and leverage to the wind. If anybody was around, they had to wonder how those scotch pines were making that kind of noise. But, to both our benefits, it was over pretty quick, and it was almost as if we nodded at each other in appreciation and came just short of a slapping high five.

"I never got to scratch you off my list last year," she said, smiling in conquest. "So I thought why not get the summer started with a bang. Kind off worth the wait, actually." She sat up and tugged the skirt back in place. "I mean, it was great sharing tips with you last year, Thomas, but ... girl's got needs, you know. So there."

"So there. Back at you." I truly didn't know what to say and had no idea what the hell she was talking about. She might have been stoned. I felt like maybe I was. *Roe versus Wade* crossed my mind for a millisecond, women's suffrage another, but mostly I was struck at how little I really knew about women, particularly women in their twenties. I wasn't quite sure how that had happened, but I was thinking it had to do with my complete ignorance of the passage of time when I was reading a good book on a Saturday night, and my ability to cook just about anything and make it good enough to enjoy a meal for one. My middle to later twenties had found me a pretty good American History teacher and very comfortable with myself as company most of the time. I read a lot, tinkered with writing a bit, both fiction and non-fiction, but nothing I wanted anybody to know about. Not yet anyway.

"I'll see you later at work," she said, hopping off the table with a quick move and shaking her long brown hair down free. She ran off to a canary yellow Volkswagen convertible, top down, and sped away. The gravel of the drive spit up under her tires and my strange mind sparked some fear she might be putting my baby at risk. This was the first time I had a real sense there was another person watching my actions, monitoring my thoughts and providing commentary. I had no sense as why this was or might be.

"Thomas?" An older familiar female voice broke into my interrupted fantasy. "Are you out here?"

"Yo…," I yelled back, snapping out of it, unthankfully. It was Connie Mulroney, *the* Italian Princess wife of the owner, annoyingly attractive, jet black wavy hair to her shoulders, dark brown flitting eyes that moved up and down a man with purpose and precision. Her lips always looked fully poised and ready. She always wore dangling earrings, always a necklace with a pendant full of diamonds, clothes that fit and formed her dynamite forty-something body and she smelled like something sweet and forbidden that lingered long after she had passed by. If she passed by. If she stood there in front of you, she became a global warmer. The worst was when she would just sit at the bar reading the paper with her hot pink, sparkly reading glasses down over her nose. All I could think of was naked librarians.

It would be about then the vision of Rudy Mulroney, Connie's husband and my boss, came into clear view. He was a mountain of an Irishman, about six-four, with board-wide shoulders, a Kenny Rogers white beard that made him look a bit older and softer than his forty-four years, and gentle gray eyes that knew more than they were saying. But you didn't ask. He roared when he talked, without trying, but on the other hand, he didn't talk much, so he was more like a quiet hulk when he was around, staying back in the tiny office in the back, running through bills, receipts and piles of paper that seemed to only get rearranged at best. An old radio in the office would be tuned in to some evangelist who talked just loud enough to be heard over the background organ music. Sometimes Rudy was humming with the music or singing softly, his lips just barely moving underneath that beard. You didn't ask him about that either.

The love of his life appeared to be a toss-up- Connie, or his fishing buddies who included Babe Winkleman and some other fish-for-money guys. He would disappear for days at a time. Connie apparently wasn't much on fishing, but she had a storied reputation of having secret liaisons that were as legendary as they were unproven. At the time, I thought she had a quiet, affected way about her that at least liked the idea of people linking her to a secret sex life.

She turned and I followed her back through the kitchen door.

4

"Need anything from town?" she asked, looking through the cupboards.

"No, I'm good, thanks," I said.

"Okay then." Her designer jeans were alive, forty-something spreading ass or not. "I'll be back later."

"I'll be here."

She turned to leave. "By the way, did you see Maria is back?" I saw he car leaving as I walked out."

"Yeah, I did. Actually. Sweet kid. And a damn good waitress. Glad she's back."

Connie nodded her head and tossed another smile back at me as she walked out through the bar. "No doubt. I could not help but notice you have either decided to start wearing her brand of perfume or she somehow accidentally spilled some onto you."

The joy in the woman's face gauging my reaction was obvious. All I really wanted to do was make sure my fly was up.

"She's my niece, you know. My baby sister's little girl." I sensed a bit of an edge to those words as they trailed and echoed off the stainless fixtures in the kitchen. I don't know why my eyes drifted up to the huge carving knife hanging right above me at eye level.

I finally got back to restocking the beer coolers; gladly, a physical action requiring mindless skills as I pondered what had just happened. It might have been the most topsy-turvy thing that had ever happened to me. *That* happened to other guys. *That story was made up by other guys. That* would never, ever happen to me and if I made that story up nobody who knew me would believe me. With each bottle I clanked in I could smell Maria on the front of my shirt. Crazy! All these summers as a bartender I never smelled anything even close to getting lucky. So what was it today? A sudden attractive magnetism? Me? I wouldn't know *cool* if it came gift wrapped.

And I'll be a son of a bitch. My fly *was* open.

# CHAPTER 2

The Fourth of July roared in as the official beginning of summer, Weather and water temperatures warming, boat traffic and beer sales both picking up a head of steam. It was another Saturday, leaving and arrival day for the families that shuttled in and out for their annual weekly stay. The road to Sunny Blue Resort came across the single lane bridge and turned into a gravel circle. The yellow house with blue trim sat at the far end of the circle with three yellow and blue cabins on either side. That would be the Walleye, the Northern, the Bass, Crappie, Perch and the Bluegill Cabins, with hand painted wooden replicas of their namesakes just above each door. Connie and Rudy tried to be together to greet arrivals, arm in arm, the picture of North Woods bliss and harmony. Greetings were full of family type hugs and cheeky kisses and stunned looks at how the children had grown in just a year.

Rudy looked massive in the sun light, that white beard, salt-and-pepper hair back and just over the ears and down his neck. He always wore a tight, pocketed solid-color t-shirt over blue jeans and hard boots. He had the look of having just showered after working out, but I never, ever saw him do that. He was physical enough, doing all the things needed to keep a small resort running, but he also had Garland Luhrsen, a tall, lean man with the strength of at least ten men, who helped Rudy with everything and anything from replacing a leaky faucet to digging up the dreaded bubbling septic field. Garland was deaf and dumb, but he and Rudy had a hand signal system that looked like it was something they cooked up on their own. One motion from Rudy and Garland was off like an over-caffeinated slave. He made little sounds like a wounded baby seal when he worked, which I was sure he had to hear, but Rudy assured me the man heard nothing, not even the sound of his own breathing. Rudy said if you really wanted to be amazed by something, you had to get down to the Heimsluth German Corner restaurant in Gull Lake on a Friday or Saturday night, where Garland played the accordion in a three-piece band. Deaf and dumb, perfectly. Polkas, Waltz's, Michael Jackson. He did it all. I just shook my head and reminded Rudy I worked Friday and Saturday nights.

It was the Creighton's from Altoona, Iowa. I was pulling bar supplies from the stock room building and watching the arrival. Actually, I was watching Veronica Creighton standing at the side of the Volvo, stretching out from the long car ride. Details are not important at this moment, but I remembered her a few years back as a very scary, alluring fourteen-year-old going on twenty-two. I was trying to do the math to figure out whether she was eighteen yet. The body stretching up to the sun, purple tank top straining to hold them back, white short-shorts flipping up a bit in the front over caramel cream long legs. Yes, I was sure it had been a long ride.

Hugs all around, flit bits of conversations and amazement prevailed, and Rudy gave everybody the big comfort smile. As awkward as that moment was for me to watch the way he hugged Veronica Creighton, I would have to admit he got his money's worth. Rudy didn't smile very much except for these little meet-and-greet driveway moments, and he had one plastered all over his face that stayed there right through his hand signs to Garland to get the bags and move them into Cabin number four- the Crappie Cabin.

Mulroney's Island Tap with its ceiling full of bras might have seemed a bit oddly placed in the middle of a small family lake country resort, but there was nothing odd about the revenues it brought in compared to the token comings and goings of the six cabins on the property. Bar business was brisk on any Saturday night during the summer, but this one also fell on the Fourth of July, making it a launching pad for watching fireworks after dark.

Maria was asking me for more cocktail napkins for her bar set-ups. Talk about looking at someone differently. A week had gone by since our encounter in the Roost and with each look at her I could feel her heels digging into the small of my back. She would turn and run off to a table and I would watch her perfect ass sway beneath her short skirt. I would stare and stagger around behind the bar like I was struggling to keep her balanced in the cups of my hands.

"Brandy-seven, vodka tonic, two Miller Lites," she said with her usual easy smile. I was hanging or drooling on every move she made, everything she said, the tone of her voice, the wisp of her hair over one eye.... And she was as cool as they came. As though a picnic table bonk in the middle of the day was no reason to change anything between us. But *everything* had changed for me. Saying "hello" to Maria had changed for me. When I looked at her, everything inside of me felt hot and wet and explosive. That is, until the words to describe it got up to my mouth. Then the surge fell back into the Thomas Cabot everybody knew- a quiet, dependable sort of guy you could set your watch by. They couldn't see the heel marks and either could I, but I could feel them both, right there. Digging, urging, pulling away. I would watch Maria unload her tray at a table, reach behind me and rub my back with both hands, and think I could very possibly live on that moment the rest of my days.

"Diet Coke with a wedge of lime," came a powerful little voice behind me as I rang the ticket. I turned to see Veronica Creighton had taken a seat at the bar between lesser desirables, with neither father nor mother in sight. I didn't need to move any closer to get a whiff of her. I was already in full swoon from the likes of whatever Maria was wearing, but whatever was coming off of Veronica moved me into full levitation. Just give the word. I was juiced up. Something was going on that was intensifying my sense of smell for, well, certain things. And whatever sensory nerve was associated with this new intensity was torturing my jeans about every two minutes. I was connected to the hard-on machine. I kept looking down to see if it was real obvious. It was to me.

I gave Veronica her Diet Coke in one of the taller, thin frosted glasses, a bit more feminine. She put her glimmering dark vermillion lips around that long red straw and I thought I was going to lose it right there. "You know," she smiled, her big brown eyes blinking up at me with less than an innocent show. "You know, Thomas, you could throw some of the Captain in there and nobody would have to know."

I knew. I knew that was coming. I must have looked like a four-year-old at the puppy display in *PETSMART*. This beautiful little child had found me, picked me up and hugged me and was begging her mother to take me home. I managed to laugh it off with an attempt of a swagger smile and a wayward look that was meant to convince her how busy I was. Thing was, by the time she had finished her drink, she had also managed to turn that long red straw into a bow with her tongue. I grabbed the glass, gave her a wink and gave it just a splash of the Captain. I would never have done that. Ever. Why then? Why, without the least bit of logic or reconsideration?

She formed those lips into a whispered *thank you*. "I graduated in June," she said, offering up an element of surprise for the taking. She eyed the crowd a bit and leaned in over the bar so she wouldn't have to talk as loud. "Graduated and popped my cherry the same night. Cool or what?" She backed off and her eyes awaited my approval rating.

Again, in less time than I had to consider my entire life to that point, I found myself ill-equipped to deal with this based on what I knew. So I just followed what came to me first. "Are you eighteen now?"

She nodded. "Love this song," was all she said, her eyes closing, head swaying slightly, short, silky brown hair bobbing. Maybe it was some old Beatle tune, I couldn't be sure with the symphony of screaming customers beseeching me for a fraction of the attention I was giving Veronica Creighton. I could hear them, see them, but it all seemed to freeze frame for me as I could only picture and *feel* Veronica's legs around me so tight I might cry out for divine intervention. What in the world was happening to me?

"Thomas!" That was Maria's voice. That was real. "Jesus, Thomas, snap out of it! What's your problem?" She gave me one eye and Veronica the other. I snapped up, poured, opened bottles, poured some more. "Sorry." I smiled and tried to make nice.

"Greedy bastard, huh?" She nodded at Veronica and moved off smoothly with her overloaded tray. She never spilled a drop and I never took my eyes off her firm buttocks. Then I got into a rhythm, my eyes finally moving on from Maria's fine ass to Veronica's wicked straw bending tongue, in between serving drinks, washing glasses and ringing tickets and cash like I was in some poetic opera. Appropriately, KISS was blaring through the jukebox speakers and I was singing along softly.

At some point over the next couple of hours, Veronica and I started eye screwing, and I decided on smiles and winks for Maria, which she returned in what came to be a comfortable routine. There were more splashes of Captain Morgan in a feminine tall frosted glass, but now I only did it when I thought Maria wasn't looking.

People were shuttling in and out of the bar, getting a glimpse of the fireworks exploding in the not too distant skies over the nearby towns of Gull Lake and Albion, then strolling back in for a reload.

"Rock and roll," came a deep voice I knew, but it startled me nonetheless and I turned to the back bar like I was on a swivel.

"Rudy! Hey!" I yelled above the crowd.

He turned to the register and put his key in to roll the numbers, stopping briefly to scan the crowd. His eyes lingered when they spotted Veronica sitting there doing the thin red straw thing again with her tongue. She avoided eye contact. He looked at me, then back to the register. "It's twenty-one to drink in Minnesota, Thomas, just a reminder in case your brain turns into dick." I could see the smirk turn up the corners of his mouth. I am sure he liked the numbers as well.

Shortly after, Connie Mulroney sauntered in from the back kitchen, circling around in her sequined designer blue jeans that gave her middle age back side just a little too much emphasis. But on this night it was the blouse that got your attention. Red and blue lightning bolts that lit up from a lithium battery power source somewhere on a white background, cotton v-necked t-shirt showing plenty of her ample cleavage, and that forever smile of glorious white teeth and a great tanned, well-cared for face. You just knew she was in the room.

"*Thomas,*" she said, in a breath, as only she could, passing behind me as I poured another Leinenkugal's from the tap. Never one to be content with just a simple pinch of the ass cheek, she reached way under, getting a handful before quickly retreating. I knew she wanted a better reaction, but that furrowed brow look on my face said I was really only thinking about where Rudy might be at that moment.

"He went outside, nervous Nellie," she whispered just a little too close to my ear. "Fireworks. … And maybe I will see you later, my sweet. I'm feeling it." She seemed to be staring at my ears, one, then the other, reaching up and lightly touching one of the lobes. Thankfully, she resumed greeting other customers in a more ordinary way and I got back to getting more beer in the glass than over the side. Rudy would like that. Keep those percentages up. Little more foam in each glass. There were huge profits in draft beer sales.

I am reeling now. My brain keeps asking the third person watching me *what the fuck is going on? No answer.* I could feel Veronica's eyes on me. What in the world was she thinking? If she didn't catch Connie Mulroney grabbing by balls from behind she had to be the only one at the bar that missed it. Maria was getting politely molested at one of her tables. She was safe. I didn't know, but if I was being honest, there was no way I figured I should be fighting off whatever this was. It didn't feel like something that was going to last very long anyway. Of course, I also figured if Rudy Mulroney even thought I would fool around with his wife, it would end rather abruptly and I would be mounted on the wall in his den next to the five-foot musky. But that was ridiculous! Why would I want to bone Connie Mulroney? Then, five, then ten or so reasons came to me. All good ones. I was in some zone.

A roar came up from across the room. I knew that one well. It meant another bra had come off. We had a long way to go, though. Three years before, the standing record of six was set on a Fourth of July. I got out the hammer and the nail and the ritual was on. First timers were either titillated or appalled, but, all in all, the mixture and reaction was usually priceless. This one was a thirty-something, from somewhere, America, with a small following that suddenly grew in size and volume as she stood up on a chair to latch her black bra to the nail I had pounded into the ceiling. As I returned to the bar and resumed the eye sex with Veronica, I wondered how this place actually looked and felt about February of each year. The dead middle of the North Woods, not a soul around, a room stilled by nature, full of hanging, historical bras. I was glad I remembered Rudy and Connie went to Key West for the winter. Otherwise, I had this picture of Rudy, his gospel music in the background, sitting on the floor, alone, a snowstorm blowing around outside, humming, looking up at all those bras.

"Don't even think about it," I said to Veronica as I set down another Captain-laced Diet Coke in front of her. I wasn't even sure she was wearing a bra, but I could read her mind. She was wearing a blue tank top that snuggled up against her lithe torso. From the customer's vantage point, they could also delight in a bare midriff with a tiny stud in her navel and a navigator's dream of smooth, tanned skin that lowered as low dared go before disappearing into the tight shadow of white, thin cotton short-shorts. There just wasn't a whole lot of material involved in clothing Veronica Creighton, or so it seemed. I doubted her parents had seen her sneak out for the evening. If they knew, they were drunk or nuts, maybe both. Every time I looked at her, her eyes seemed to get a little more liquid, lips getting licked, mouth agape. Just snugger and tighter until I thought I might explode just pouring another Leinie's.

"Whoa," she said, pushing back on the drink. "Whoa, horsy…" She giggled and gazed up at me, setting her chin on her hand, those big brown eyes like setting pools.

Veronica's family had been coming to The Sunny Blue Resort ever since she was able to walk. That thought haunted me like a nagging injury as I tried to make like I was interested but too busy for conversation.

I could feel Rudy's eyes on me again from somewhere. He never said much, but I always seemed to know what he would say if he felt the need. He always looked like he was way ahead of anybody, and he could make his facial expressions do all the talking. He made you work at figuring it out before it was too late. Sure enough, he had come back inside and was leaning up against the wall just outside of the kitchen, arms folded across, following Connie's sequined ass as it swayed across the room with purpose. She would stop to talk to customers, occasionally dipping the cleavage for effect. That particular look on his face? I wasn't sure if that was one that said he was going to bone her as soon as he had the chance, or toss her through the meat grinder he used to make deer sausage. Sometimes, I suspected you really didn't want to know what Rudy was thinking.

Rudy, for whatever reason, never poured a drink or drank a drop. Though he didn't talk about it, I got the feeling he drank pretty heavy at one time, had his share and that of a few others before he called it quits. And just for the record at this point, I was no prude. I enjoyed my beers, smoked an occasional joint and was no complete stranger to a hash pipe.

"Thomas." Veronica motioned me over. Somehow I felt like I had nothing better to do than to treat her like she was my only customer than night. She tried a shy smile look on for size. "Do you remember when you tore a hole in the backside of your swimsuit that day when you were helping Rudy fix the dock a few years ago?"

"As I recall, I caught it on a nail getting out of the water."

"As I recall, sitting there in my lawn chair, reading some stupid novel because that's all my parents would let me do when I was fifteen, this vision of the perfect man's ass comes into my view and do you know what?"

"I am afraid as hell to ask."

"I've had a few dreams...."

I don't know what she said after that. It seemed to catch in her throat and make her giggle, and the rowdies at the other end of the bar were working up some steam. The problem with her giggle was that it was not a young teenage girl giggle at this point; it was that of a sexy young woman who seemed to know exactly what reaction she could get with it. In fact, most of what Veronica Creighton did and said seemed a precise calculation aimed at maxing her options for the evening. Years ahead of her time. And all of it was working for me.

"Ok. I have to do this. Let me see your driver's license," I said finally. The noise level right before closing was sometimes deafening, and on this night it was no exception. Another bra was going. I could feel it. "I just can't believe you're really eighteen already. It seems I still remember you playing with beach toys and a diaper for a swim suit."

"That was my little brother, sicko!" she shot back, reaching into her little purse on the bar and producing an Iowa Driver's License. Eighteen, with about a month to spare. Whoever nailed her on graduation night had been right on the edge. "Dude...," she uttered in a way that was potentially damaging to my fantasy. It seemed whenever a guy and or girl uttered the word" dude" these days, they were all still shooting to imitate a young, glossy-eyed and stoned Sean Penn in *Fast Times at Ridgemont High*. To me, it always came off sounding like snot-nosed drivel unless it came from somebody that really *was* glossy-eyed and stoned.

I suppose what kept me out of situations like this most of the time during my eligible years to date was I would begin to sense the awkward

13

process that set in when all the flares had been sent up, then sexual chit chat had confirmed the intentions and it now boiled down to making the first real move to make it happen. These were the moments when I needed to be cool and look like cool came natural to me. Flip the hand, nod the come on, and brush by her, and touch her casually in just such a way to get all the expectations turned to what was yet to come. I sucked at that. That's why the Maria encounter was so incredible to me, and now, Veronica. Maybe aggressive women took away my fear of confrontation and failure- my natural state. M reality suggested I was just a history teacher whose idea of a great time on a Saturday night was hiding from everybody else under a good book and a fine dinner prepared by yours truly *for* yours truly. Dinner for one. Plenty of leftovers.

"How long 'till you close?" she asked, putting the license back into her little leather purse. I think she yawned. Naaah.

"About midnight, looks like. Maybe a little after."

She nodded her head, resumed on the straw and smiled, looking away for my benefit.

When I gave last call, the place went up for grabs. Another bra flew in the air, this one a traditional white, no lace, slightly padded. This girl had some stones. It got up there with the rest and the take was five for the night, missing the record by one.

# CHAPTER 3

She might have been as tired as she claimed to be, but the glares I was getting from Maria seemed to say my species was in grave danger.

"I'm exhausted," she said, and to be honest, that's how she looked. In sort of a hair wisping all over, slightly ruffled up way that made me think about how sturdy picnic tables are made. It wasn't hard to work up the thought of the evening ending with her bra on my head again. I wasn't the least bit tired.

"Great night for the house. Bigger questions is… how did us little people do?" I asked the walls. Seventy-five bucks in tips would be a pretty good Saturday night for me. I counted out eighty-two with a smile.

"A hundred three," she announced, not thrilled, lips pressing, sticking the cash in her purse and taking another sip of her White Russian through a green straw. It was as if she was watching herself and just caught up on things again, pulling up onto a bar stool by her set-up station and pushing her hair back off her face. "What happened to Delilah?"

I tried to read her face. "You mean, Veronica?" I asked with a benign snarl.

"She looked like a jailbait Delilah to me," she said, toneless, tossing her straw at me with intent to kill. "Sorry. My tongue's too tired."

"I checked her I.D. actually," I said.

"That's hilarious, Thomas. Let's see, you knew she wasn't twenty-one, even though you keep slipping her some rum, so why would you check her I.D.? Gee, let's see if we can figure this one out." With that came some mumbled sarcastic emphasis and body language, then she grabbed her purse, stood up, flipped me the finger and walked out.

I took another look at the cash I had counted and considered the first totally quiet moment of the evening. It was about quarter till one. So, let me check the early returns on this year's Sunny Blue experience. My tryst with Maria was ancient history, evidently, because now she was pissed at me-over another female- who had gone out for some "air" over an hour before closing and had not returned. The exquisite work I had done on my sexual fantasies for the evening had culminated into this very moment. Alone, with my money, sucking down a Budweiser, staring up at the newly hung bras, wondering where everybody had gone. From the way things turned out, it seemed the closest thing I had to real excitement for the evening was Connie Mulroney grabbing my balls and whispering that eerie promise in my ear. I took another couple of swigs. Funny, through it all, I could still smell Connie's perfume from somewhere. It was compelling enough to remember, but why? It was a scent that seemed about right for a middle-aged woman that took great pains to make herself subtle and sexy, with just a touch of an experienced Paris hooker.

All in all, it was time to take myself back to my room and call it a night. I was tired, too, now that the motivation was stripped away. I checked around, every bra in place, turned out the lights and locked up. The moment I hit the quiet, night-scrubbed air outside, the scent of the pines and the sounds of crickets and frogs were in full sync while I hummed some melody that would set up in my head from time to time. For years, the same melody, about ten or twelve bars, and my mind demanded I either hum it or whistle it over and over until the thought passed and I was allowed to stop. It was part of my occasional thought process that reasoned all people were likely insane to a certain degree, and I was no exception to that rule.

In the short walk past the docks to my room, I had reconciled life had given me some curious looks of late, given me pause to think there might be more to all of this than I thought.

I opened the door to my room and flipped the light switch. I had managed to rip my shirt off over my head and was unbuckling my jeans before my sight line picked up the partially blanketed outline of a person lying in my bed under the covers and pillows. I froze at my belt buckle, scanned the rest of the room and looked down at the wide old upholstered chair in the corner that caught most of my clothes and throw-offs when I came in. It didn't take much to connect the little crumpled bundle of blue material that would stretch out into a tank top on the lithe young body of Veronica Creighton. And those white short-shorts thrown on the floor, and the white tangle of shoelace that would have been the why-bother thong.

I hesitated, disappointed that the picture of Mr. and Mrs. Creighton came into clear focus at that precise moment. There they were, on the doorstep of the Crappie Cabin, her arms folded across her chest over a large machete while he stood straight, tall and broad shouldered, a meat cleaver dangling in each hand at his sides. First, I rebuckled, flipping the end of the belt back through the side loop on my jeans. I approached the bed and pulled the pillow up, revealing a very gorgeous, very passed out young lady so incredibly and beautifully unspoiled it would make an artist weep.

I sensed once again, I had no real training or instincts for what to do in a situation like this. Plan A- follow my heart, or below, give the thong a good sniff, get naked and jump into bed next to her and wait for her to wake up- or better yet, *wake* her up with the reason she snuck in my room in the first place. I also realized at that moment there was a reason I rarely locked my door at the Sunny Blue Resort unless I was in for the night. Decisions. Plan B- Of course, I could not follow my heart in a situation like this. I suppose I was technically still on the payroll. Screw the blood letting I would get from the Creighton's. If Rudy Mulroney found out about this I would be opting for a quicker certain death. He had informed me about the golden rule the first summer I worked- If they spend money here- don't fuck with it. My record had been perfect on that account until this year, and already in the first month I mangled that clipboard with barely an once of guilt laying heavy on my soul. My new mantra was *go with the moment* - mainly because there *were* moments. Not something I was used to, but given time, I was sure I could get used to it.

"Veronica," I whispered firmly, leaning over her at the edge of the bed, reluctantly pulling the blanket back up over that firm flesh otherwise awaiting me. I could feel heat radiating from somewhere. Up from her. Down from me. I didn't dare crack a window. "Veronica," I whispered louder, giving her shoulder a little shake She moaned through her lips which nearly sent me over the top and back to Plan A.

I sat down on the edge of the bed and tried raising my voice just above conversational level. "Veronicaaaa... ." I listened, watched, waited. The only thing that was happening was I could hear snoring coming through the walls, the common wall between my room and the main house where Rudy was apparently into his twenty minute ritual. I overheard Connie telling someone Rudy snored twenty minutes out of each hour, on the hour, every night, except Sundays. I didn't have the guts to ask him if it was true, but I knew there were times I could hear him, like right then, and other times when it would just suddenly stop. It wasn't always loud enough to be heard through the walls, but at times he could shake the rafters pretty well.

Suddenly, Veronica shot up into a sitting position, letting the blanket fall to her sides, looking at me with a sort of cocked craziness in her puffy eyes, her proud little breasts pointing the way to me. She smiled and put her head onto my bare chest. I held her only moments when she stiffened, then lurched upward trying to redirect the projectile vomit that hit me square on the Adam's Apple. I twisted and turned but got the best of it in my left ear before I could recoil enough to simply hold her head until she finished.

Looking mortified and quiet, Veronica slowly got her bearings and staggered into the bathroom to finish off a couple of aftershocks. When all was calm, I could hear water running, splashing on a face, then silence. Meanwhile my reality expanded to notice how quickly puke got cold.

Cracking that bathroom door back open had to be tough for her. I was sure she thought if the bathroom would have had a window, even a twelve-inch square, she would have made her escape and pretended this never happened. "I'm sorry," she whispered, barely audible, shielding herself with the door. "Could you please hand me my clothes?"

I hustled right to it, trying not to show her I was still trying to dig chunks out my ear canal. Yes, my hands did touch the thong. That, apparently, would have to carry me.

I offered to walk her back to her cabin but she just shook her head and held up a hand and gave me a look like she might puke again. She went quietly, but I walked outside and shadowed her back to make sure she didn't fall in the lake or worse. From my safe distance, it looked like she got inside the door without any lights popping on. I hoped for the best, for her, and for her parents, and for me. They had six more days to go. My guess is I wouldn't be seeing much more of her at the Island Tap. That might be a good thing.

I was wide awake at this point. Book reading? I still had the vision of her little pile of clothing on my floor. I could still feel a silky warm thong on the pads of my fingers. So, I did what any normal person would do under the circumstances. I finished cleaning the vomit out of my ear, changed the bed sheets and took a shower.

Within an hour or so, I had settled back into some normal world view and my eyes stopped blinking long enough to close. Not for long. I was dreamless and sound asleep when I was jarred awake by the sound of the lock rattling on my door. It swung open in the dark. Standing there, a shadowy figure in silhouette to the moonlight filtering down through the pine limbs. It walked inside quickly and shut the door. I threw off my blankets and as I got up to pose for battle, the undeniable scent of Connie Mulroney hit me full up both nostrils. "Connie?" I asked, incredulous. I made no further move.

"So, what is it with you this year, Thomas Cabot? What is it that is turning me on like this? You look a little different. You carry yourself a little different." I could hear the rustle of soft fabric as she walked over to me in the dark.

Another question without an apparent answer I was prepared to give. "I... I don't have any idea.... I am a year older."

"Deep, sweetie. Very deep." She was standing in front of me now, my head swooning from the perfume. I could feel her full breasts press up against me with only the thinnest of nightgowns between us as she took my hand in hers and moved it down between her legs. "See what I mean? Like I said earlier today, baby, I'm feeling it. Now you feel it."

Hot. Hot and wet. More hot.

We were falling onto my bed in slow motion with her shifting in a position to straddle me, holding my hand in place. She began to writhe and moan in whispers, words I could not really figure out, sounds that didn't seem to match up, maybe another language. In less than a minute she had replaced my hand with my rock hard cock and I was buried inside of her. By the time she moved my hands to her breasts, we had found a rhythm and the crazy words and sounds stopped. Our breathing seemed to compete for the available oxygen in the room. The pace was increasing, her hands moved to my ear lobes and stayed there, stroking, playing and pulling firmly as she began a harder, angled grind and again short, crazy sounds like vacuumed-packed lids being opened came from her lips. I was right there with her when she stiffened and I could feel her inner thighs vibrating and shaking it down through the rest of her. "Ohhhhh... fuuuck," she rasped, then began laughing quietly, little girl snorts coming out of her nose, gurgled amusement at the back of her throat. She held still above me, my earlobes still tight in her grasp, laughing through a shudder. She finally got a grip, and we listened together as Rudy began his twenty minute sonata through the wall.

In another quick move, she was off me, moving across the floor, the door opened, closed and she was gone. If I had a put a stop watch to the whole thing, it might have taken all of seven or eight minutes, about the same amount of time it had taken Maria and me to accomplish the same thing in Smoker's Roost. Other than the major difference in age, size and marital status, I noted the biggest difference was one came hard, biting her lips to keep from making too much noise, the other shook like a paint can being mixed at Ace Hardware, cussed at the wind and laughed in giggle snorts.

I lay there in a surreal, suddenly quiet darkness, thinking about getting up to fasten the safety chain lock on the door. Why? Thought I. Who in the hell knows who could come in the door next. On balance, unless someone was going to slip in and kill me in the middle of the night, I liked my odds.

After further review, I considered the fact I had broken more rules, written and unwritten, crossed the lines of moral and ethical boundaries, actually broken the law by serving liquor to Veronica, and potentially set myself up for a retribution that might include physical harm and/

or death. I felt no remorse, no fear, no sense of impending doom. No. I think what I felt was *alive* suddenly. My cocoon had cracked open. My wings had begun to flutter. The only thing that concerned me, really, was looking Rudy in the eye. But in reality, Rudy never looked at you when you talked to him. He was a scanner, always looking left, right, or ahead of you. There was more going on there than anybody knew. That was a given. And as for Connie, Connie was... Connie was a ball grabber. I could hardly wait until morning.

# CHAPTER 4

I had thoughts maybe things might revert back to a mundane, yet wonderful string of Minnesota summer days; however, I admit to being saddened that my emerging status as a sexual object apparently had stalled in its development. The rest of the Fourth of July weekend had been uneventful, the usual amount of bras going up, the usual silliness ensued, the take for Rudy and Connie rather normal- very good, but normal. Blue Heron Lake was giving up a few large fish to some of the guests and Rudy had done his best to make a big deal over each one, even if they weren't so big, taking pictures, making sure the Sunny Blue Resort sign at the top of the circle was in the background of each one.

I was retrieving a Dad's Root Beer from the pop machine near the front docks when I spotted Veronica Creighton lying out on a beach chair, oversize sunglasses angled down at a hardcover book across her waist. I felt something stir down low as I watched her occasionally look up to watch a passing boat or jet skier.

"Hey gorgeous," I said, and meant it, as I casually approached Veronica. This was new to me also- having the guts to give a girl a tag instead of a real name. It felt good, a little dangerous, a little Lash LaRuish.

She looked up at me through the huge dark sunglasses, the sun flooding tiny prisms into the sun tan lotion covering the taught skin on her stomach. "Did you... ."

"I wouldn't tell a soul. Are you kidding?"

"Thanks. I'm telling you it's been like walking on egg shells around my parents. I might as well had my brains fucked out by some perv as far as they are concerned."

I considered commenting but left it alone. "What happened?"

"Well let's just say I wasn't done puking my guts out yet after I got back in. And... I must have dropped my thong in the kitchen when I was walking through. They found it on the floor in the morning. Not a good scene."

"You didn't put them back on?"

"Kind of a stupid question, dude?"

I scratched at the side of my head and shot her a smile of some sort, a heat shard of embarrassment crawling up my back side. Another boat roared by with a skier behind cutting the wake on a slalom ski just outside the no wake buoy about a hundred feet out from the Sunny Blue docks. "Great day to be out on the lake."

She pulled her glasses down a bit and I could see the same eyes I was looking at the other night. "Screw the lake, dude. I need to get laid."

After absorbing the shock, which took a few moments, my head bobbed out of the water for breath.

She turned a page and shot a glance back at her cabin. "This fucking place really got small this year. God, there is nowhere to go without people watching your every move. ... Shit."

"Very true. In the daylight... ."

"Don't think I can wait until tonight."

"No?"

"Uh uh."

"Okay, then." I smiled at her. No argument here. "Give me a few minutes. I'll think of something." I turned and walked away as if I had purpose and direction, but mostly I needed some air and a view without her in it to think straight. There was some kind of air at the Sunny Blue Resort this year, to be sure.

I began a perimeter check, scanning and looking at every possibility as though I had been set on the property for the very first time. Smoker's

Roost was out, not to toy with chance there again in the middle of the day. My room, forget it; the door faced the main dock. The storage shed, the old garage… this *was* a *very small* fucking island, turns out. The walk-in cooler in the bar kitchen… you'd have to be joking. Okay. So, big man with the big ideas said he would come up with something. Better hurry. Strike while it's hot. I had the feeling though she would not be subject to cooling off for awhile. My guess is the guy with her on graduation night never knew what hit him. He was probably still trying to figure it out.

I set my gaze towards my secret little wooden fishing boat sitting by its little pier on the far side of the shoreline. The view was mostly tall reeds, willows and pines, but I knew it was there, waiting for me. That slope down to the dock was pretty steep, but definitely out of the line of sight. Soft grass, maybe the quilted cover from my bed for a blanket. I had not seen anybody walking around down there. The best views and access to the main lake were on the other side.

"He's gone," came a sing-song voice from behind me. I froze, then felt the now familiar firm hand grip on my balls. "He's gone," Connie sang again. She moved around in front of me, moved her hands up to my ear lobes and smiled, wet-lipped and wide. "Off with Babe and the boys for two days. Or so he says. Meet me up at the house in an hour?"

I had to admit, as middle-aged women went, she was a stunner. Funny, though. My recall of our sex was that I more of a willing and able accessory. In the dark, for me, it was more like having sex with her heady perfume than anything else. "What can I say?" I laughed. "Rudy wanted me to…"

"Rudy's gone, sweetie. I'm going to take some bedding over to the Bass Cabin and I'll be back in a flash. I can feel it…." Even in the bright of mid day, this was a compelling woman with dark, wild eyes that could defrost a freezer. She played with my earlobes, flicking them back and forth between her fingers, bit her lip, and walked away exhaling nothing but sexy.

I wasn't sure about this balls and earlobes deal. But, if I were to protest, to whom would I protest? Instead, I moved in a cautious, deliberate circle, kicked a few rocks into the lake and veered left towards the bar to get a beer. We didn't open Mulroney's until four on weekdays.

I had about three hours to kill before I resumed a simple life protected by my employment. But if I was going to figure this whole thing out now, I would need a beer. Maybe two. And I had the keys.

Before anything in the way of a game plan or solution came into mind, I was dizzied by the absurdity of my options, picking among the fantasies and possibilities like a child with a gift certificate in Toys R Us. I reached the back door and went inside. Whenever I walked into the bar to open, I always had the same first thought- a bra had to be happier hung from a ceiling than folded in a dark, top drawer. Just a thought. Then that ten-bar melody would set up in my head and play through a few times until it was done with me. Crack a Budweiser, set up the bar. Good to go.

I twisted the cap off. Deep swig. Icy cold, shot at the back of my throat and ran bitter to sweet. Life was good. Now…. The question was imposing enough. Was Connie sexier than Rudy was scary? The quick answer over an ice cold Bud was that sex with Connie as I knew it could be set by an egg timer and being dissected into a slow death with one of Rudy's fourteen-inch hunting knives could last for days before I was left for dead in the forest. I pictured myself laying there, drawn, quartered, my penis and ball sack hanging above me, swinging from a pine bow on a piece of twine.

"Wow… hitting it a little early today, Thomas?"

My ears deceived me, I was sure of it, but I turned to face the voice anyway. "Maria, Maria. Maria….," I began to sing West Side Story. "I just met a girl named Maria… ."

I expected a blast of indifference, but instead she responded in song, same melody, continuing… "And suddenly … I realized… I lost my new diaphragm somewhere in here last night." She hit the high note pretty well.

I stopped. "What?"

"Damn thing keeps falling out."

"Tell me not with Bobby?"

"Last night, right around here…." She walked slowly, looking down, then stopped and reached underneath a table and picked something up off the floor. "I knew it." She smiled, walked around the back of the bar where I stood by the cooler and ran the rubber object under the hot water, adding some soap, rinsing. Air dried it about four inches in

25

front of my nose. "Can't take the pill. Makes me homicidal. Fucks up my hormones until I think I'm Freddy Kreuger."

"I see."

"And no, do you think I would fuck Bobby Southers? Give me some credit."

"He stalks you. He never takes his eyes off your ass the entire time he sucks down his beers by himself at that little table over there." I pointed to the smaller table very close to the one possibly involved in this crime.

"Gosh, Thomas. Thanks for mentioning it before."

"I thought you knew."

"They all look at my ass, Tom." She took a Miller Lite out for herself and leaned into the back bar. "Except you. You are a very busy boy, these days. Here I set you up as my summer fuck and the next thing I know I have competition coming from everywhere."

"What?"

"Oh give me the look? How about Connie Mulroney grabbing your balls in front of all the fans. My God! And Veronica? How does that taste, big boy? So what do I do? I hatch this plan last night that I'm going to nail you again, just like in the Roost, up against the wall in the hallway maybe , just as soon as the last customer leaves last night. Then, what happens, you get on that cell phone while I'm wiping down tables…. I'm waiting, waiting, then you yell across the room you're coming back later to lock up."

"It was my brother, Rondell. Drunk and dialing. He does that a lot. Jesus, Maria, I had no idea…."

"I guess not. Anyway, so my diaphragm, useless as it was, fell out while I was wiping down a fucking table, and the rest, they say… is history."

"It *fell out*." I didn't like the visual on that one.

Maria looked at me like I was idiot. Accurate, as that might seem. "It *fell out* of my *pocket,* numbskull. My God, Thomas, here all I was trying to do was bed you down and you got me screwing Bobby Southers and wearing my diaphragm while I'm serving tables. Now I understand why you were so quiet last year working here. You're this great looking sexy guy until you open your mouth and give me a glimpse of what you're thinking."

"Easy, lady. I'm just trying to get a grip like everybody else. Hey, Bobby Southers, i.e.NASCAR driver, a local legend with the ladies around here. You have to admit it's a pretty good guess."

"Well guess this. The real story on Bobby baby is not that his career ended after the accident. The real story is when he is behind the wheel; his brain only lets his body make right turns. ... So think about it... racing cars without being able to turn left. You're fucked unless you go around the track the opposite way."

I gave her a puzzled glance and fought off looking at my watch.

"And he is a lousy fuck."

"I thought you had a thing for him."

"Hardly. But he will continue to tip well as long as he thinks so."

The banter lost its steam and we were in the midst of the dreaded awkward silence, sucking down beers, touching things, shifting weight. The thing was, since it appeared by every unimaginable imagination that I had a choice for an afternoon sex partner, unless I figured out what to do, the windows were all going to shut pretty quick. So the unimaginable took on a thinking process, a selection process of sorts, with the American History teacher who was a virgin until he was twenty taking up the notion that he was to choose from a sexual menu the likes of which he had never thought possible. Every item on the menu had one of those little asterisks which led your eyes to the bottom of the page where you would find the words- *Everybody you do or eat may be hazardous to your health.*

Maria finished her beer and tossed the empty in the recycling bin.

I walked over to her and hugged her tight. She tensed at first, but as I breathed in the wonderful light sweetness of her hair, she relaxed and let her body slack into mine. "I'm flattered, you know," I whispered to her. "It's just a little overwhelming for me that you would be that interested."

"Purely physical," she whispered back.

"I'm very okay with that. I spent most of last summer lusting for you."

"Without making *one* move," she finished for me.

I drew her head back and looked her over, the sparkling eyes, little nub of a nose, just right. "Who, me? Make a move? I've never made a move in my life."

"It shows," she smiled. "You need some training."

"Yes, master."

"Now we're getting somewhere." She reached up and kissed me on the cheek. "So what would be your next move, assuming you could make one."

There was no way I could share that with her. I didn't know myself. I took a shot. "How about you sneak into my room tonight, after work. I'll leave the door open, and… I'll kind of be ready for you, like you were for me at the Roost."

She nodded. "Not too bad. It's a start." She smacked me on the ass and grabbed on with both hands, digging her fingers in for moment before retreating and turning to leave. "Gotta go."

"See you tonight. … Maria… I just met a girl named Maria…" I sang, while she kept moving away from me. "I'd be happy to hold on to your diaphragm for you if you like," I said, a little too loud.

She flipped me the bird over her left shoulder.

I looked down as I heard the screen door bounce the door jam, threw the empty bud at the bin and looked at my watch. "Shit!"

# CHAPTER 5

"If it isn't the idea man," Veronica said to me while pushing her sunglasses up off her nose as I approached. I was still not sure what I was going to say or do, but hoping the moment would appear somehow. She nodded with more of a twitch at the young boy of around twelve that had sat down in one of those wide sweeping white wooden lawn chairs I had helped paint the first week I arrived. "Idea man, meet DS man, sometimes known as my barely tolerable little brother, Shawn."

Shawn seemed rather perturbed he needed to stop playing with his Nintendo DS to shake hands with me. He nodded his disapproval and was immediately back to his mass murdering and nuclear annihilation.

I could see she was reading *Crime and Punishment* by Dostoyevsky. "Taking a light reading break from Nietsche?" I had to ask.

Her answer was hiding behind the sunglasses. "So it seems it is my job to make sure my little brother doesn't drown in the lake while my parents go off to wherever for the next couple of hours," Veronica said with valley sophistication. "He makes a move I don't like; I'll wrap him in duck tape and throw him in the lake myself. *Just* to watch him die," she added, with a hint of a smile. He didn't flinch. His eyes a pair of lasers trained on that tiny screen ten inches in front of his face. She mouthed the words- *I need to get laid*- at me.

My moment was at hand. I thought, then, if I had my Palm Treo with me, I could start using the scheduler to my advantage, but then- what- give up the spontaneity? No, I was better off, so far, allowing this bubble I was living inside of to move me around with the wind. And I mouthed- *later*- to her.

She gave me a curt smile, a deep sigh, and for a moment I thought she was going to start without me, brother or not, but she was just turning a page of the book on her lap and maybe accidentally caught one of her fingers in the top elastic edging of her bikini bottom. There was such a wonderfully wide expanse of oil glistened tan flesh between her navel and the top line of her suit bottom. Any wider and it would have been illegal.

I moved away slowly, really not wanting to take my eyes off of her, thinking small talk with the brother would be good, but thought otherwise when I gave him another glance. They both seemed to have a look of intensity that matched up, possibly a family facial feature thing. But I was certain they had different things on their minds. At least I thought so. Then again, I was twelve not all that long ago. I remembered seeing Mary Jo Regorovitz in her red and white bikini, sunning in her back yard, a high fenced postage stamp of grass next to our postage stamp of grass in Chicago. She was putting on the tanning oil. I was watching her pulling her straps down from her shoulders, rubbing the Coppertone everywhere, not missing an inch of exposed flesh. I was stunned and frozen and as erect as quickly as any twelve-year-old could be. Then, without any warning, she pulled what looked like a beige-colored nylon stocking out of one of her bikini cups, reworked it, and stuffed it back in, just so, giving her cup size a huge boost. I went soft and mowed the lawn, like a good boy. I never looked at her the same again. Worse, my best fantasy, the one that had begun to serve me so well, was damaged beyond repair. Thanks be to Christine Johnson on the other side of the alley for leaving her bedroom curtain open just enough to get me going again and sustaining me until I got to high school.

The front door was never locked at the Mulroney home. It opened into a big kitchen-den combo and served much like a motel office, people coming and going for general information, a brochure on a local attraction setting in a stand along the wall, or to report a clogged toilet in their cabin. I could smell her the moment my hand turned the knob.

I walked through the kitchen area, a tribute to the late 1950's, gray-white swirled plastic counter tops and matching center pedestal oval table large enough to seat eight, muted pink and gray patterned wallpaper and white appliances. The den was knotty pine walls that were darkening very well with age with a fieldstone fireplace along the back wall. Above the heavy pine mantel was a large picture of Connie, Rudy and their German shepherd, Erskine, who they had to put down the year before at age twelve.

I could hear music, could have been Garth Brooks, or one of those country music marketing sound-alikes with one syllable names like Clint Flint or Gray Black or Chase Case. It was almost like I could see her waving me up on stage as I edged along, pushing through the louvered swinging café doors that led into the never land. I was floating on the air of Connie's perfume, whatever the hell it was. It was as if they came up with a formula that matched up to all my endorphins, tingly spots and hard drivers. It was something so indescribable for me because it turned my mind to mush and the rest of me.... There you have it.

"Hi," she said, watching me walk into the bedroom as though Alice had dropped through the matter horn.

"Hi." I stood there trying to stretch or buy a moment, taking it all in. Connie was lying on white satin sheets, two pillows behind her head, an alabaster satin cover twisted and tucked around her breasts and down underneath an exposed bent leg and a foot that teased the smooth fabric with perfectly painted dark pink toenails. Back up to her eyes, they danced, they played, they knew. No one could set this stage any better. I stood there, as if I didn't know what to do. I mean, I knew what to do when it was it was pitch dark in the room, time was short and the urgency was high. But this whole scene would imply some obligation· to legitimate love-making, for lack of a better term. Time here would require a fulfillment, not a theft. I could tell by the look on her face, just observing my awkwardness had to be worth it for her. The rest of the room was a blur as I began to undress. While unbuckling, I wondered just how far away Rudy was on this fishing junket or whatever. How *far* away? Maybe as far away as my guilt instincts. I was settling for spontaneous necessity and confusion over guilt and fear. Who would have thought I was even capable of that? Connie, possibly.

"Be a dear. Go back out and lock the door and put that little "no vacancy" sign in the window by the door. I promise I won't even breathe until you get back."

Unlike the abrupt screwing we engaged in during the middle of the night, time left us alone as we made love in a manner previously unknown to me. There was no grabbing, no agenda, no urgency. Not right away. There was a deliberation and quietness about each movement we made. Soft touches, gentle teasing, whispered requests, new explorations; this was something so new to me, so unbelievably intense in its simplicity and patience, I was unable to speak. Every move I made came from an instinct I didn't know I had. She responded, she initiated, and she did everything a man thinks a woman might do to him or for him in a lifetime.

My mind was as limp and damp as the rest of me as I stilled for what had to be the last time, my arms wrapped around her shoulders, her legs still tight around me, heels locked into the small of my back on either side. I could feel spurts of blood in my veins everywhere, my heaving chest slowing and finally coming to rest and meshing with her large wet breasts. If you exclude the dimensional nature and moral judgment, I could not remember defining a better still shot for me- *right then, right there*- lying still against a woman's large breasts, soaked and exhausted from sex that drained every last ounce of my bodily fluids. I would not chance describing it for Connie, but it seemed like she was, in a word, ravenous, and might have bitten off both of my earlobes while she gave me nearly constant progress reports.

"Jesus! What the…!" I yelled and jerked back out of her hold.

"Oh that's Twinkles," she scoffed quietly.

"Yeah, right, well, that was Twinkles tongue that just licked my ass!" The weightless chihuahua the size of a beanie baby had made its way onto the bed and evidently decided to get in on the action. I rolled over and tried to angle out of Connie's arms.

"Twinkles! Out! In your bed!" she barked. She caught her laugh and threw her head back on the pillow while I suspended and tried to pretend that didn't happen. "It could have been worse," she said, trying to regain her composure. "It could have been Erskine!"

So what was unquestionably a moment to never forget for all the right reasons was followed by perhaps one of the creepiest moments of my life. No matter what stage or world view I was operating under, I would never be able to totally erase the fact that a Chihuahua had frenched my ass. Even if it were to be in the cards that I would have sex with a midget or a quad amputee, this would undeniably stick to me.

I don't think I spoke ten words the entire time I was with Connie Mulroney that afternoon, but I knew when I was walking out the door into the bright summer sunshine, I felt differently than I had ever felt after having sex with a woman. There was no way to pin it down, label it, call it something or another. It was just different. I felt light headed but not dizzy. Rested, at peace, but warmly exhausted. Full, complete, yet drained of all possible body fluids. I smelled her perfume and her sex all over me. If it wasn't for that damn dog, I might have been unapproachable the rest of my days.

Garland was fiddling with a stubborn lawn mower by the porch near the door to the house as I took a deep breath of whatever great air they were selling. He stopped his fiddling and looked at me funny, cocking his head, making that baby seal sound, and I thought I could detect a slight movement of his head from side to side as if he was reluctantly passing along a negative ruling. He couldn't' speak, or hear, but he could see, and he could smell. Now, what if he had been sitting in that kitchen, or worse, had he peeked into the bedroom? I was sure he had a key. Real strange look, I thought. Back in those sunken dark eyes, maybe a thought to taking that crescent wrench in his hand to my nuts.

Some of the exhilaration left me then as I plodded back around the building to my room to catch a quick shower before I went to work. Puzzled, but moving ahead, I stopped in my tracks when two hands scrunched into my sides from behind, finding, with uncanny accuracy, two tickle spots that nearly crippled me to the ground.

"I ditched him!" Veronica announced, her voice as excited and as playful as it could be. "Where have you been?"

"Uh…" I caught my breath and readjusted my ribs. "I had to take care of some things for Connie."

"Whatever…" she breathed, staring me down with those big, eager eyes. I could almost see the red swizzle stick folding in thirds.

"Right. Well, at this point, don't get me wrong… you, standing there, wow… but I have to get a shower before I get to work. That gives me about twenty minutes until we open."

She looked around. "Perfect." She shrugged.

The decent thing to do was shower Connie off before I put Veronica on.

Twenty-one minutes later, a bit shaky, I unlocked the Island Tap and threw another thought Rudy's way. Then I cracked a Bud and looked up at the bras, let a shudder works it way down out of my Nike's and found myself gathering back into a normal breathing pattern while I began comparing vaginal characteristics.

"Hi Maria," I said, soon after, watching her walk in wearing her trademark fringed denim skirt which would always and forever remind me of Smoker's Roost. "What's going on?" I was acquiring a certain sense of rhythm, but my head sang with reoccurring words to describe the physical specifics of initial vaginal contact and entry.

"Should be busy tonight. Bikers are in town."

"Shit!"

"Remember the last time?" She asked, rhetorically.

"If it's the same guys, how could I forget? Among other things, the guy who mooned at the end of the night. How can you forget where that tattoo was…."

"You mean the *WOW?*"

"*I MEAN the WOW!* The *O* in *WOW!* Oh yes, who could forget that." Bad visuals of the asshole and cheeks classic combo were not a pleasant remembrance. But the guy was big and bad enough to hurt a score of people that dared take exception to his antics at one in the morning. Rudy probably would have clocked him half way across the lake, but I expect he was sawing them off pretty well by that that time. "Don't you think wearing that skirt tonight might be kind of risky with that crowd?"

"Hoping…," she cooed, going about her business setting up her work station. "Actually, I didn't have time to change. So there."

I gave her a Miller Lite and smiled at her.

She played with the neck of the bottle to tease me and then put her mouth and tongue around the top just so. "Your ass is mine tonight after work. We clear on that, Thomas?"

"Wouldn't have it any other way, Maria. Maria…."
*"Don't start singing!* You'll ruin everything."
She looked more attractive than ever, which scared me half to death. In the moment, I felt ten feet tall, invincible and strong as iron. Bring it on. Fuck American History. I *was* American History in the making. Just give me a few more days like this. And more bodily fluids, please.

# CHAPTER 6

"**A**nother pitcher of *STRAWBERRY* Margueritas," Maria shouted over the ascending laughter and buzz.

I made a decent Marguerita, and on occasion I had requests to make them up by the pitcher, but this was some rare occasion.

I shook my head and sprung into action and kept my glances working over at the massing of bikers. It was close to midnight and the rest of the customers had been gone for over an hour. I figured it wasn't the bikers themselves that scared them off; it was the one everybody was calling Moses. It was obvious Moses was the leader, how they played up to him... and with him. This was not the same group of bikers Maria and I remembered. The choppers looked the same for the most part, but these guys were as gay as an Elton John entourage covered in tattoos.

"Moses, baby," one yelled out, reaching around to grab Moses' big shaved head and swallowing his left ear.

I would turn away at that point, and many others. This either worked for you or it didn't. The chemical mix whirling around in my brain threw out hot pokers of nausea when I got a look at that. But beyond the obvious antics and behavioral ticks, they were fine by me. Nice enough guys, really, that apparently had a great time and never caused any real trouble. I couldn't imagine Rudy putting up with much more than an eyeful and a few bucks worth of this, but then, he wasn't around, or so I was told. And I was believing that really hard.

Anyway, I thought he would have a rough time with this. He was all of that masculine sinew stuff rolled into one, inside and out, all man, all the time. At least that is what was on display day in and day out. I had not seen a splinter in that rather wooden approach to life of his in all the years. Not unpleasant, not arrogant or stoic, just a man with some infinite man-looks and coolness, and one just assumed he was very much into being a man's man. His chemicals told him to be that way. That quiet gospel music thing was kind of eerie, though.

"You suppose Moses will be parting the sea any time soon?" I asked Maria while I set the pitcher of Margueritas on her cork lined round tray. "How you holding out?"

"I'm ok. I hope they tip well. We'll see. You?"

"What, are you kidding? We haven't put up a bra all night. My tips suck, and I'm watching gay guys clean out each others ear canals with their tongues. The place smells like ass. I'm doin' great." The moment I finished my editorial, I was dumbstruck with the thought. I assumed *Twinkles was* a female dog. I never asked. Little shit. If it had a dick, it would be the size of an eraser on a number two pencil. How could you tell? Not a good night to be messing with my sexuality.

Maria added bar napkins and another salt shaker. "I like the competition tonight."

As she walked off, she knew my eyes would be fixed on her rear. She gave a little extra shake. Much appreciated. Her comment did remind me I was surprised Veronica didn't manage to sneak into the bar during the course of the evening. And I had seen Connie only once earlier. She came around the bar, pulled the keys to check the take, gave my balls a quick tug, blew in my ear and off she went with a single, silent wink.

They were marginally in control of the place by last call. The volume was cranked and the white noise buzz even felt wrong. A guy answering to Cochise, featuring sleeveless faded pink denim under a hot black leather vest and matching riding leather pants, was on all fours on a table, the others gathered around whipping him with cocktail napkins while he sang the National Anthem and lit a series of farts with a Bic lighter. The last one trailed up his crotch and it took a joyful effort by a compatriot to put it out before the pants flamed up. That was just too much fun for me, and I flicked the lights on and off twice to remind them it was last call.

Maria was truly an amazing looking young woman who took on a sexy aura of sorts when she was a little disheveled, her hair falling over her big, tired eyes, almost like they were being held up by her high cheekbones. Her distinctive waggle had slowed to a shuffle. She was usually humming something when it was quiet enough to hear, but when the tips were less than expectation, there was silence. You could hear the pins dropping everywhere.

Her lips were tight as she counted out. "Fucking pricks stiffed me! Ten bucks for three hours of that shit. Give me a break."

"A total wipe out," I added, pointing to the meagerness in my glass beer stein by the register that usually held much more for the effort.

"Screw this." She dropped her small stack of cash into her purse and looked across the bar at me.

"I got a better idea."

She brightened considerably. As did I, likely just at the notion I had taken the initiative. It felt good, as if I had redeemed myself for my obviously shallow behavior. I really wouldn't go that far, but nonetheless, this *boldness* of presumption was new to me and felt like a sin. At the time, I totally disregarded the fact that Maria had made a reservation earlier.

"So where do you suppose Rudy is this time?"

"Fishing with the Babe."

"That's a crock."

"What makes you say that?"

"I can see it in his eyes. He's lying sure as he's breathing. Most men lie pretty well, but the eyes lie long after the words are spoken."

"And you're how old?"

"What's it to you. You can figure it out."

"Right. Pretty young to be that jaded, I'd say."

"Okay, I'll give you that. Jaded, I'm not. But every man... so far. I'm working on the jaded part."

"*Every* man?"

"Every man capable of pulling down his pants and getting inside of mine."

I would have gone and asked her if that included me, but I thought I was miles ahead by staying away from that bomb. I shrugged and waved the white towel I was using to wipe down the bar.

She knew it. She read it. In my eyes, miss smarty pants. She shot her tongue into her cheek and tried to suppress the knowing smile.

Maria's hips had enough left in them to move with such deft precision I was largely just on for the ride. I hadn't noticed it so much during the quick and dirty on the picnic table in Smoker's Roost, but with a mattress underneath of her she caught a rhythm that had my eyes rolling into the back on my head. She was riding so high on me her heels were locked *above* my shoulder blades. The flames on the pair of apple spiced candles she brought and placed on the end table were bouncing from the vibrations we were sending out on the air waves. I was just about there with her when I pictured Connie walking through the door. I nearly went limp but quickly stashed the thought when I looked down and gently brushed Maria's face in the candlelight. She caught two of my fingers in her mouth, ran her tongue around them, then bit gently as she brought us home.

"How far do you live from here?" I asked, as she curled in under my arm and reached up to offer me a hit from her joint. I really couldn't recall the last time, but it seemed like the right time. I took two hits.

"My mother's place is about two miles from here. She's got a little house in Gull Lake. You know Connie is her sister, right?"

"Sort of. I mean, I think I heard that just recently."

"Yeah. Connie has always been sort of a big sister for me. When my father boogied about five years ago, Connie was there for me while mom went through a nervous breakdown and nearly killed herself. I was lucky I had my music scholarship to get me through college. My father is a schmuck. I haven't seen or heard from him in over a year. He was suppose to show up for a performance of mine at a Christmas show last year and never made it. He might be dead, or he just might be in Tahiti sucking down Mai Tai's. Not much in between for my father."

"So he's a liar, too."

"Big time. Your father ever lie to you?"

"My father?" I hadn't thought about my father in awhile. "My father was too paranoid to lie. He thought everybody was lying to *him*. Thing is, he was probably right. He died of a heart attack when I was pretty young and my mother married the guy he thought she was having an affair with all along. The local high school football coach. The local *black* football coach."

We both took a few more hits. "The world is swirling in man lies," she said.

I nodded, and was barely conscious when the door swung open. Connie's profile seemed to sag into the door frame with a groan. "I just bet Twinkles twenty bucks it was you, Maria. I win. Hah!" she laughed and wobbled across the room to the old mismatched corduroy sofa chair and flopped into it like its new throw pillow. Neither of us moved, but Maria was going to have to do something soon with the joint because it was down to her fingers.

"That's the best damn part," Connie said, pulling herself out of the chair with great effort and taking the joint from Maria's hand. Maria used the opportunity to pull the sheet up over an exposed breast. Connie maneuvered her lips over the joint and sucked it dead in three hits, choking and gasping and throwing her head back into the chair. "Wow, that's some good shit," she said, as we remained an adoring audience of two.

I had partial thoughts of things I could say, but nothing bubbled up ready. As coherent as I could be, I was sure Connie noticed I was struggling.

"See," she began, "I was out at the Fireman's Annual Cookout for Kids and when I got back... late... I did my usual lady things and then went to bed. I could hear those crazy people at the Tap. What in the world? All the bikes? Bikers talking like that? My God in heaven. Anyway, these walls are rumored to be quite thin.... But I thought the decent thing to do was wait until all the commotion you kids were making died down. And... here I am. I got a great idea. Let's go over to the Island Tap and have a drink. We can chat there. This is growing just the tiniest bit uncomfortable for me."

None of us needed a drink, but I couldn't think of a better way to get out of the situation and at least into neutral territory. Connie studied us for another moment and got up to leave. As soon as the door closed, we threw our clothes back on and wandered over to the Tap. Connie was already there, turned on a small light behind the bar and motioned for us to pull up a stool.

My head was heavier than the rest of my body but I bravely sipped from the bottle of Budweiser Connie put in front of me. Even if I was all there I don't think I would have been able to come up with anything snappy to say.

"Do we have to have a big scene with my mother over this, Aunt Connie?" Her voice suggested she might not want the answer.

Connie poured herself a Cuervo Gold, straight up. "You're what, twenty-three?"

"Two."

"Hell, girl, when I was that age, no sailor in sight spent the night alone."

I could have done without hearing that.

"No scene," Maria confirmed.

"Hello, I was just pissed off you guys woke me up. So now you have to have a drink with me, that's all."

I thought Connie was winking at me when Maria wasn't looking, but I couldn't be sure. Hell, I wasn't even close to being sure about anything. Connie began to talk and went on about the great country western band at the cookout, and the lead singer with the great ass. "Reminded me of your ass, Thomas," she mused, bringing pointed yet differing reactions from Maria and me. As she went on about a laundry list of things, I could start to hear a central theme. She was taking me right to the edge, dangling me over the top, then pulling me back by a belt loop. "He had that deepness in his voice, too, Thomas, just like you when you.…. I'm just kiddin'."

I kept looking over at Maria for any possible connection of dots, but her face was angled with exhaustion and whatever else had been thrown in. She made faces at me when Connie wasn't looking, mouthing the words *crazy lady* more than once. I was listening to Connie go on endlessly and joyfully, with Maria the mime occasionally adding emphasis when Connie wasn't looking. I was a nervous wreck.

"What is going on around here?" came a voice from the kitchen. In walked Veronica Creighton and my nightmare was complete. "All those bikes starting up woke me up and I couldn't get back to sleep. So I thought I would take a walk. Okay if I come in?"

"Sure, dear," Connie said. "Pull up a bar stool and join our little party. But I *know* you are not old enough to drink. But you know what? Neither are we!" Connie thought that was hilarious. I went along with it, but Maria crossed her legs and rolled her begging eyes.

"I really need to get home, Aunt Connie."

"Nonsense. You aren't driving anywhere. I'm sure we can find a nice warm place for you to snuggle, don't you worry." Connie seemed pleased she came up with that one as well. She was enjoying herself. "Scene? If I send you home like you are, there will be a scene alright."

Maria didn't look up for the fight. She crossed her arms and wrapped herself up and shrugged. "Your call."

"So, little one," Connie sighed. "Veronica. Not so little anymore, hon. My goodness I can remember you running around here on my beach naked as a little bird… and that was just yesterday afternoon." We all felt obliged to laugh. At least Connie was only sipping the Cuervo, but it would appear she had an early start to a long evening. "Rum and coke, right hon?" She moved around behind the bar and mixed Veronica a drink. One and done for you. And probably the rest of us too. I think I've peaked for the evening. And I know these two worked their little fannies off tonight." Connie slammed her hand down on top of the bar. She was killing. The queen of comedy striking yet again.

Veronica took the drink graciously, nodding her thanks, and began twirling the red swizzle stick. She wouldn't dare, I was thinking. The thought did occur to me that I ought to be considering some resolution, if not accountability to all of this, but honestly, the idea of a resolution never entered in, and I decided accountability was simply out of the question. Maria was right. We shared a world of swirling man lies.

"What *is* that?" Veronica said, pointing out the window to a bright orange glow that seemed to be reflecting off the glass. Connie turned her head in the same direction and studied it for only a moment before she bolted out from behind the bar.

"Fire!" My God!"

# CHAPTER 7

The only thing to do was to follow Connie as she flew out the door and around the side of the building. There was no mistaking the flames coming up through the soffits at the edge of the roof along the side of the house with the sleeping rooms including mine. Smoke was billowing from the edges of window frames and you could see an orange bouncing glow inside. In the dark it was hard to see everything, but it appeared heavy smoke was pouring out from different locations of the building as well.

*"PHONE! CELL PHONE!"* Connie yelled, fumbling for a cell phone that wasn't there. A purple robe over a night gown, but no cell phone. Mine was in the room. We rushed towards the fire then back towards the front of the house in a blurring that suspended the reality of what was happening. The air was full of heavy acrid smoke, there were sounds of wood popping and sparks were shooting up in the sky.

"Here." Maria had her cell phone in her purse. While Connie stopped walking long enough to shakily dial 911, I ran off to the hose bib located by the supply building and turned the water on full blast, pulling and uncoiling the hose as a I worked in as close as I could. There was a nozzle on the end of the hose that gave the stream some added distance-it was the only thing I could think of doing- but it was no match for the growing inferno it was trying to reach. The heat was so intense I couldn't get close enough and the water pressure from the

43

well left a lot to be desired. I remembered there was another bib and hose on the front side of the house.

"Maria! Come here and hold this on the fire. I'm going around the other side to see if I can get the other hose going." Maria grabbed the hose from me and I ran to the front side of the house where guests had started to congregate in their pajamas and robes. I spotted Veronica standing next to her little brother, holding on to him.

"God, no! Please, God, no!" I heard Connie screaming.

"Don't go in there, Aunt Connie," I heard Maria yelling.

I couldn't believe Connie would have gone back into the house. "Mr. Creighton!" I shouted. Would you mind manning this hose for me while I check on Connie?"

He ran to me immediately and took the hose.

"Connie!" I yelled. "Where the hell are you?" I ran inside the house and the smoke hit me in the eyes and nose at the same moment, sending me down to me knees. I coughed and wiped at my eyes, then moved along lower with my hand over my mouth and nose. "Connie!"

"Here. Take these files out of here. Now!" She handed me an armful of manila files full of paper and followed quickly after me with what looked like a large jewelry box and some other smaller boxes. I dropped the files into a pile on the ground safely away from the fire and she did the same with her load. "Everyone, *please* stay back. The fire trucks are on their way." With that she went back inside and I was right behind her. We grabbed everything we could but by the third trip out, we were both gagging. The back of my throat felt liked it had been seared and I couldn't seem to grab any air and force it through my lungs. I was hunched over when I saw Connie collapse on the grass and two of the women guests ran to her side.

"What else..." I said, trying to gather for one more trip. I looked up and saw flames starting to lick the highest part of the roof at the ridge line and I knew this old frame structure was feeding on itself and wouldn't last much longer.

"Twinkles!" I was sure I heard Connie cry out. "My Twinkles!" I don't know if she passed out after that or what, but I took my tank top shirt off, wrapped it around my nose and mouth and headed back in.

I crawled across the kitchen floor. "Twinkles! ... Shit!" It was notably hotter and the smoke too thick to see less than a foot from the floor.

I moved into the den area and I could see the flames leaping across the bedroom down the hall. "No way..." I said a few times, flattening out my hands, trying to see if the dog was cowering somewhere in a corner or, possibly hiding. " Ouch! God dammit," I yelled. Twinkles had found me, my thumb that is, as I reached under a chair in the den. He had his little jaw powered up and hung on for all he was worth as I dragged him out against his will, sinking his teeth a little deeper as I maneuvered along the floor on my back and spilled out the door and tumbled onto the ground outside. I was spitting up black gunk as he let go and I watched the little bastard run to his mommy.

I was still shaking my head clear when I began to hear the sirens. It seemed like a day had gone by before they got there. The pumper truck fired up while a flurry of men dropped intake hoses in the lake and flew in all directions. But it was way too late. There was no such thing as fire hydrants in these parts, but it wouldn't have mattered. Within another hour, the house was nothing more than a flattened, smoldering mess of charred timber around a blackened fieldstone fireplace that stood tall, and alone. The firemen had managed to keep any of the other buildings from catching fire. There was some roof damage on the Walleye Cabin from falling ash and debris, but nothing that couldn't be fixed in a day or two. It was an eerie scene, with an audience that had grown with others from surrounding resorts. Connie stood there holding Twinkles as a man the size of Andre the Giant joined at her side and slipped a massive arm around her.

Maria and I sat crossed legged on the grass, flipping small handfuls of blades in the dark. She was looking at the same thing. "More there than meets the eye," she said with a yawn.

"Old friends, likely, like everybody else around here, I expect."

"Thomas?"

"Maria?"

"Did you blow out the candles?"

I had to part the heavy sea waves tossing everything around in my head. "No. That leaves you, and you already asked."

"So now what. I mean, we don't *know* that's what started it."

"I think we have a pretty good idea."

"But if Connie doesn't butt in... ."

"And maybe if Connie doesn't butt in, maybe we get too stoned and too tired and die in our sleep?"

"Or maybe…" Maria said, "she gets us out of the building like she did so she can burn it down while Rudy is gone for some insurance money thing, but nobody gets hurt. Or maybe Rudy burned it down…."

"Or Garland," I said. "Who the hell knows what he's thinking about. He gave me a look earlier today, or yesterday I guess it was… something straight out of Stephen King."

I looked at my watch. It was just after four in the morning.

Sitting cross-legged on the grass, covered in inches thick soot and filth, my heart truly heavy for Connie and Rudy, there was my groin sending me the all-clear signal, bypassing the heart, and setting up a place in my head for me to think about how twenty minutes with Veronica was just not enough.

"My superman, Thomas," I heard Connie say. She was standing over me and gently touching my shoulder. Maybe I had passed out sitting up. "Thomas, I want you to meet Chief Fortnight. He's an old friend as well." Connie's voice broke.

"I got up and began to apologize for the filth on my hands but he shook my hand anyway, nearly breaking every bone. It seemed like the bottom bone in my hand collapsed under the weight of the one above it. It was my first handshake with sound effects. Never had I shook hands with a man with a bigger, stronger hand. I always thought mine was pretty good until I met Rudy. Rudy's was a handshake to prepare for, but this guy had a grip like a janitor ripping a steel cutter through a combination lock on a student locker.

"Nice to meet you, Chief." Fricking Godzilla. It was dark except for the few spots the fireman still had on, but I had to take a shot. "I'm sorry, but… WD-40? Wahoo Doyle Fortnight?" It had to be.

"The same." His voice was a dump truck of hard gravel.

"I'll be damned. It hit me right away because you played for the Chicago Bears your last season before you retired. The knees, right?"

"You got it."

Wahoo's head without a helmut. The honest thing to say anybody who ever followed pro football could ever forget seeing. He had perhaps the largest head in the northern hemisphere. The hair all pulled back into a pony tail down his back, the eyes bulging from the sockets like they were already full of human remains, this was a defensive end for the ages in his prime with the Minnesota Vikings. A great story, a local boy off the urban Indian reservation in St. Paul, attended the University of Minnesota, first round draft choice in the NFL. "WD-40," they would chant, "WD-40!". As time went on, he garnered a reputation for being one of the dirtiest players around, biting halfbacks in the calf at the bottom of piles, twisting ankles when he could get away with it, and he had a unique talent for getting every drop of a fermented luge through the face mask of almost every offensive tackle he faced in the league.

Some years had gone by but this was still a mountain of a man whose voice even sounded like he hurt people in his sleep. He wasn't dressed in his Fire Chief's outfit right then, but I could only imagine he would be one imposing SOB with any fireman's hat sitting on that big hunk of skull of his.

"Fine thing you going in there to save Con's dog, Tommy." Wahoo said.

I looked at the dog settled in between Connie's breasts, back up at Wahoo, then the dog started cheapshoting me with tiny four second growls.

"Oh stop, Twinkles," Connie said. "I can't begin to thank you, sweetie. You saved her." Connie leaned over and gave me a peck on the cheek. For whatever reason, she did not grab my balls this time around. At that moment, I was thinking it was pretty likely someone like Connie knew someone like Chief Fortnight in much the way I knew Connie and Connie knew me.

"Connie, did you get a hold of Rudy?" It just came to me to ask.

The two of them looked at me like I had three eyes. "He's out of cell range where he's at up in Canada," Connie said. "If you can believe that."

"What do you mean?"

"I mean, Thomas, I tried to reach him and his cell won't pick up. I get his voicemail. So I left him a voicemail. You want to know what I said? I said, 'Rudy, your house is on fire.' Then, I left him another voice mail, 'Rudy, dear, I know you must be out of range, but just to let you know, your house has burned to the fucking ground. Please call when you get back in range'. How's that? See, Tom, if he is out of range in one of those remote fly-in camps, he can't get my message. And, if he got my message, he can't really call me back either, can he."

It was most interesting to check out the facial movement on Wahoo while she was talking. Like he knew about all of this, knew what was going on, knew the role he played in all of it. I was just guessing, which is all the experience I had in these things- being a decent guesser.

Twinkles continued that pit bull want-to-be growl at me. I did my best to repress the memory of our most intimate moment together, reached for my thumb and remembered I should probably get something to clean that wound up. Connie and Wahoo drifted off back to the ruins while I checked back on Maria, and my thoughts resumed and zoomed in on Veronica sliding up and down my body in the shower. I was a fucking mess. I hadn't even given a thought as to what I might have lost in the fire. Really, the only thing that I could focus on was the last thing Veronica said to me as she left my room after that incredible twenty minutes.

"Tomorrow. You and me, Genius. Screw marathon. Nine a.m. starting time. Right here." The door slammed. But now, no door. No *room!*

*Here* no longer existed. So, even though there was maybe some change in agenda with this fire event in the mix, my focus needed to be on getting a shower, a few hours of sleep and coming up with an alternative location. As sick as that was, I was not insensitive to Maria's plight as well. What plight was that again? She was staggering and making her way to her yellow VW and I figured even if she wasn't in the best shape to drive, she was better off leaving this mess than staying. "Goodnight, my love," I managed in song as the ignition turned over.

Connie? Connie was apparently in good hands. Hands! Are you kidding me? The guy probably had a dick the size of a fire hose nozzle. On the other hand, if he had been into steroids- and with a noggin that size it would figure- his junk could be more like the little garden hose nozzle that pretended to put out the fire.

I was talking to myself like an idiot as I made my way to the Island Tap. I could shower in the kitchen, sort of. I could extend the spray nozzle from the kitchen sink and use the soap there. I could stand in front of the sink, hose down, and even though most of it would hit the floor, it would go down into the pitched floor drain. I turned on a light and caught a glimpse of myself in an old mirrored Schlitz Beer sign on the wall.

"Mammy!" I cracked. I passed for black for a few moments, convinced myself none of that was racist, and moved on into the kitchen. I got naked, pulled open the top of a plastic bottle of Palmolive dish washing liquid and poured it over the top of my head. The green goo mixed with the black soot and made a beef stew-like gravy, but after I got the water as hot as I could stand, I began to spray and sponge my skin free of the black man I had become. In about twenty minutes, I was once again free and white. Then it hit me. I had nothing else to wear. The sum total of what I had to call my own was the filthy pair of khaki shorts lying on the floor. No underwear. I had gone commando, getting dressed quickly to meet up with Connie in the bar after her visit to my room. I had about eighty bucks in cash in the pants pocket, a Master Card in my wallet, a thin mini Swiss army knife and a Listerine Cool Mint Pocket Pak.

# CHAPTER 8

It wasn't like any other Thursday morning at the Sunny Blue Resort, to be sure. The vibrantly clear Minnesota air had been replaced with an undeniable bitter stench of damp charred wood and there was a pall about the Sunny Blue Resort that anyone would expect. Guests, neighbor resort owners and the unrelated curious who saw the orange flames in the middle of the night coming from somewhere filed by and snooped, the other resort owners offering Connie anything she wanted or needed. She was gracious and kind, but tired, haggard and generally baffled by what the daylight had brought to reality. She thanked people for their offers and words, but her real focus was on sifting through the rubble that had been her home for the past twenty-two years. She would find little pieces of things forever ruined as she tromped around the mess in her purple robe and calf-high yellow rubber boots on loan from Wahoo. I don't know if she slept at all, or where. I grabbed a couple of hours in a booth in the bar and followed her around, lifting and tossing things, acting like I knew what I was doing and why.

It was almost nine. Exactly at nine, Veronica Creighton emerged from the creaking screen door of cabin number four and stood there on the top step with her hands on her hips, dressed in hot red Nike short-shorts and a matching red tube top. Her hair was pulled back under a black head band and she looked all the part of a young woman with a soul on fire and an agenda to prove it. She looked around, spotted me on the rubble pile and stood her ground. Let there be no doubt that whatever had happened, she was on a mission and would not be denied.

After she could see clearly that I had a necessary agenda of my own, as unfortunate as that might seem, she slowly walked my way and found a moment during one of Connie's wails to whisper in my ear.

"We're supposed to be fucking." She looked at me, and I suppose I looked like lunch in her state of being. Filthy khaki shorts hanging low on my lean six-two frame. Not muscular, but I was fleshed out well enough to look like a man that had taken decent care of himself, but anything I had, I came by without the benefit of training or working out. This particular summer it seemed like it was enough to generate some serious interest. I was not to be fooled into thinking one, that it would last, or two, that it was anything but an anomaly, coincidence, or simply timing in casually brilliant style that had brought me to the sudden sexual peak of the ages. The fact that I was surrounded by provocateurs; lusting women who considered me no more than a sexual object or a humping post was the biggest turn on of my life. I would be an even bigger fool to not enjoy it while it lasted.

At least, that it the logic the prevailed for me at the time.

"You see what's going on here, right?" I asked. My tone was gentle, my hands waved over the evidence. "I don't know what we're going to do next. I'm thinking Rudy needs to be here..."

Veronica looked around as if she was trying to spot up a better option. "God, I hate this fucking place. I'm not coming next year. That's it." She looked over at Connie, considering the ratty get up. "So what am I supposed to do? Sit around and cry about some crummy old house burning down?"

"Easy does it. Come on, Veronica. Tell you what. Give me an hour or so to sort this out and I promise you..." I looked at her and tried to get her big eyes to hold still for a moment. "I promise... before high noon.... I want it as bad as you do."

"Okay, okay," she said. "I'll just go back into the cabin and watch my parents play cribbage and talk about my Aunt Beth's irritable bowel syndrome. Or, some more of the poor Rudy and Connie stuff." She turned to leave but leaned back to whisper in my ear once more. "If

Rudy was here, I'll bet I could talk him into fucking my brains out in thirty seconds or less."

I decided not to challenge that comment, but I had to wonder, as I watched her tight little torso walk away. Did she mean she could *talk* him into fucking her brains out in thirty second or less, or did she mean that thirty seconds or less is all it would take to get the back of her head to orgasmically explode against the wall. I wasn't sure if it mattered, but I enjoyed the process of thinking about it. I wouldn't for a moment make it seem like I wasn't there for Connie. After meeting Wahoo, I just wasn't sure where to stand in line for Connie. It was awkward, at best, trying to figure out what to do or say without Rudy there.

Connie finally sat down on a bench by the pier. I sat down next to her and put my arm around her. "Is there something else I can do?"

"No, hon," she said, blowing her nose and trying to make it seem like she could never look this bad. "The insurance guy will be here sometime this morning. I just need to figure some things out. Rudy isn't here. I need to get used to that. I thought I already had. That's all."

"You know, it could have been the candles Maria and I were burning in my room. I need to tell you that."

"No you don't. People burn candles all the time, not just when they're fucking. But they don't do it to burn their house down. Don't worry about it."

"Well, Maria and I...."

"Thomas, let's just say Maria quit. She won't be working here anymore. Okay. Her mom never liked the idea, anyway."

"Whoa... that was fast. When? How?"

"I just told you. Let it go, sweet."

That was the bitch in Connie. I was very aware of that part, had seen it in action many times over the years, but I was still taken back by it. I guess she had her reasons. There was just too much going on and swirling around me to try to make sense of people's motives and actions. I was in no position to comment or criticize. Nonetheless, emptiness filled out my stomach as I tried to imagine not seeing Maria or her swaying backside running around the Island Tap all night long. And I couldn't help but think part of this was my fault. Maybe most of the parts were my fault.

Connie had been working the cell phone in between her discoveries and breakdowns. She called me over to take a look at what used to be the computer hard drive in the little office. It looked like a metal twisty cone from Dairy Queen. I dropped it back into the rubble and froze as the thought finally occurred to me that my own lap top was in my room, which of course meant it didn't look much different than Connie's.

"And just so you know, Thomas. I just got off the phone with Bo's Flying Service up in Canada. Rudy Mulroney was a no show for his flight up to the remote fishing camp. Guy says he flew three guys including the Babe up yesterday, buy Rudy wasn't one of them."

I was baffled, but that had become a natural state. "So where is he?"

"I have an idea. Tell the truth, I would go after him myself, but… look at my life here… what the fuck am I supposed to do now?"

"He's due back, what, tomorrow, right?"

"Sure. Tomorrow. Surprise!" She feigned an enthusiastic greeting and held out her arms for all to see. "This is really crap on a stick. I *know* he's down in St. Paul. He's with the Doctor's wife. As we speak, he's sucking her big tits. You remember the Doctor. Doctor Zolanda and his wife Figi."

"No way. Figi Zolanda? That red headed bombshell? They come up the first week in August."

"Rudy starting banging her last year. Evidently the once a year thing wasn't going to be enough with this one."

"No kidding. I can imagine it would be hard to ever get enough of that." I don't know why that came out, but it did, and Connie gave me a swat on the ass and a glare that went with it perfectly.

We both thought about what we wanted to say next while we kept sifting. For awhile, I didn't understand a word she was saying and I responded with a series of nods and grunts.

"Fiji Zolanda. Married to the gynecologist." Connie played with the words. "I mean, that's got to be weird, I give you that. 'Hi hon, have a nice day? Oh, what, you're tired of staring at pussy? Okay. Please wash your hands before dinner.' Yeah. It's got to be weird. But this one kind of worries me. Rudy usually finds some young thing to buy all of his Kenny Rogers look-alike bullshit, gets his rocks off and acts like nothing has happened. This one. This one's older, almost my age. He might actually *like* fucking her. Could be dangerous."

"Well I think I am hearing more than I wanted to know, but...."

"Oh hell, Thomas. You're in it up to your you-know-what. So cut the innocent young inexperienced guy bullshit on me. You fuck me, and beautifully I might add, then you burn my house down while fucking my niece, in the *same day!* God, I wouldn't be surprised if you didn't fuck that little tramp Veronica Creighton as well. She's like some toy poodle looking for a leg to hump, and you're the leg! Jesus, Thomas, what is with you this year?"

"Me? Christ.... Me?" I laughed and shook my head. Connie gawked at me like I was nuts as I started prancing around like Jerry Lewis in the *Geisha Boy.* When I could finally settle down again I took a deep breath and hitched up my sagging dirty shorts. "What the hell are we doing here, Connie?"

She stopped and smiled up at me. "Do you really think anybody who thinks about it too long has any idea what the hell they are doing?"

"Not sure."

"Exactly. Knowing is just too fucking painful. My guess is smart people aren't any better off than rich people, largely miserable and bored with how the world continues to disappoint them. It's better to be baffled, Thomas."

"I qualify then."

Connie's cell phone rang. The poor thing. She looked like a bag lady in pastel. She and I both needed a shower. A smile crossed her face as she hung up. "That was Chief Fortnight. He's arranged for me to get a big motor home cruiser from Chambers RV Sales out on Highway C. All I have to do is pick it up. It's got everything, brand new, and won't cost us a dime. We can live in it. Two bedrooms, one for me, one for you. We can flip for Rudy if he shows up."

I gave her the glare this time. "You're serious?"

"Of course I am, hon." But you know what. I've got to stay here to wait for the insurance guy to show up. Can you drive over and get it? It's only about a half-hour ride."

"Sure, Connie. No problem. But the sleeping arrangements are still on the table."

"As if you have a choice."

"Maybe I can get somebody to go over with me and I'll drive it back."

I could tell Connie was already thinking about something else. "I'm going over to cabin one. The Carlson's offered me their shower and they are going to be gone until later today. "I'd ask you to join me, but… let's leave that for another day. Actually, the Creighton's are just leaving, looks like." The Creighton's Volvo was backing out of the parking spot by their cabin. "They offered as well…. On second thought, I'll use the Creighton's cabin, you use the Carlson's. I don't want you sniffing Veronica's bikini on the line over there." She nodded towards the short length of clothes line strung from one corner of Cabin Four to a white birch tree. Alone, and taking up precious little room on the line was what had to be Veronica's bikini parts drying in the sun.

I needed a shower so bad I didn't argue the point. It was senseless to argue a point with Connie anyway. We both deserted the still smoldering pile reluctantly. It would have seemed the respectful thing to do was spend more time going through everything that was left, but there wasn't anything left. The sooner the mess was cleared away the better. I was lightened by the thought the insurance would apparently put things back together again, but mainly that Connie wasn't going to swear out a warrant for my arrest for some form of sexual arson. I figured she likely knew the police chief as well as she knew the fire chief. One could imagine how that would work out.

One of the better showers of my life was interrupted by the naked likes of none other than Veronica Creighton. "Dude, we have to stop meeting like this," she said, slinking in underneath of me as I tried to open my eyes under a lather of shampoo. I nearly had a heart attack this time, but before I could account for the missed beats, she had dropped to her knees in front of me.

"Jesus, Veronica. I thought you just left."

"My parents and my brother just left to go play golf. I stayed behind and watched you and Connie. I figured out what was going on when I saw you walking down to the cabin. And when she walked into ours, I hid in a closet, waited until she got into the bathroom and walked out the front door. Do you need to know any more? I'm kinda busy here."

I honestly wasn't sure what she was doing.

"Can you... show me how? Teach me?" Her voice was soft and different. I rinsed the shampoo out of my hair and eyes and looked down at her. She was searching me with those big wide eyes while the water ran down her face. An honest, eager face, waiting for me. "Please? I really want to learn how to do it. All Billy wanted to do was fuck me until he came, which took about thirty seconds, then he zipped up and went back to the gas station."

In a very short time she proved a quick study, adapting her own very effective technique. She stopped for some reason, stared at it, then up at me. "Why do they call it a blow job when all I'm doing is sucking?"

"Oh you're doing more than that," I assured her. "You're about to find out why it's called that in about a minute or so." The teacher? The master? Heady stuff indeed. Truth be known, my learning curve was maybe just a short jog ahead of her. "Don't bite," I added. And *that* was the extent of my higher learning on the matter.

No dream got better than this. I was rigid and deliriously lost when I heard her start to gag. She coughed and spit and crawled right out of the shower stall and finished clearing her throat at the bathroom sink. "Oh my God!" she said. "I'm going to need to work on that." After a shudder ran down her body from shoulders to toes, she returned to the shower. "Can I have the soap?"

"So what else do you do in Altoona, Iowa?" I asked, moving a wash cloth over her back and shoulders.

"I live on a farm. Did you know that?"

"No."

"We farm two hundred acres of corn and soybeans, raise some beef cattle, pigs and chickens. It's the real deal."

"Wow."

"Yeah, dude, like you're impressed. Little white farm house, gravel roads that go forever. We live in the middle of fucking nowhere."

"Sounds like the heart of America to me."

"You watch too many Chevrolet commercials. It is quiet and nowhere in the middle of the day and quiet, black and nowhere at night. It sucks, dude."

"So how did you develop this... appetite of yours?"

She turned around and laughed at me. "Very funny. But, okay, check it out. I got off sitting on the clothes dryer when I was probably four. Just kidding." She worked the wash cloth over my back. "I was maybe twelve, thirteen."

"Asking you if you're serious seems like a waste of time."

"Visions of a big cock between my legs... it gave me chills. Then after I turned eighteen, I grabbed my high school chum Billy Dean and put my legs around him until I got him to do it. So then I'm thinking... this can't be a big cock. I'd seen the pictures. And, this couldn't be fucking. The dude was spazzing. Then, I met you."

"What?"

"Well, twenty minutes... in a shower. I liked what I saw but I needed some convincing. That's why I thought up the marathon thing."

"Veronica. It doesn't have to be a marathon to be good."

"Then show me that."

# CHAPTER 9

B y the time I was done drying her off, she had it all figured out. "We drive your car over, find some place to park, do it in the back seat, pick up the motor home, find some place to park it and break it in...."

I was not against the idea, and I did need somebody to take with to bring my car back. When she reassembled into her red outfit and stood there waiting for me, I knew this was a good idea, even at the risk of catching Connie's wrath. I told her all I had to wear were the same shorts. *All* I had, really, was the shorts. And, of course, this new found sexual prowess foisted on me by women to whom I would be eternally grateful. I truly had a sense all this was not remotely possible, that I would never be able to pull it off, even if it were. Along with it, an even stronger sense that whatever this was would vanish from my life momentarily and the real Thomas Cabot would reemerge somewhat enlightened yet happily reclusive and unapproached.

Therefore, enjoy the ride, Thomas Cabot, I said a bit too aloud.

"We'll stop in town and buy you some clothes, silly. Throw them on. Come on, let's go. I've been watching. Connie hasn't come out of our cabin yet."

"She's likely asleep on a couch. Poor thing."

"Better yet."

I started my Subaru and off we went, apparently missing Connie's watchful eye. "Just to set the stage, young lady, I have to be back to the Island Tap by three-thirty. Connie and I already decided we're not closing down."

As we drove through the woods and past other small resorts and motels, Veronica began to talk about what is was like growing up on a crop farm outside of Altoona, Iowa, raising a few pigs, cows and chickens. How, simple life seemed, and how, for the most part, you got used to the smell after awhile. Then, there was that night of graduation with her legs wrapped around Billy Dean.

"I swear, the moment he popped me, I began to think of my life differently. Everything I knew got really small and insignificant. Dude, it was like it didn't matter what it was; the unknown was what I wanted. I didn't want to feel small and familiar with stuff."

"What are you going to study at college?" I really wanted to tell her to stop using the word "dude". The imagery I had set up around her shook like an earthquake when she used the word. I had never picked up the habit, as it seemed to roll out of my mouth in an odd sounding way, as though I was embarrassed by using it just to use it, while others around me seemed dependent on it to describe everything that happened to them.

"I really haven't figured that out yet. See, that's the thing, dude. I want to do what I don't know. I want to learn, figure things out when I get there. And if all that turns out to be crap, I can still fuck my way along. I *do* know I have a lot to learn about fucking." She smiled over at me and touched my thigh.

"What in the world makes you think I would be a good teacher?"

"Dude. If I never had sex ever again, two times in the shower with you was enough to convince me."

Any words I came up with would either erode at the mythology or serve to change my lofty status. So I just smiled, for the time being, enjoying the ride.

"It should be fun for you, too. I mean, it seems like you're enjoying it so far," she said.

Again, smiling seemed the appropriate response. It was obvious to me she had not done any background checks on me and I was enjoying a sensational safe harbor.

"So, can we do, like, positions and stuff? I mean, I probably know all about everything but *doing* it is different." She giggled and moved her hand up my thigh. She knew *enough*.

"Sure. Why not." To give her the idea I was not as worldly and experienced as any 28-year-old male probably should be seemed unimportant to relate at the time. My own virginity came crashing down when I was nineteen, on the floor in the basement of the DeWitt house with their daughter, Stacy. I met Stacy at College and agreed to spend a Thanksgiving weekend with her at her parent's home in St. Louis. What I was stuck on remembering was being hot, bothered with getting the condom on, then letting her do most of the work out of necessity while I tried to hit some stride. In the midst of that I heard-

"Wrong hole."

I immediately rectify the situation, only to hear next-

"Can't you go any deeper?"

It was, probably as awful as Veronica's Billy Dean experience, but I do not remember having some epiphany telling me I could right the wrong by fucking my way through life. I made some mental crib notes about trying to keep my hips from trying to break my sex partner's ribs, and getting smoother on the initial thing and the importance of directional accuracy. Stacy DeWitt complained about a possible cracked rib until the day we broke up- some two weeks afterward. That saved me from having to buy her a Christmas present. In my mind, I had already picked out an Ace Bandage and a sixteen-inch dildo the circumference of a Coke can. Turned out Stacy had been around. A lot. And unless you had a horse dick, she was on to the next.

There was no series of women to follow in this story; only an occasional relationship that yielded some generally awkward sex. Sex in my twenties to this point could have been categorized by most as sporadic, uncomfortable, with lots of gagging, spitting and hating the smell of slimy latex. The best and worst could have been Jody Franco, a beautiful checkout girl at the Jewel Food Store who helped me pick up a broken bag of groceries one day. We dated a few times, and on our big night, we made outrageous love several times, but each time she would climax, she was loud, then farted. Bad smell farts, like wet, runny sulphur. Took the edge off of the relationship. I tried to ignore it, hiding my head under a pillow until the coast was clear, but the next week on another night, the same thing happened. Her only comment after was that it "was a good one". The break up was very hushed on my part. I just sort of crawled into a hole for six months and acted like I didn't exist until she probably thought I was dead. I got my groceries at Dominick's from that time on. I didn't even look for another Jewel store, thinking it possible she could be transferred without my getting notified.

"And we gotta hurry because I leave tomorrow."

"Tomorrow?"

"Saturday. Tomorrow is Saturday. You'll get some new blood in here. But today I own what you got." She grinned from ear to ear. "What *is* that on the radio?"

"Chicago. The band. It's a really old CD."

"Kinda weird. Doesn't seem to fit you."

"There's some other stuff in the glove box if you want to take a look."

"Nope. It's cool. Hey, this looks like a good spot, don't you think?"

Ahead off to our left was a little clearing in the trees and an edge of water visible through some scattered tall pines and white birches. I wasn't sure if it was me turning the steering wheel or her left hand all the way up my shorts that had me agreeing with her. The back seat of my Subaru flipped down and it turned out just wide enough for her to get her tiny, lithe body fully extended underneath of me. Everything worked wonderfully well. Except it suddenly dawned on me as I was doing my part that she was shaved as clean and smooth as warm silk. It was like reaching down in the dark to put my shoes on and finding only smooth cedar shoes trees. Odd thought at the moment. Why try to compare this to anything at all? No similes. No metaphors. Maybe I could just get used to it without trying to intellectualize it or compare it to anything. Leave it as it is, like all of this was- a *new* experience without precedent or the need for either historical significance or a page number. No history lessons. No homework. Just wild fucking. As if I was a machine that was designed to do one thing and one thing only.

At some moment in the midst of what would be the final grind for the time being, with me by then on my back, legs flexed, Veronica rocking away at a dizzy pace, I pictured Connie and the insurance man, wondering what was being said, if his head was nodding for *yes* or *no*. If he was summoning the local police or the FBI, if evidence was pointing to my room, and me. Would they, could they arrest somebody for an unintentional act like that? Would they reason the fire occurred only due to an intentional sex act, therefore…? None of it made sense. I snugged her hips tighter, going in the extra inch as she began squawking like a parrot. I checked her ID, honest. Twice, I think.

I wondered whose clothes Connie borrowed after her shower. Maybe she was blowing the insurance man. Maybe the cops were already there and she was blowing everybody.

Veronica and I wiped our brows in unison and climbed back into the front seat. I started the car without another word and in less than ten minutes we pulled into the Wal Mart parking lot just off Highway Six. They had a big sale going on Reebok apparel and Veronica insisted on picking me out a new, makeshift wardrobe. I fought and won the battle to add two pairs of pre-washed blue jeans and a few cotton t-shirts, but most everything I would be wearing in the near future would say *Reebok* on it.

"Don't buy underwear," she said. I want to remember you without underwear. You can never, ever wear underwear again, dude. I swear."

Veronica was growing on me by the minute in some strange, unexplainable way. There was something so unpretentious, spontaneous and natural to even the way she wiped at her nose when it dripped snot that made me smile and go along with just about anything this little woman would come up with. Actually, I couldn't wait to hear what came out of her mouth next. I was the one who was completely nuts, of course, and I was getting some excellent help in keeping that notion running unbridled in my head. When I watched her picking out the clothes, I was actually thinking about what it might be like if she invited me to the farm in Altoona for Thanksgiving dinner. I pictured that scene in *The Wedding Crashers* when the character played by Vince Vaughn gets jacked off under the dinner table by the deliriously nutty daughter. Moreover, her earnest facial expression while doing it. This would be my Veronica. All she had to do was ask. I would be there. We were two pieces of the same fruit cake.

We were third in line at the checkout and I had pulled out my Master Card. "We should get a few things for Connie," I said. We turned and went back to women's apparel. Veronica made quick work of a couple of velour jogging suits and some shorts and tops.

"I'm guessing at the size," She mumbled. "She's got a pretty big ass. And big boobs." She stopped and struck a pose to show me what she might look like if she had big boobs, pretending to waddle and fall over while trying to cradle them.

"You're terrible. The lady just lost her house!"

"Who's terrible? You're the one fucking her."

A quick thought hit me that if she already knew that somehow, or even if she was just guessing, the best thing to do was laugh it off. "Right." I laughed, or at least I should have looked like I was laughing. After all, whatever she knew wasn't slowing down our adventure any.

"You think I'm some dumb farm girl, dude?" she asked as we walked back to the check out.

"No. Actually, I think you are an amazing girl who happened to grow up on a farm."

"The things I did to pass the time until recently would scare the shit out of you. Trust me, dude."

"Like what?"

"Gang banging chickens, pigs, stuff like that...."

I nodded.

"I worked for a little bank in Altoona since I was fourteen."

"Fourteen?"

"Oh yeah. After school. Saturdays."

We got through the check out and back into the car.

"Anyway... for whatever reason, I think you're the one to share this with. Why is that, dude?"

"People say I have an honest face. My brother, Rondell, says I have the most honest face for a white man he has ever seen." She gave me the usual puzzled look. I hadn't meant to go there right then, but I was there. "My little brother is black. Okay? It's a long story. I'm more interested in yours right now."

"Whoa. That is awesome! How cool would that be?"

"I'm very cool with it, but he's got major issues. Trust me."

"No doubt. ....Anyway, so if I tell you this, you are sworn to secrecy as my first real lover."

I smiled, then bit my lip to keep from laughing when I saw the serious look on her face. I adjusted a bit too late.

"Fuck you, then."

"I'm sorry. I'm just happy you feel that comfortable around me. Just a little sudden is all."

"Well, what do you expect? Billy fucked me. You make love to me. That thing in the car you did… oh my God." She shuddered and poked me in the side. "How long until we get to the RV dealer?"

I tried not to get ahead of myself. She was so easy to please and so eager, I was enjoying the new edge of somebody else's coming out party. I was even jealous, in a way. Most of all, she was fascinating me and I was starting to not want it to end.

"So anyway, I'm going to tell you this, because I've got to tell somebody, dude."

"Okay, then. I'm here for you."

"I was at the bank about three months. I did all sorts of things, including taking care of the corner office of the president, getting his coffee, making sure he had fresh flowers every day, stuff like that."

"Fresh flowers?"

"Oh yeah. Carnations. He loved the smell of carnations. When I was there, I would run and buy three for him at the florist on the town square down the street."

"Okay."

"Yeah. Okay. So anyway, he started sort of going out of his way to *brush up* against me when nobody was looking. Long story short, within a year he was finding ways to get me in his office behind a closed door and jamming his nubby little fingers into my panties. I still wore them then. He would rub my pussy and start panting like a zoo animal at feeding time. It was, like, totally disgusting, dude. This little, fat, balding man with dandruff all over the shoulders of his suit coat dropping to his knees and shaking like a leaf. When he started to do himself, too, that was it for me." She gazed out the side window for a few moments. "I could have taken him down, you know. But I had a better idea…."

I looked over at her, not sure I wanted to know any more, but sure I was going to regardless.

"I now have, let's call it a cash trust fund- right in his own bank. When I saw how this moron reacted to a little touch of pussy, I learned something then that I still believe to this day- the world turns on an axis of pussy. Pussy rules. If you have the pussy, you rule."

So I am thinking about Sampson. History.

"He's still president of that bank, and I still stop in and pick up my little envelope on a regular basis. Truth is, dude, I will soon be a young wealthy woman unless he wants to cash in his chips. Five kids, twenty some years of marriage, I figure my odds are pretty good. I get nothing by becoming some martyr for the cause of all women. I'm just using my pussy for what it is- a pussy."

I was without a word. I started to say something, but the words crumbled and I acted like the driving was my focus. I nodded my head at her, but I am certain I was not able to disguise my amazement. She was how old when she came up with extortion?

"But now… you come along. Maybe it could have been somebody else, maybe not. Anyway, you are my first lover, Thomas. And you know my secret." Her left hand started again on my thigh and was soon in familiar territory.

"Here we are," I said. As I pulled into the small lot, I could see a shiny new, silver-gray Winnebago motor home at least fort-foot long awaiting us out front.

"Dude! If that's ours, it's got to have at least two beds!"

# CHAPTER 10

As I angled the Winnebago around the circle in front of the remains of the Mulroney house at Sunny Blue Resort, there were four people appearing to standing guard at the edge of the smoldering ruins, apparently awaiting my arrival. I told Veronica to keep my Subaru a mile back and I would call her on her cell phone when it looked like she could sneak my car back into its space on the back side of the property. Connie was the one with the face of stone, I assumed the insurance adjuster was the tall, thin guy in a yellow golf shirt, Garland Luersen, hands shoved deep into his bib overall pockets, looking as stiff and mean as always, and what might have been Rudy Mulroney himself, except for the clean shaven face and head to match, dressed in some flowing white smock over a pair of white jeans and white Nikes.

Through the darkened one-way windows, I could see their heads begin to turn to the sparkling new motor home as I brought it to a halt. I got out of the driver seat and took a quick walk back through to make sure Veronica and I didn't leave any obvious traces of our inside tour. Everything looked showroom except for an obvious mark on the back facing window above the bed there. The sun was coming through at just the right angle to show the perfect outline of a narrow footprint. I pulled out the tail of my Reebok shirt and wiped it down. Veronica had this interesting way of finding additional leverage wherever she could. At just the right moment, she had told me she was a floor routine gymnast in high school. She said she thought some of that training was coming in handy and I had immediately agreed.

I walked out of the motor home and found this group now ogling the new Mulroney temporary home. "Rudy?" I had to ask.

"It's a long story, Thomas. One which I will be more than happy to share with you later." Seeing Rudy smile on that hairless face and head was like watching some newly concocted bizarre character appear on *The Simpsons*. Even his voice was different, the deep canyon edge missing. His rounder eyes looked like they were wired into his bald skull for effect. But when he walked up to me and hugged me, I knew there was something more to this than a new wardrobe and hairdresser.

I got my look in at Connie while Rudy and the guy I guessed the insurance adjuster went inside the motor home to look around. I couldn't tell what she was thinking, but it looked like one part heartbreak, two parts anger and one part completely baffled. She was dressed in a printed tent dress she would never own, let alone wear, obviously borrowed from Mrs. Creighton's farm wife collection. A little make-up, hair tied back, solid dark red tennies with thick white laces, double-tied. She looked like a bad caricature of herself. Her eyes and head moved just slightly in the direction over her back where the Creighton Volvo was pulling in next to their cabin. Three got out of the car. My Subaru, driven by Veronica, followed right after, moving on to my parking spot on the other side of the property.

Connie turned back to me, a tight smile crossing her face. Then she gave me the finger.

Garland was probably watching all of this. He was making that weak baby seal noise. Connie gave him the finger, too, and stomped off down to the docks by herself.

I always felt uncomfortable around Garland. He just had a look, like he could or should have been in *The Texas Chainsaw Murders,* or possibly they may have based the story on his life. He walked away from me and pretended to be interested in fixing a broken pine tree bough. When he walked, his shoulders barely moved, his black construction boots seemed to glide underneath of him, hovering in the air just long enough to move that lanky frame along. But it was the angry eyes that seemed to spook even the birds. No matter what direction he was looking, those sunken orbs seemed to be looking at you, dark, deep pools hiding deep, dark secrets, pin pulled, grenade ready.

The air was pungent with soggy char and it looked like it might rain out the last of a Friday afternoon. Guests leaving Saturday morning expected more than that from their last day. I took a deep breath and waited to see what my Veronica would have to say. Fascinating little woman, that Veronica Creighton. I felt myself being drawn into the world she lived in. It felt like something beyond the insatiable sex drive. It was more like a comfort zone that I was starting to feel when she was around. I wanted to hear what she had to say next. I wanted to get another glimpse into what was going on in that crazy little mind of hers. That wasn't like me. I liked safe, predictable, missionary style women that would not threaten to expand my safe, straight line horizon. When she got within range, she threw the car keys at me. "Fucking busted, dude. They drove by me while I was parked in your car down the road. My mother doesn't miss much." She giggled and skipped her way off to the cabin. "Thanks for calling." She didn't bother looking back, or who was looking, but she gave me the finger as well.

I gave in to a moment of perspective- I had been hugged by a strange looking man and been flipped the bird twice by two women I had been intimate with, all within the same, oh, twelve foot circle, all within about ten minutes. Oh, and add in also, the murderous glare of the deaf mute I was getting the whole time. Priceless. But, less I get too caught up in such drivel; I needed to be at work in twenty minutes.

"Thanks for everything you did to help," a subdued Rudy said as he came out of the huge Winnebago.

"Yep," added the tall thin man. "Art Golden, Gopher State Mutual." I shook a hand that felt like bones and veins and seemed cold and clammy for the middle of the summer. Art looked a lot older up close, probably in his sixties, like maybe he played enough golf or spent enough time out of doors to get the tanned, wrinkled look of a youthful old person. A wide smile dwarfed his thin face. "No way to save these old frame homes once they get started." He handed me his business card. Art Golden, Vice President, Claims Adjuster, then a few sets of capitalized letter acronyms that I am sure were meant to assure those with a need to know that Art had game. Said so right there on his card.

"It seemed like it only took minutes," I said.

"You saved the cat," Rudy said. I wasn't sure his flat tone meant anything. Another look at him spiked a shudder down my spine. "Twinkles," he repeated.

"Connie says you were a real hero," Art said, raising his thick, wild eyebrows. Then to Rudy, "Rudy, you sure you're okay with the motor home here? We can put you up anywhere you like in town. That's part of the coverage."

"No. Thanks, Art. This will be fine, I'm sure. I need to be on the property, so this works out great. Leave it to Connie...."

I am sure Rudy was stunned and upset by all of this, but how he got back, how he looked and how he sounded- like he had been painfully neutered- just filled my strange-happenings cup to the top. "Art, nice to meet you. Rudy, I've got to get the Island Tap ready. I'll catch up with you later?"

"Indeed, my son."

Oh, *fuck* me.

By the time I got everything set and flipped on the neon beer signs, it was three minutes after four, the first time I had ever been late for a four o'clock door opening. It didn't matter there was no customers waiting; it was just something I always did. But then this was a summer of many firsts. Up until this year, my working summers at Sunny Blue were largely uneventful, save catching an occasional large bass or dealing with some drunk trying to pull the bras down off the ceiling. This history teacher's summers were just fine rowing around the bay at night, kicking pine cones around during the day, or just pouring Leinenkugal's for a few bucks and laughs. But my observer seemed to be telling me that this summer was to be different than the rest. Any remembrance of all the lean years of my sex life would be crushed. My natural reliance on the sense of time, place and proper behavior and accountability would be trashed. The tall and meek mannered Thomas Carlisle Cabot would come to loosen his grip on the small, safe world he lived in and jump head first into the unchartered waters of the unknown, propelled by forces he neither understood nor could alter. Knowing little if nothing or why, or wherefore, he moved to the pace of this new world with surprising pleasure and a feeling of grace, despite feeling he was being manipulated by those that can,... well, manipulate.

My observer was of few words, setting the example I followed. Who was I to question such astonishing collisions of fate and pleasure? I, in fact, had serious thoughts that I might be a budding male nymphomaniac. Not knowing the first thing of the symptoms or qualifications, at least I thought I might *want* to become a male nymphomaniac. There was an underlying current to all of that though that bubbled up the idea that I was likely just becoming another male with a piggish idea of sex.

The first customer walked in at four-sixteen. A young, bearded guy in a professionally tattered black t-shirt and baggy jean shorts. I carded him. He was twenty-one by two months. He looked like he was going to tell me he really needed a beer.

"Man, I needed that," he said, on cue, downing half of the ten-ounce frosted glass.

Earth to Thomas- unless Connie was just being snide about it, there would be no Maria to wait tables- on a Friday night. I was used to a very orderly, methodical thought process which could sort through everything and continually guide me through the insanities around me. Even on my worst day, my mental notebook rarely missed giving me timely reminders of what to do next, or what was coming next. Trash that. My brain was in overdrive. "Tough day at the office?" I asked.

"The world… is a chair of bowlies." He belched, finished the beer and ordered another.

My mental Kodak kept cranking out the snapshots of the romp in the Winnebago. Did it really happen that way? I had to ask myself after the pictures just kept rolling in. At one point, with Veronica braced at the little kitchen sink, me behind, she was whispering it felt like it was hitting the back of her throat, and in the next moment she was grabbing back for me to make sure it did. I didn't need much more encouragement than that. Then, when the shudder in her legs subsided, she yelled "Time!" and we moved on to the back bedroom, where she ultimately pulverized me before finally getting her feet up to the window to brace for another finale. We took a millisecond to catch a breath. Then, "Time"!

"Merciless vultures… I tell ya," he said. "How you doin?" he asked.

I stared at him for a moment, thankful he jolted me from my redux. "Well, let's see. I've had sex so many times in the last two days I've lost count, both of the number of times and with the number of women." I poured a short glass of beer for myself.

He looked at me sideways and his nostrils seemed to flare. "Awesome." He said. "I gotta get me one of these bartending gigs."

I smiled, and put Veronica aside, just for the moment, but there was apparently little that could disturb my preoccupation. Even with all that had gone down, there was an undeniable part of me climbing over the barbed wire, already thinking about when and where we would do it next. My world, as I knew it, was now colored with crimson and a craving I had never thought possible. I had to wonder if it was something wonderfully contagious I caught from Veronica, like the Altoona flu.

I think my customer was rattling off some nonsense about delivering office supplies to the Green Gables Conference Center up the road when Connie rolled in from the kitchen. She was wearing an orange silk oriental kimono, hair up and back, make-up perfect. She edged up to the side bar wait station, planted her elbows and settled her chin down onto her hands. She smiled.

"I'm your slave tonight, master," she said.

I wasn't particularly surprised to see her. The dress, yes. I had a few jokes to crack about how she got it, but I figured that could wait. How do you figure her mood at this point?

"I'm the hired help. Do with me as you will. You're pretty good at that. Very good, actually."

As awful as she looked only a little while ago, Connie looked both exotic and enthused by the idea of looking exotic. I don't know if she was on something or reeling in shock, or whatever, but she was a knockout. Her eyes had the sparkle and bounce that commanded a second look from any man. I have to admit to being such a slob that I completely shelved the Veronica idea for the moment. Impossible. Which fit me perfectly, it seemed.

I wanted to ask about Rudy, but I was guessing that could wait, too.

"Rudy's gone." She shifted moods without as much as a twitch.

"Gone? Again?"

"Gone. As in, his mind, gone. The old Rudy, gone, caput, fried. He's back on that Hare Krishna thing again. Turns out he wasn't down in

St. Paul. He was right down the road at the Green Gables Conference Center for a retreat. This time they got to him. Shaved his head, gave him the garb. Asshole finally turned his phone back on and got the message the house was burning down- this morning."

"So he's not really gone again?"

"Oh, hell no, I wish the hell he were. I wish the hell he was with the red head. Now I have to put up with this crap? Are you kidding me?"

"He's done this before?"

"Oh yeah. But he told me the first time. This time, he tried to hide it from me because he knew I wasn't buying any of that bullshit. He starts talking again about selling the bar... actually he talks about selling the bras and the idea... then shutting the bar and the resort down and turning it into a little retreat for these goofs."

"Selling the bras?"

"Rudy figures somebody could buy the bras, the idea of the Mulroney's, the name, the whole scheme and just move it out of here lock, stock and barrel. And here's the thing... Wally DeMere, DeMere's Lakeside Resort? He's supposedly already made an offer six months ago to bring it over to his place. He's got that little island thing going for him, too."

"Well, Jesus."

"And now... the house burns down... while he is gone... then he comes back having gone over the edge with the skin head thing and all that. Christ!"

I tapped another glass of Leinie's while Connie walked to the back bar and poured herself a Korbel brandy straight up. She took a couple of healthy swigs. She was close enough to me that my nose was picking up a familiar fragrance of raspberry dreamcicles. Absolutely *not* Connie. It *was* absolutely Veronica.

Connie hovered near me until she was sure I had enough to fill my lungs and short term memory bank. "Like my new perfume?" She asked. "Borrowed it," she said, not waiting for me answer. "The dress came from Lorraine Carlson. What a sweetheart she is."

I had nearly forgotten our only customer. I turned to see him staring up at the bras above his head. I poured him another one on the house.

"Connie. This is crazy. You don't need to be here, tonight. I can handle it. Really."

"And what else would I do, Thomas? Just what in the hell would I do?" She reached up and toyed with my earlobes. "Everybody worth fucking is either taken, or busy. And you might say an evening in front of the TV watching Rudy fall asleep on the couch is out as well. After the new guests get in tomorrow, I'll drive down to Minneapolis and buy a new wardrobe and try to get laid. Until then… you get to watch me slink around in this thing. Actually, it feels wonderful against my skin. What do you think?" She stood back with her brandy in hand and did a little spin, getting the attention of our exclusive patron as well. It was a little snug around her hips and her big boobs were forcing some of the material to puff out between the front running buttons. Overall, it was either an exotic thrill or Halloween, depending on your mind set.

Our customer finished up and left with a wave.

"Perfect," she said. She moved back to me and took my left hand in hers and moved it under the dress. "Should I buy panties or not, tomorrow? … That is the burning question. But for tonight… we are not going to have to worry about panty lines, are we?"

It was quite apparent to me Connie was not going to let the house fire and Rudy's mental departure take away what came natural to her. Forcing an issue, exerting control, making life respond to her. That was her style. As I played along, willing enough, three young guys came into the bar. Connie time was over. For now.

She let go of my hand and rustled up and away. "Surely you recognize the perfume, dear?" She asked. She was never coy about anything. I got the point before. Nonetheless, playing games with my sensory notions was a cruel joke. I would never confuse Connie with Veronica, or Maria, for that matter. As I saw it, part of the absolute power of women- other than the obvious- was there were never any two alike in any but the most subtle and irrelevant ways. Their relevance and uniqueness was in everything they said, everything they did, how they went about their intellectual and sensual business, and if, and how they cracked the sexual whip with the lesser men in their lives. And how they smelled. No two alike? No two alike. So Connie was really fucking with me. She was very good at fucking in general, but I suspected she was at least as good or better at fucking *with* people.

By the time I flipped the lights on and off for last call, the tally was as follows: Connie had grabbed my balls nine times, stuck my hand up her dress three times, and touched my earlobes more times than I could count. All this while we had a pretty good night. Two new bras up and a pretty good take. Good tip outs. All in all, if you included the stop watch blow job she gave me in the men's room right after I locked the doors, I would said I had a day.

"Hey hon," she said, cleaning up. "I would lift this dress right now but I don't want to press my luck with Rudy. He walks in, he could go psycho on us."

Why hadn't I thought about that? He could have been listening on the other side of the door, for all we knew. Throw one of those guns from his collection into the picture with his Billy White Shoes outfit and the Kojak hair-do, I saw nothing but blood spattered everywhere. Mine- just to *get* to hers.

"How about we see how it works out in the motor home later," she said.

"Right," I said. "Maybe Rudy can take some video before he kills us."

Connie ran out back through the kitchen and I proceeded to finish the closing and clean-up. A strange feeling came over me, and I didn't recognize it for a least a minute or two. It was called silence. Peace. Quiet. The absence of conversation, noise, clatter, commotion, confrontation, pretense or orgasmic activity. I was alone with myself. This had become my usual and preferred state of being and mind for many years. It had worked rather well in my book. I would not have believed it could be oddly disconcerting in any possible way. Yet here it was. Being alone, with me, had become quite a jumble of colliding thoughts with stabs and misses at reality. I laughed out loud after a bit. I had never, to the best of my knowledge, ever laughed while I was alone unless I was watching TV at the time. Some Saturday Night Live skit, most likely. Or Jerry Springer.

I don't know if the smile was yet off my face when I finally turned the key and closed the screen door behind me. It was raining like hell.

"I'm not sure we said good bye properly, " came a familiar voice from close by in the dark.

# CHAPTER 11

I guess walking pneumonia in the middle of the summer turned out to be some sort of blessing. It slowed me down to a crawl and brought my old reality back. Not that I minded a single bit the roll I was on, but it was pretty obvious I could not keep up the pace without the risk of serious injury or embarrassment. Having never been sick a day in my life as best I could recall, I attributed my sudden collapse to an acute change of the liquid chemistry inside my body. Too much outgo, too much stress on my immune system. That was it. Of course, it also gave me some down time to consider how much I was going to miss Veronica. A good-bye grope in a rainstorm seemed fitting in some ways, but I wasn't convinced I had seen the last of her.

As weird as things got and stayed with Rudy, it was a given to do everything possible I could to stay away from his wife, no matter how she doth protest. I was beginning to wonder if there was line she had crossed as well. In the worst of it, I lay there in the little middle bedroom on a square Winnebago idea of a bed, wheezing and coughing, considering life without a lap top, stuck with Connie's "saved" collection of Nora Roberts paperbacks.

Once Connie walked by in her white lace bra and high-hip riding panties. "Let me know if you need any help shoving a thermometer up your keister, hon." I thought that would be it, but instead, she looked around to make sure the coast was clear, then darted in and went directly under the covers for my balls. I recoiled like a napping rattle snake in the sun on a log. She got the point, but lingered a few moments, twanging my earlobes with her forefingers while her vibrating boobs held court in front of my nose. Temporarily mesmerized, I only became aware Twinkles had hopped onto the bed when he began knawing on my big toe through the blanket.

"Twinkles, knock it off!" Connie yelled, then turned and took her boob show with her.

As it was, the motor home was impossibly small for the three of us. Four, if you counted Twinkles. And you had to, the ungrateful little fucker. None of us were meant to be together.

By the time I was really feeling normal again it was the middle of August. The week my brother Rondell would be arriving with his new wife, Sara. He used to come with his first wife, Catherine (the Great) but they divorced two years before after a celebrated incident in which they got drunk and naked and chased each other around the yard with war surplus machetes. Rondell would love telling this story and coming to the punch line in which he would tell you just how much more he had to lose than she. They decided, actually quite amicably, that they were just not right for each other. They both drank like fish.

Rondell liked to come up to Sunny Blue because it was the perfect place to get away from what he normally did for a living- Rondell was *the* young, black attorney in an otherwise all white, all Jewish law firm of Derwitz and Schwartz, in downtown Chicago. A second team Big Ten All-Conference offensive tackle his senior year at Michigan; Rondell was just a year out of the University of Michigan law school. He made no apologies for his young cosmetic presence in the firm's cases that called for a proper loud, obnoxious black attorney in lieu of a proper loud, obnoxious Jewish attorney. He lived in a swanky, heavily mortgaged, forty-first floor condo on the Magnificent Mile with spectacular views in all directions, which he now shared with his new wife. I had met Sara just once; at the small wedding procedure in a well-known judge's chambers. That was in February- Valentine's Day. Rondell had said then, no matter what, he, or they would still be coming up this year.

"Tommy, Tommy, Tommmmmmeeee!" Rondell screamed as he entered the Island Tap with Sara on one arm and cradling what looked like a multi-colored parrot in the other arm. He ceremoniously walked up to the bar, set Sara on one stool, the, yes, it was a live parrot, on top of the bar, and stood between them. Then he ran around the bar and hugged me, picking me up like a sack of oranges with all the might of his six-four, two-hundred-forty-pound black hulkiness. He wasn't all black, of course. Our tiny mother's skin was so white you could see through it. Coach Johnson, Rondell's father, and subsequently my stepfather, as he liked to think, was almost charcoal. Rondell looked like the coach. The only thing that came through white on Rondell was around his big saucer brown and black eyes.

"We're late, but we're here," Rondell yelled in my ear as he set me back down. The quiet hush around the bar tried to revert back to pre-Rondell levels. "We got a late start getting out of the city and ran into some Goddam marathon thing going across Lake Shore Drive. Asinine plan." Rondell smelled of gin, which was no surprise. I guessed they had stopped for dinner along the way and he had his usual pair or three of Bombay martinis. In Rondell's world, any sitting of any type was an occasion for the martini. Short of that, finding himself in barbaric conditions in which there was no gin around, a beer, wine, anything would really do. I had made sure we had a case of Bombay on hand for the week ahead.

"And...," he led me by the shirt sleeve to the picture window that looked back across the circle drive at where the house used to be. "Looky there."

In the last of the day's light, I could see a massive red boat sitting on a trailer behind his white Ford Excursion.

"We be water skiing tomorrow, big bro. Just like the old days." The old days were the days of our teens, when Mom and Coach Johnson would bring us up to Sunny Blue and rent a ski boat and pull us around Blue Heron Lake until we couldn't stay upright any longer.

"So what's the story with the Mulroney house?" He asked.

"Burned down," I said. "I stay with them in that motor home over there next to your yacht. What's with the bird, Ronny?"

"Big, ain't it?"

"The bird?" I asked.

"The boat, moron."

"Ronny, everything about you has always been big. You even had big snot."

He grabbed my nose between his fingers and squeezed a little too hard. "You remember Sara?" She had quietly taken up a stool at the bar. We weren't that busy but those that were there had moved up an inch on their seats. It wasn't often in these parts of Minnesota you saw a large black man with a white woman walk into a lake resort saloon. Folks mostly thought that happened elsewhere. Like Mars.

"Of course." I leaned over and gave her a kiss on the cheek and got an air-kiss back. She was more oriental looking than I remembered. A bright, round, Polynesian face, dark black, shiny short hair and a great big perfect smile. "Good trip?" I asked.

She nodded, then looked up with Rondell hovering over her. "Six months today," he said, massaging her shoulders. Rondell was always into touching everything, or everybody. He was a *big* toucher. Few ever took exception, less they underestimate or misunderstand the menacing look that just came natural to him. The Rondell I knew was a big old pussycat who would have had a great career in the National Football League except for his rather immense soft side. He spent more time helping people up off the football field than he did knocking them down. His father, Coach Johnson would still look at his son, Rondell, and shake his head at the waste of talent. He would quietly mutter the term "wimp" when he didn't think anybody heard. I did. When, at age twenty-two, Rondell's first marriage of one year ended in divorce, with him citing mental and physical cruelty in the petition, both Rondell and I heard the term "pussy" being thrown his way by the coach more than once. Not in the good way.

"So, where's my damn drink!" Rondell yelled, vibrating some of the bras just barely above his head. "Is there a decent bartender anywhere when you need one?" All in all, there were lots of parts to Rondell, including some of our mother's quiet peculiarities, and many times, none of the parts seemed to go together.

I loved growing up with Rondell, despite the inevitable racist collisions we faced. It was almost comical watching them sweat. How could it have happened this way? Someone as meek as our Mom, Eloise Cabot (now Johnson), has an extramarital affair with a black high school coach, gets pregnant, then has the horseshoe-up-the-ass luck to have her then current husband, George Cabot, drop dead of a heart attack. She marries the Coach six months later. Two days before little Rondell was born. Tricky math for most.

The coach was a piece of work. He always seemed to give me a hall pass, afraid I would say something that would make things difficult. Send me walking off down the hall while he pictured ways he could legally torture me. He expected Rondell would be the *real deal* anyway, but when the high school teams Rondell played on that his Dad coached won but two games in four years, he began muttering things about Rondell behind his back, almost like instead *he* was the unwanted white kid in the family. Rondell fixed his nuts good by getting an academic scholarship to Michigan and then making the football team as a walk-on.

Neither Rondell nor I had much contact with the Johnson's these days. A couple of years back, Rondell and I got a few drinks into us while watching the Chicago Bears take another beating on a Sunday afternoon. After the game, we left the bar and while laughing through old stories, made a strategic decision to drive over and surprise the folks. We knew where the hidden key was and it was still there.

Giggling like school kids on a prank, we snuck in the back door, walked through the kitchen and into the living room where he we found our parents, doggy-style, a black penis up our mom's ass to the hilt. The grunting barely stopped long enough to acknowledge our presence. We were gone in a flash, but that Kodak moment was on paper that would last a lifetime.

George Cabot, by the way, did not entirely escape the wrangles of being considered an odd parent either. As he died when I was two, I knew nothing of George except through my mother. We did not take photographs in our family while I was growing up, for whatever reason, but she painted the picture to me of a kind man, on the short side, overweight, with a big warm face, smelled like cinnamon and had a great singing voice. He was very fond of putting together plastic model airplanes, World War I and II replicas mostly, and he was a great player at solitaire. She would get misty talking about watching him play solitaire while she gave him reflexology on his feet- which smelled like cinnamon, she said.

Growing up, Rondell could have cared less about who and why George Cabot was, but once he figured out that his own father was truly an asshole, he cut the George Cabot story some slack and said on more than one occasion that George was probably cool. Just a guy with a bad ticker that smelled like Cinnamon.

"Wrrrroocck Wrrrroocck!! Somebody's gonna get laid tonight. Wrrroocck!" went the parrot, finally. "Holy shit, look at the tits on that one! Wrroocck!"

"Cute bird, Ronny," I said. "And the reason being… ?"

"I'm watching him for my boss, smart ass. He's just warming up. I taught him a whole new vocabulary on the way up here. The bird loves me."

Three martini's later for Rondell, two vodka tonic's for Sara, a couple of beers for me; we were all taking turns telling stories, laughing- I even had Rondell and Sara helping me deliver drinks to tables. Connie was off to Minneapolis again to shop for a day. She had thanked me for the "quick boning" in the Ladies' Room earlier and said she hoped it would get her through the weekend because the last time she had gone to Minneapolis right after the fire she ended up with an older hunk who was having a bad reaction to his Cialis. He told her his erection felt like a hard, painful zit that wouldn't pop. Even Connie dried up with that one. She told him he could squeeze it all he wanted on his own time. She was out of there. Unless things looked more promising this time around, she would be back by midnight.

"So tell him," Rondell said to Sara, clearly amused and clearly getting martini-ized.

"Tell him what?" She asked.

"Your middle name. Tell him." Rondell shook his head. "He will love this."

"It's a made up name, Ronny," she said. "Stop it. Sometimes I don't believe you."

"Ain't nothing made up about 'Lovelace', baby," he said.

They both laughed and pushed at each other.

"Lovelace." I was afraid to make it sound like a question.

"Ok. Ok, already," Rondell said, giving into her flush. "Another story for another day. It's your job, babe. Nothing wrong with that."

I backed off pretending to see a customer in need. Sara resumed her evening seemingly happy to listen to Rondell and I go on and on about some of the best and worst things we remembered about growing up black and white brothers. We shared a bedroom until I was fourteen. Though I was often angered and saddened by the way people looked at us, and how at times Rondell was treated because he was the black one, our days growing up were remembered mostly in the ways we spent our time together; playing catch, wiffle ball, building forts, snow igloos and defending our ears and minds from the ultimately bizarre relationship that existed between our mother and the Coach. There was no physical violence that we knew of between them or towards us. Sometimes they barely spoke a word to each other over dinner and the early evenings. But later, and sometimes in the very middle of the night, we could hear our mother wailing and we could hear the Coach grunting like a wild hog, which, at first, scared the living be-jesus out of us. Rondell and I flipped a coin. I lost. I would be the one to ask mom in the morning about the noises we heard.

"We were praying, honey," she finally said. "And when you hear noises in the middle of the night, it is God's way of answering prayers."

I left it at that. I was pretty sure what was going on, but when I tried to explain it to Rondell....

"I think they have sex a lot," I told him.

"People make noise like that when they have sex? You think it hurts that much? I don't want him hurting momma."

"No, Rondell. They make noise because... because they are happy."

"How can that be?"

"You have to trust me on that one for a couple of years."

"Gross," Rondell said.

I nodded in agreement.

"Thomas?"

"Yes?"

"Our parents are weird, aren't they."

"No, Rondell. They're just people that get really happy in the middle of the night."

"What a crock of shit."

Though our souls would forever be close, we didn't spend as much time together as we would have liked. To say we lived in the same town was to say we lived on the same planet. Chicago was a big place with a lot of lives colliding and a lot of living going by like speeding trains going opposite directions on parallel tracks. When we caught up to one another by cell phone, email or a quick lunch at the Weber Grill, we tried to slow down long enough to remember, but it was usually a conversation that quickly paced itself within the framework of the world around us and what we were doing to keep up with the insanity.

On a gorgeous spring day in late May we decided we would each pick up a bag of lunch somewhere and meet at the courtyard outside the Chicago Tribune Towers on Michigan Avenue to catch up. I had not seen him since his Valentine's Day wedding day.

We chatted about a few things and I was digging into my Subway club sandwich when this young tall guy in a grey pin-striped suit began pacing a few feet away from the bench where we had set up lunch. Within minutes, like the scene in the movie *The Birds,* it seemed people were pacing everywhere, glowing blue dots in their ears, talking as loudly as possible, oblivious to others talking as loudly as possible. I was just sort of chewing and looking at Rondell when I heard one slam the cover of his cell phone down, shove it in his pocket and proclaim "what you kill, you eat." And walk away.

"People arguing with the air they breathe," I observed.

"Satanic," Rondell said, chewing.

It was almost eleven-thirty when Hunter and Boris walked in. I had seen them arrive earlier in the day in their black Infiniti SUV pulling a Nitro Bass Boat with a ruby red metal flake paint job that was catching every ray of sun in the sky. You would have never known they drove all the way from Indiana. There wasn't a speck of dirt anywhere. The likely truth was a quick stop at the Wee Wash down the highway before they got in.

"We meet again," Boris said with the unmistakable deep bravado I recalled from previous years. He stepped up and over the bar far enough to give me a big smooch on the cheek. He still smelled like freshly applied Polo cologne, which still produced a gag reflex in me. I made some vague reference to my walking pneumonia which ended up working to my advantage the entire week. The closest he came to me was a wave for another drink from a distance well back from the bar.

"Good to see you guys again," I said. Hunter was always within a few feet of Boris so it was easy to address them as a pair- which they *were.*

My brother Rondell remembered them as well since they came up at the same time he was at Sunny Blue the year before. "I'll be damned!" Rondell walked up and gave then each his own brand of a hug- *relax*, go with it, or risk a cracked rib. "Honey," he called to Sara, "Come on over here and meet the best gay bass fishermen in all of North America." He said it a bit too loud, but Boris and Hunter were good hearted laughers and very much in love, and very proud of their success as national tournament bass fishing partners. There was no such tournament scheduled on tiny Blue Heron Lake, but they loved to come up to this secluded spot a couple times a year to try out new gear, and, just well, you know....

Sara reacted the way most beautiful women do when they are around gay men, like a long lost favorite sister.

The drinks poured and the Mulroney's till filled massively. I tried last call three times, but Rondell claimed he would cover the legal fees for staying open until dawn. Nearly ever person in the place was game, and drunk. I was pretty loose as well, but babbled to myself I was just some kind of enabling parent. My tip jar was jammed with cash and the bottom of the cash drawer was so full of twenties and fifties the drawer would barely close.

"Ronny, we have all week," Boris said. Boris and Hunter were easily the class of this lot, their thin, loose fitting fabrics still looking freshly pressed and shiny. "Hunter and I have fish to catch in a few hours. We have work to do."

"What'd you guys clear last year?" Ronny asked, dipping at one more martini.

"A half million, give or take," Boris answered without hesitation or pretense.

"Asshole... catching fucking fish?" Rondell winced, and just as he was about to give a position paper on that, he turned to the rising cheer from the left over crowd and watched Sara remove the last bra strap from underneath her blouse. She was swiftly offered a chair. Up she went, and waited patiently until I could get a nail up there for her.

Another cheer went up as she presented herself. My shit-faced brother Rondell shrugged off the guy who was holding Sara up on the chair.

"Wrooockkkk Wrooooockkkk! Fuck her, I did! Wroooockk!"

The bird crapped on the bar and, as if on cue, Rondell turned his head and with a roar, sent his puke running and splashing down the bar top, complete with olive pimentos.

Wow, I was thinking. Orientals really *do* have big nipples.

# CHAPTER 12

If there were a person that ever lived that snored louder than Rudy Mulroney, my guess is he or she was unceremoniously shot at dawn in some town square. As I lay there in my square bed, freshly showered and feeling my heart beat along, Rudy would inhale, and it was as if each fastener in the aluminum siding rattled in the midst of a category five hurricane. He would subside, I would drift off, then he would come back with a vengeance, as though we were in a two-man pup tent and he had turned my way. Sometimes he would seem to stop abruptly in the middle of it, maybe scaring himself shitless, then he would start again, louder, uneven snorts and gags and wet moaning cackles that made me nauseous. It was like listening to a vacuum cleaner with a bad motor collect snot.

There was another sound I knew well. The little swish and vacuum of silence created when my sliding door opened and shut. I waited.

"You know what, Thomas?" I could see a shadow lean into my narrow doorway. "I'll bet there is more history in those damn bras out there in the bar than in any history class you've ever taught."

"No doubt."

"My God Almighty. Will you listen to that?"

"Been."

"I gotta pee. Jesus."

There was a flush, a rustle, rapid footsteps, and then a very warm naked body along side mine under the covers. As had become our routine, when Rudy was in mode, it was an easy shot.

"No luck in the Twin Cities, huh?"

"God, no. They all looked so old to me. Gray, pasty goofs with bad breath and tiny dicks." She nuzzled into me. Unusual. It had been almost two minutes and her hands hadn't pulled on something. I believe she actually wanted to cuddle, if that was possible.

"So how old do I have to be to fit into that category?"

"Age is overrated. Dick is underrated." Apparently, she could cuddle and pull, or maybe she was just making her point.

"Ah."

"Let's talk about dick," Connie continued, "Men think with their dick. Women love dick, real or otherwise. I mean, if its not real, it at least has to look and feel like dick. So it's dick. Everything revolves around dick. So, you know what that means?"

"Can't imagine."

"Oh sure you can. It means pussy rules the world, Thomas. Here. Feel."

I was along for the ride.

"See. Wet, right? Now... look, in exact proportion... you're hard as rock. Gee, what a surprise."

"Got me there."

"Got you? Are you kidding?" She wheeled up and got on top of me, guiding me inside her with precision. The spreading wet heat was so intense I could feel it down through the small of my back. She made a slight move forward and down, then spread her knees apart and sat still, with me in as deep as deep could be. "I could just sit here and rule the world, you know that?"

"I believe it."

"Really believe it?"

"*Really*. Really, really. Take me to your kingdom." I cupped her breasts while she arched her back. We both seemed to take a moment to make sure Rudy was still cranking, then began.

I don't know what is was about that night. I couldn't tell you how many times Connie and I had sex up until that point, but we hit something together that night that had us gasping for breath and unable to old each other tight enough as she collapsed on top of my wildly arching hips. It could have been minutes, it could have been an hour. I was lost in her. Every touch, every lick of my ear, each time she moaned. I could feel her convulse around me almost from beginning to end. I wasn't sure who was getting the better end of this, but neither of us seemed to be keeping score.

She got her breath and played with my earlobes. "See?"

"That... was world peace." Then I had another thought. "Where's the damn dog?"

"Locked in the bathroom with a chewy toy about as big as he is. Don't be mean. You saved his life which means you two will always have a special bond."

"More like a special nightmare."

"Meany."

"I never got a dog growing up. I had a gerbil and it died after three days. My mother said she couldn't take it. So that was that."

Rudy was snoring up a storm.

We did a complete barrel roll without losing suction. I noted there was no apparent hurry. Connie seemed to really enjoy hard, quick sex. Lots of it. This time I tried to slow the pace with slow, even strokes.

"What the hell are you doing?" she asked.

I thought it out quickly. "I'm fucking you."

"Bullshit. You're trying to make love to me. Come on, kick it in."

She might have been right. Sometimes you had to decipher her tone or body language- her *Wikepedia* eyes- but Connie was usually right. If I was trying to figure out the *making love* aspect to all of this, those ideas were quickly dashed as I tried to catch up with her rhythm. When she tapped my chest a few times I knew I had caught up. She gave the all-clear and we made a final lunge at each other. I felt whatever I had left make a valiant effort for elevation, but I suspect it was but a final drip.

She lay quietly on my chest for the moment, then began. "Men, Thomas, like to fuck. Even the smoothie slick-hairs, those pretty things they throw up on the movie screen with the deep macho whispering routine and romantic cover? What a crock! Put a dozen in the room, not a single one is going to look across the room at me and say 'boy, I would really like to make love to that vivacious woman. To the man, in his soul, he says, 'I'd fuck that tramp in a heartbeat'. Sooner and quicker, the better. So you know what I do? I fuck them back- but just the ones I want to fuck. So who has the power?"

"Connie... you are... an amazing woman. Thank you for being in my life." I leaned over and kissed her cheek. She eased out from beneath me without another word.

"I'd go again but we better not press our luck, big boy," she said, pulling on her night gown.

"Agreed."

"Who's tighter, by the way?"

I said to myself- *trick question*- and let the air suck up my answer. She was about to elaborate, I was afraid, when she put a hand to my chest and we held still, listening to the silence. Rudy had stopped snoring. Somebody pulled the plug on the snot collector.

She back away easily and disappeared into the little bathroom around the corner. I heard one yelp out of the dog and I am sure she gave him a look that would drop him dead in his tracks.

I looked at my watch. Almost four a.m.. Hunter and Boris would be getting up soon, making coffee in the copper espresso machine they brought with them, and whatever. I had nothing but good things to say about the gay people I had met in my life, except a few of the bikers when they got out of control. Engaging, positive people in most respects that usually brought energy and class to any situation. But the visuals always bothered me. It wasn't a matter of being right or wrong with me, it was pictures I had to deal with, and those pictures didn't go in any album I owned.

"Jesus. God! Thomas, come quick!" I heard Connie yell.

I fell out of bed, my feet tangled in the blanket, regained my footing and dashed in the direction of the voice.

"He's not breathing! Call 911!"

"Not breathing?" I ran back to get my cell phone. I placed the call and ran back into the back bedroom where Connie was all arms and legs over Rudy's motionless body. She had flipped on the lights and I could see his lips were blue and his face ash gray with large dark circles around his red-rimmed empty eyes. His mouth was wide open and rigid.

"Move!" I yelled and firmly pushed her aside. I know CPR." I began to work on him, pushing on his chest and breathing into his mouth with all I could remember from the class I had picked up at the junior college a few years back.

"My God, my God, my God," Connie gasped frantically. "Not like this. Please, Lord."

Some things you just do without thinking, other things you think and never do. I was just doing. I looked down at his empty eyes, fixed, pupils dilated. His skin was cool and stiff. When the paramedics arrived, they flew into action with the paddles and tried nitro, adrenalin, everything they had. In the end, they simply looked over at Connie. "Very sorry, ma'm. He's gone."

Connie didn't say anything. She covered her mouth with her hands and stared ahead, then dropped both arms to her sides.

Outside in the dim intermittent light from the red flashers, a full audience had assembled to put a punctuation mark on the first night of their summer vacation. The ambulance drove off with Connie and Rudy in the back.

Back inside, avoiding them all, including my brother Rondell and Sara, I peeked back out through a small window and watched them all quietly disperse as the ambulance took off silently. My head was a kaleidoscope being hand turned in one of those optical twist-and-turn scopes at Sharper Image. Each quarter turn brought an entirely different combination of colors, angular cuts and reflections. I could hear myself breathing, my heart beating in the deafening quiet. I sucked in air through my nose and smelled what I thought was the damp crimson rot of death. I paced the small walking space through the kitchen, then tried to sit at the kitchen table, holding my head with both hands, trying to push the kaleidoscope out through my ears.

My observer jumped down off the microwave shelf and sat next to me for a few moments, watching me on the edge of losing it, coming back, losing it again, then somehow getting a grip as the colors began to slowly fade.

Get in the car, drive to the hospital. Connie will need a ride back.

"Thanks," I said aloud. I got up and got dressed.

As I walked to my car, it was dark, but there was enough moonlight to see somebody was waiting there, angled up against the driver's side door. As I got closer, the figure stood straight and still, giving me just enough room to open the door. I heard the baby seal sound, but this time it had a growling end to it as Garland Luhrsen stumbled back and away from the car.

I waved at him, opened the car door and got in.

The hospital was forty minutes away. When I got there, Connie was sitting on a bench near the front entrance beneath a mercury light, with the arm of Wahoo Fortnight cradling her tight. He sure did get around when it came to Connie.

As I walked up to them, I felt his eyes on me, as if he knew everything there was to know. But, then, what was there to know? It could have been him fucking Rudy's wife while Rudy died less than half a Winnebago away. He was grateful it was me. I could see it in his eyes. Nodding. Very pleased. besides, this was not the CIA, this was a frigging Fire Chief.

"You remember Thomas?" Connie's eyes were rose red and puffy. She clutched a man's white handkerchief in one of her hands.

"Of course," Wahoo said. "You saved Twinkles in the fire," he said a little too ironically.

I nodded. My fifteen minutes of fame at the hands of a butt licking Chihuahua.

"Too bad you couldn't save Rudy."

"He tried," Connie said. She was completely on empty, her face sunken onto her chin, her distinctive beauty lost in sudden age and gravity.

"I tried. I... what happened to him?"

"Doc Albright thinks he might have died of a heart attack, maybe brought on by sleep apnea, of all things." Wahoo explained. "You know. Rare. But, you just stop breathing in the middle of a snore. Wham! Just like that. Evidently, the shock to his system shut him down. He pooped."

"He what?"

"Pooped. Shit his pants. Sorry, Connie. His whole system gave way internally. They'll do an autopsy to make sure somebody didn't kill him."

I waited for the sarcastic smile that should have come with that, but it didn't.

I nodded, turned, and took a walk inside the hospital lobby. I found the men's room just in time. I spun the scenario. Fire Chief knew the

Police Chief- both boning Connie. Special arson investigator knew the police chief. Special arson investigator gets to know Connie. Bones Connie. I get accused of arson and murder. I go to jail for life. They all bone Connie. Connie's happy. God, the world I was living in was bringing me a mental process that produced delusions in real time. I didn't have to wait for the nightmares. But then this was preposterous. There was no arson investigator that I knew about, but it seemed there might be many things swirling around that I didn't understand.

It seemed perfectly harmless to be rolling with my own little sexual revolution, albeit, a little later in life than most I would guess, but things were getting complicated. At least in my mind. While I was at it, I could try to visually conceive of just letting these things roll together as the lives of others. I was the bystander, and yes, a willing sexual participant when asked or allowed, but nonetheless just a bystander to all of this. Within two weeks I would be back in my little apartment in Lincoln Park, looking at a new lap top, listening to the L-Train rattle by, enjoying perhaps a Starbucks and a low-fat blueberry muffin. So I saved the fucking dog. So what? I was still a bystander. And, a question for my observer. How *many* guys were actually boning Connie Mulroney at the time of Rudy Mulroney's death?

# CHAPTER 13

I was sure Rudy's death was destined to hang in the air at the Sunny Blue and Mulroney's Island Tap for quite some time. Maybe forever. It wasn't so much that Rudy had put a personal stamp on everything as much as it was how people coming to a place like this hated change of any kind. Some returning resort guests may have thought of nothing else for fifty-one weeks of the year. During that time they had the place pictured and pegged down to the garbage cans and they looked forward to things just being the way they were supposed to be. The bar patrons came to a place like Mulroney's in large part because it was everything it was supposed to be, right down to the last and oldest yellowing white bra hanging from a rusting nail.

Connie had insisted on keeping everything going. No official mourning period, no canceling schedules and people's vacations. She wanted hustle bustle, happy returning guests, slightly over-served bar patrons and a few bras on the ceiling. She pushed Garland around where she needed him and she had me keeping things under control in the bar. There were probably decent caring folks who thought Connie was keeping herself busy and keeping the place open because Rudy would have wanted it that way. The truth of it was she did it because Connie wanted it that way. I could follow that.

Nights during the week in August got quiet. I didn't need a server to help me out, to say the least. To think in another couple of weeks I would be back in the classroom teaching would usually start entering my mind about this time and find a comfortable acceptance and growing eagerness. But not this year. My mind scrambled for room, begged for space, overwhelmed with a recent snap shot of one thrust after another. And loving it. Save a house fire and a death, who in their right mind would want this to end? My thought process waged war with my old logic system and the inevitability of going back to being who I was before this summer. What would that be like? Jesus.

That attractive tall glass of water was approaching the bar for the third time. She apparently spent most of her time outside, returning only when her long neck Miller Light needed replacing.

"Nice out?" I asked

She leaned sideways into the bar and watched the four male companions she walked in with hours before assisting a portly young girl with a definite four-snapper to the ceiling to hang her ware. When she let that last snap go, her white t-shirt looked liked it was shielding illegal squirrel fighting.

"You have *got* to be joking," she said as she shook her head in disbelief. "I want to blame the species, but she looks like she is having more fun than anybody else."

I leaned over. "You just have the wrong species. Women with big breasts are a species of their own. They know *exactly* what they are doing."

She looked down the flat run of a shimmering emerald green blouse she wore and gave me a killer look.

She continued to watch as the boys eased the girl back down, taking their sweet time, and cheering her on as those t-shirt covered orbs continued to enjoy their freedom. They motioned for drinks all around and I was happy to oblige. That was the idea. And, if I was counting, that was the fourth bra of the summer for that girl. As far as I knew, there were no house rules forbidding multiple hangings. Neither did I recall ever seeing her buy her own drink. Once again, bad skin and a decent jelly roll of a waist notwithstanding, she was the most beautiful woman in the world. And there wasn't a guy around her to the man that didn't think he was going to end up porking her before the night was over. The news I had for them would not be good for business.

"Thanks," the tall one said as I set another Miller Light in front of her.

"You know, I'd have to apologize for too many of us...," I added, then moved on to fill out their next round.

As I was ringing up on the register on the back bar, I could see her reflection in the wall mirror, head in hands, looking for something to look at or do until the boys were done being boys. I figured there was something about being out here in the woods, in the summer, beers, women and bras that got everybody a little goofy. I wasn't immune to it, either. Whenever a "hanging" as we called it occurred, I got a little extra step in my shuffle, a little more animated in my serve, and I am sure I had a smile on my face very time.

"All in good fun," I said to her over wiping down the bar. I insisted on a clean bar.

She looked up at me and smiled, just a little. "Silly me. I didn't wear a bra tonight," she said.

I shrugged over the noise and laughter. Odd moment.

"Too bad nobody can tell," she added. Her smile broadened and she shook her head. She had a point. She looked every bit out of place but somehow like she could use being out of place to take some of that furrowed brow off her otherwise attractive face. Big, dark brown eyes, full lips, and dark brown hair that was cropped short, but fit her features and curved around perfect ears with studded pink stone earrings.

"I have no follow for that," I offered, setting up my hands against the bar across from her. "Thomas Cabot." I coaxed another smile from her.

"Mattie." She offered her hand. Firm handshake, business like, but a notably softer hand. "I knew there must have been a reason these guys would drag me out into the middle of nowhere for a beer," she said.

"Hey, you can't go wrong with forty years of bras, can you?"

"I'd really like to get off the bra subject but it does beg the question how something so neanderthal like this got started."

"You definitely would prefer the short version versus the ones that get told around here after a dozen beers."

"No doubt. Let's hear it."

"As the most common legend goes," I began, "the current owner's father, who shall remain nameless, came into the bar to clean up one morning after a big Saturday night. He was all hung over and blurry-eyed but he spotted a bra lying on top of the pool table. His mind racing to remember and I guess he did, when he hears his wife coming down the walk. No time on the clock, he picks the bra up and throws it, not knowing where it landed as she walks into the bar. She spots it right off, hanging over that stuffed eight-pound walleye mounted on that wall over there. She looks at him, he shrugs, she proceeds to unsnap her bra and hangs it over that stuffed fifteen-pound Northern Pike mounted over there on the other wall. Then she walks out on him and that's the end of that. She moves to San Francisco. He hangs both bras up on nails off the ceiling in memory of that fateful day and it kind of took on a life of its own after that. Then, sometime after that, I suppose when felt pens started to pop up, signing got to be optional."

"Fascinating." Mattie took a decent swig of her beer.

"There are other versions...."

"I am sure. Male obsession with female underwear. Explain that."

"Can't. But... actually, I think it's the breasts, not the bras." I nodded as the chubby one seemed to get my cue to stand up and give them another colossal waggle.

"Oh my God." She shook her head and eyed me like I was whale shit.

" What the hell *are* you doing in here?" I asked.

"Short version?"

"Whichever one is better."

"Okay. I am giving an investment strategy seminar at the Green Gables Conference Center near here."

"You said *giving,* right?"

"Right. Good bartenders are good listeners."

"I have other qualities."

"Like?"

Not the new ones, jerk, I told myself. Don't go there. "Night fishing."

"Fishing or fishing stories? Any underwear involved?"

I put up my hands to show her I was clean.

"Actually, " she said, "you can believe *I am* quite the fisherman. Bait my own hooks...."

"You don't say." I marveled a little too much. "Let me get these people over here another beer and I'll be right back."

"And… I am rather adept at fly fishing. I landed a four-pound rainbow trout during a trip to Idaho last year on a yellow tailed spring fly. In hip waders… how does that grab you?" Her face seemed to move easy over words, showing little change whether she was trying to make a point or not. Her dark eyes floated and sparkled above it all, a slight smile on her supple lips leaving the truth hanging in the air for speculation. She wore little make up, appearing to need even less. Her skin was clear and kept from the sun for the most part, with just a hint of even color to let you know she was healthy, young, maybe thirty going on twenty-five, and a tall, slender glass of water that drank her beer out of the bottle.

I hurriedly took care of the customers in need. One of the guys who came with Mattie appeared to have been over-served somewhere else before he got to Mulroney's. He was bent over from the waist, pushing up against the bar for support, trying to mouth a Cheryl Crow song coming out of the jukebox and staring without shame at the nipples au jour.

"Have you ever tried popping for bass in the moonlight?" I asked, anticipating the answer.

She considered her response, twirling a swizzle stick she had grabbed from my station mat. "Pretty good line. Some points for originality, anyway."

"No, no… That's my *other* quality thing. When the moon is at least a quarter, I get out and kill them after midnight. They hit for just about an hour usually."

"So where I come from, this is a move."

"Ok dammit, call it a move. Whatever. I'm trying to tell you how I fly fish. I use a fly rod, floating flies we call poppers around here, and we run a small boat into the weeds and stumps when the water is still and the moon light gives just enough glint on the surface to see a bass splash for the bait. Not much of a line, is it?"

She shrugged, but seemed more interested.

"It's a beautiful thing. Nobody else around, quiet, then you hear this tight break of water and if you pull back just right you got him.

Big ones hang around the stumps and they aren't as spooked as during the day. You should try it sometime."

"Like tonight?"

I shrugged, but my smile was a dead give away.

"Let's see," she said, joining in the smile. "Mattie comes out to a place in the middle of God knows where and jumps into a boat in the middle of the night with a perfect stranger. Sounds a little goofy to me. You think?"

I shrugged. "You know I never considered myself a perfect stranger. Strange, maybe, and flawed, certainly. Not perfect in any way, really."

"Killed anybody lately?"

"Lover, not a fighter," I said as uncomfortably as I knew how. What kind of shit comment was that?

# CHAPTER 14

If it gets to be after midnight, and all they are doing is ogling as opposed to drinking, I yell out "last call" and usually get the place cleared, spiffed and locked up by a little after twelve-thirty. Mattie was right. I think the chubby braless starlet seemed to be having more fun than anybody else, which was usually the case, but it was largely at the expense of a few men putting on a display of one of the more pronounced defective genes in the species. In the end, she would go her way with her girlfriends while each of the men would go home once again unable to taste the forbidden fruit they thought surely in their grasp earlier.

Flashlight in hand, I led the way down a familiar path, being so bold as to hold her hand with the other, strictly for security purposes. I could walk this in the dark, but didn't think there was any need to show off or risk her breaking an ankle before we even got to the boat. I took notice and acknowledged my gratitude to the star-splashed sky and full moon for being in the perfect entertaining mood on this night.

"I gotta be nuts," Mattie muttered mostly to herself.

"Not much further," I assured her.

"Let's see, Mattie," she continued, "you let your big safe body guards go and take off in the pitch dark to go fishing with a goof ball in the middle of the night... alone... probably a serial killer... chop me up into little pieces and use me as bait... ."

"That's an idea… ," I countered. I stopped walking for a moment, dropped her hand and put the flash light under my chin shining up into my nostrils and eye sockets. I tried a little blood thirsty Monster Mash laugh.

"I carry mace… ," she said, reaching into her purse and proving it.

I changed my laugh to something less menacing and gently grabbed her hand again. "Something tells me with you the mace would be the last thing I would need to be concerned about."

"What does that mean?"

"Well, you might just have the most beautiful eyes I have ever seen, and I would bet you don't get those without also getting really good at devouring your prey when necessary. Like unwelcome advances from creepy men."

"Right, bucko. And the book is still open on you, just remember that."

I cautiously led her down the embankment to the dock. "Here we are… ." My treasured little secret wooden row boat was tied up, fly rod and tackle box tucked inside, just waiting for me, and maybe a guest.

"Not exactly the QE2," she deadpanned.

"Hey for somebody who has fished in *hip waders* before, this is pretty plush. Actually, this is as good as it gets. Flat bottom wooden row boats make virtually no noise in the water, particularly calm water like tonight, and even if you hit a stump, which we likely will, no vibrations under water like aluminum or fiberglass. Other than being tipped over on shore for the winter, and an occasional coat of marine paint, this little guy has been in the water of this bay every summer for probably fifty years."

As I helped her in and the flash light panned around, she could get a feel of how small we were and how big everything around us seemed to be in the darkness. "Small… no motor?"

"None needed. Just the oars." I urged her down into the front bench seat and took my place on the middle seat and grabbed the oars. "We're only going a short distance in the bay here."

I could almost feel her apprehension. "I was thinking you looked like somebody… maybe that actor, Matt Dillon? No, that's not it. Somebody…. somebody when they were younger."

I couldn't remember anybody ever saying I looked or reminded them of anybody else famous or otherwise. Of course, if they saw me with my brother Rondell, or my stepfather, Coach Johnson. Enough said. I had just started rowing and stopped. "Stop thinking and listen. Just listen."

As she held still and silent, a fish broke the surface close by. Then another. Then a lunker splash that caused her to jump slightly welcomed us to the midnight feeding world of the mighty largemouth bass. She was on alert now, head up, shoulders square, quietly listening to the symphony, like muffled gun shots, almost one after the other. "Wow...," her voice rolling back to a whisper. She caught on quick.

"So," I whispered back. "Even if I were to cut you into little pieces for bait, my guess is the big ones prefer the looks of the bass popper. So relax, and enjoy this, Mattie. It's a special time and place not that many people know about."

She was simply silent for what seemed like at least a minute. "Okay," she finally said, peacefully.

"We're heading out and around that point out there and back into some stumps and lily pads, just at the edge of where the duckweed gets too thick to hear or see anything. They'll be there."

"What's that smell?' She asked, not sure if she liked it or not.

I took a deep breath and considered it. Clean, crisp, no doubt, but the slightly bitter tinge of the duck weed probably got her attention. "Minnesota," I replied.

She might have been nodding. At least she had stopped bristling. The way she talked implied some edge and confidence, but more than that, I couldn't really get away from the idea she actually had the guts to get into the boat with me. Hell, I wouldn't have gone out with me.

Once we were around the point and headed back into the stumps, any breeze was blocked by the pine trees on shore and the boat coasted to a full stop as I tucked the oars back along the inside of the boat. I pulled out my old Shakespeare fiberglass fly rod, unhooked the yellow and black bass popper in the eyelet, stood up and began stripping some floating line. "I'll give this a go a few times to give you the idea...," I said, making like Zorro and getting the rod into a ten o-clock two-o-clock rhythm. I made four swirls back and forth and then sent the line screaming out into the dark in the general direction of the tree stumps.

"How can you see what you are doing?" She asked, noting the obvious.

"I can't. That's the secret. It's all by sound and feel. You get a feel of where the popper hits the water, then listen for a splash from that direction. If you set it right, and pull back just right, you've got yourself a big bass. Like that!" I almost yelled and yanked the rod tip up and back only to have the line come flying back at the boat in a whirling mess that landed mostly on and around Mattie.

"What the...," she was startled but didn't move for fear of a hook being somewhere in the tangle.

"Hence why most of the time I fly solo, and why there is only one fly rod to a boat in my world. Just hold still. I'll have you unraveled in no time. No harm. No foul." I was slinging the rod back across the darkened water and had another big strike on the very next cast, but missed him. Some of the line caught Mattie again, not as much, and she didn't seem to mind as much either. On my fourth cast, a two-pounder came up and nailed the popper. I set the hook, playing it gracefully while it circled and slashed its way to the boat. We both thought it might be larger, but it was big enough to get the adrenalin going.

"Ready?" I asked her, double checking the popper to make sure the fish hadn't damaged it.

"Maybe."

I handed her the butt end of the fly rod and showed her how to work the basic manual crank reel. "My Uncle Eugene gave me this fly rod when I was ten. It's logged in a lot of fish so don't be shy."

Mattie stood and I sat. You don't want to be in the passing lane of fly line when it is being laced through the air, day or night. The hook on the end has a way of finding the backs of heads, earlobes and even an occasional nose or eye. She looked like she probably knew what she wanted to do but was having difficulty getting the line to stretch all the way out on her backswing. Net result was most of the line ended up around Mattie's waist and feet and the popper itself slammed against the back of my head.

"Okay. No big deal," I assured her. The hook barb had missed me. "You just need to give it a little more hesitation when you get it stretched out back. The line's a little heavier than what you use trout fishing so you give it just an extra two-count to stretch out before you wing it forward. You can do it."

A quick study, she had the rhythm figured out in a couple more tries and she laid the popper out there while I grabbed the oars and moved us ahead slowly towards the area of the back bay that was full of stumps, submerged trees and enough under water structure to provide an attractive home for every largemouth in the lake. Sunny Blue Resort sat on a small piece of land that was surrounded by water on three sides and technically was an island because you needed to cross a forty-foot wooden plank bridge to get to it from the fourth side. It was a broken tip of land at the end of a peninsula in the magnificence of Central Minnesota's lake country; God's full set of footnotes on how to carve out pristine waters teeming with fish amongst tall pines, white birches and red maples.

I heard the huge splash first. "Set it!" I yelled. Mattie yanked the rod tip back and pulled the butt end of the rod into her waist. "Pull some line in! You can't let him run deep!"

She hadn't made a sound as she was peering into the dark at what might be bending that fiberglass rod nearly in half. Surface. Splash! Splash again, closer to the boat now, the fish could see the boat in the dark from his perspective and made a run at it, Mattie pulling line, keeping that rod tip high and tight, butt end wedged into her side. "Don't give in to him. You're doing great!" I yelled. I had disturbed anything that might have been asleep within miles. It dawned on me at that moment that when I was by myself fishing out here at night, I was just like Mattie when I had a fish on- quiet, enjoying the whole thing privately. Here I was, kicking up the dust and acting like a ten-year-old with a fish on his new fly rod from his Uncle Eugene. So I shut up. For a moment.

The drag began to scream as the fish took off for another run back towards the stumps. Mattie held her ground, giving him some, but not all he wanted. "I can't see shit," I heard her mumble under her breath.

I tried to row the boat a little closer to the shadow of the stump I could see ahead in the moonlight. "God, he's a big one, Mattie. Hang on!" I felt the boat bump up against a log underneath and slide off to the side. No big deal..., happens all the time back in here. Another splash! This was a *big* fish. The lined continued to sing out against the drag. I was afraid she was going to lose it the way I had lost the biggest ones I had on- the fish taking a final run and wrapping the line around an underwater log or branch until he created enough slack to toss the popper out of his mouth. If I could get the boat close enough, I might be able to dip the landing net in deep enough to get him in for her.

"I'll get him!" I told her. "Easy, now, hold him firm; don't let him get any deeper. I can hear him swirling right over a log." I eased the boat forward and set the oars down, picked up the landing net and got myself in position to try a swipe at the fish from the side of the boat. Big scoop, his tail splashing water in my face, but I missed. The boat moved on me and I switched positions to the bow. I could hear him in the water right below me and got up to get better leverage before I took another stab at him. Just as I reached down and into the churning water right beneath the bow, the boat bumped up against another log, and without hesitation or any resistance, over I went, head first. Water is always cold when it is dark, no matter where or what time of year.

I am not quite sure which set of ideas came into mind first, but I for one don't think well upside down. As I surfaced, the only thing I could think of was keeping the opening of the net above water. Even my light weight New Balance sneakers needed to do some heavy slogging to keep my nose just above the water with the net held up higher than my head. My sense was the fish was in the net and I wasn't going to let all of this be for nothing.

"Good God, are you alright?" I think I heard Mattie yell out.

"Hold on to the rod!" I yelled back. Just... hold on to... whatever." I grabbed the side of the boat with one hand and reached inside the net.

"I lost him," she blurted. "Shit!"

"I don't think so," I said pushing the net up and folding it over the side into the boat. I heard the huge largemouth slapping about as he spilled out into the bottom of the boat and I could feel Mattie's hands trying to help me as I got a grip on the edges of the boat and pulled myself back up and over. "Get the flashlight!" I thought I could hear her snickering as she did while I tried to pin the flopping irritated fish down with the palms of my hands. By the time she got a light on it, I had my thumb and index finger around the bottom lip and we were admiring a seven-pound largemouth bass most people would put above their fireplace in the den.

"Is he big? Looks pretty big," she said.

"Huge. I have to say bigger than anything I've caught up here in ten years!"

"Or… maybe you just don't catch the big ones…. . Wasn't that hard… ."

It was difficult to gauge a person's sense of humor in the side glow of a flashlight. "Right. Well, all that may be true, but I got a news flash for you… you didn't catch the fish, Roland Martin. He was *captured!*" I cleared the water dripping down my nose and pushed the hair back off my eyes.

"Whatever you say."

I looked up at her and we both started to laugh, as though we both figured out at the same moment what this would look like to anybody else. "It's a beautiful fish, though, isn't it?" I asked.

"Actually, it's kid of gross, that big fat belly and all. Trout are much more graceful looking."

"Enough, already. Let's get him back in the water."

"Wait… can you get a picture for me… with my cell phone…." She pulled the cell phone out of her hip pocket, set it to camera function and flash, and handed it to me. "Now… how do I hold it? Will it bite me?"

I assured her she was safe if she kept her pretty fingers out of the gills and held it just like I was, then I stood back and snapped off a few pictures for her. "Now you should set him free."

"You don't want to eat him or stuff him or something?"

"No. He belongs in the lake."

"How noble…."

"We all belong somewhere, right. Some of us just don't know where that is."

"So deep, Thomas." She put the fish down over the side of the boat and let go. He flipped his tail at her with a flourish and was gone in the dark.

We sat there for a few moments and gathered the serenity of the night back in. I expect she could hear me trying to sort of squeegee my shirt sleeves.

"And you are soaked," she said easily. "But you know what? At some point during that whole thing, I stopped thinking you were a serial killer. Now I think you are just as vulnerable as the rest of us. Thanks for saving my fish."

I untangled the fly line mess and cranked it all back up into the reel. "I can tell you one thing for sure. You may have caught the biggest bass in the bay, but we have also managed to spook any other fish out of here for the foreseeable future. But you are welcome to try again, if you like."

She laughed quietly. "It is beautiful out here." I imagined she was counting the same stars I was counting.

"The most you can get for free anywhere on the planet," I suggested.

"What is it you do, Thomas? You don't belong to that bra infested bar, do you?"

"And if I did, anything wrong with that?"

"Gee, I don't know, but something in your deep blue eyes tells me your life is about more than serving beers and hanging bras on nails."

"Okay. I teach American History at a junior college outside of Chicago during the rest of the year. This is my summer vacation. Has been for the past ten or so years. And you?"

"Me? Oh my goodness, you didn't *know*? I am a commercial real estate analyst for a big company out of New York. I look at billions of dollars worth of shopping centers, office buildings and condominium projects and pronounce them fit for consumption. I'm actually giving a seminar on the very same at the Green Gables as we speak. The thing is, those boys I came with tonight thought I was a little too prim and proper over some cocktails earlier this evening and bet me I wouldn't loosen up and go out with them slumming. So here I am, loose as a goose, slumming... ."

"I suppose it's a long way from there to here," I said, aimlessly, sitting there, thinking swamp ass.

"You know what I suppose?" She asked, a tone in her voice I couldn't really figure, but she moved towards me, and in the next moments my soaking wet blue jeans were at my ankles and to my even greater surprise, as she straddled me on the seat, her dry ones must have been in the bottom of the boat as well.

Crickets crick. Frogs bellow. Flat bottom wooden boats sway ever so slightly while those inside work into an easy glide against each other under approving stars. Her tiny breasts smelled like tropical flowers as I kissed my way around. She arched and reached and I held on.

# CHAPTER 15

"And so it is my goal to give you enough of an educated process here to get to you to challenge the historians, to ask your own questions, to develop and rethink and look beneath all that is said and written and form your own opinions, and if necessary, to rewrite American History as you understand it. Then share that with the rest of us. It need not be so deep a burning question that only an intellectual can understand it. It can be something that keeps popping up into your head. Something that demands an answer. Such as the question a student posed last spring semester- 'Mr. Cabot, is Monica Lewinsky's dress in the Smithsonian Institute?' And the follow up. 'Then, where is it?'

"Does this demand an answer? Maybe? Nonetheless, this student was determined to come to an understanding about the relevancy of the Clinton Presidency, and then place it in historical context."

A student near the back raised his hand. I pointed to him. "Will that be on the final?"

I was back at doing something that now seemed so easy and non life-threatening that I was amazed I may have ever taken it for granted. But as I dismissed this first class, all went blank as I watched the young blonde in the micro mini in the first row uncross her legs and get up. The riveting drama, then, snap! The Kodak was working. For the rest of the day, my lectures were given with a slant towards pink panties.

Had my summer frolicking jaded me forever? Would I succumb to the idea Connie floated that falling in love was really for suckers? And staying in love was for the smallest of gene pools? I actually liked my recently acquired interpretation of being in love, for that matter. The version I was espousing was largely based on a physical appreciation of the female form in it entirely; its curves, temperature, smell, sound, the way it moved, and even its unique reaction to life itself. Womanhood itself. I was in love with that. Size and age seemed hardly a matter of discussion. Even comparing them in sexual performance was to say one apple tree in the orchard yielded more apples than the next. They all yield the same kind of apples, and when you tasted them, it mattered not which tree it came from.

My observer noted I was beginning to acquire a life philosophy that might guide me more years than I could know. We'll see, he concluded.

But as my first day back rolled through, I came to realize this was the first time since my first year of teaching that I felt out of synch with what was going on around me. I felt detached from the podium, from the students, from my little cubicle of an office. My hallway greetings to fellow teachers and former students seemed more like a rehearsal of the real thing. Odd, unfamiliar sounds coming from my lips. And theirs. I wondered if my face hinted of an untold story in the same ways theirs did not.

Head abuzz, a disjointed day behind me, and lost, that evening I nursed a beer at a familiar neighborhood saloon on Lincoln Avenue called Harry's. I asked old Harry how in the hell he had been.

"Another summer come and gone. Jesus Keeee- rist almighty," Harry answered. His whipping strands of white hair were in there usual format- straight up over the dome of his balded top. "But... would you know it, Thomas. I won the frickin' lottery in July. $300,000 lump sum."

"No kidding."

"Oh ya. Wanna buy a bar?"

Nothing else he said stuck, except the idea. Why not? Why not me? I never had so much as a reason until that moment, but the damn crazy idea stuck like glue. Harry was laughing softly, like he floated that little one out for fun at least once a night since the day he won. But I was right there. I hadn't the slightest clue what a bar would cost, should cost, or if Harry's was the right one to buy, but it was the oddest damn thing this was jumping around in my head like, well, like lottery balls.

"How much, Harry?"

Harry looked at me with a quick glance like I was just another bad checkers player and turned to the television set up in a corner above the bar. The Comedian Ron White was doing a stand-up routine on Comedy Central that evidently was a favorite of Harry's. Ron White was a fat guy that drank scotch and smoked cigars while he spun out countrified swill that made people laugh even though they weren't really sure what they were laughing about. I looked up and watched. Within moments I was laughing with everybody else. I don't remember why. Harry Dombrosky was doubled over.

When he recovered, I got another beer. "If you *were* serious, Harry, how much?" I asked.

Harry gave me another hesitation, then his evidently pat answer. "Well, let's see. I'm sixty-seven years old, Thomas. Today I'd sell it just to be able to sleep through the night without pissing in my pants. And, let's say, one nice easy crap. Short of that, inventory, payables and about $150,000 cash. Done deal. Why? You know somebody interested?"

"Maybe so."

My third floor, two-bedroom converted condo on Halsted Street seemed just about as oddly uncomfortable as the Harper College campus had earlier. I had purchased a new lap top at Best Buy and instinctively turned it on just for the blue glow it added to the room. I flopped into my oversize tan leather recliner and began channel surfing. Direct TV. Everything. Nothing. When all else failed, I usually settled into the soft porn for a good laugh. Women looking like they pulled tight plastic bodies over their own with tits of shiny concrete with tiny scars at the base of their nipples. The men. Now *that* was easily the funniest thing about it. I mean, I think I could understand not getting an erection while pretending to fuck anything while you were on a stage with a dozen morons trying to film it, but the work that went into the camera angles and body positions to make sure neither penetration nor bodily fluids appeared on screen was amazing.

There she was, an oriental looking woman pretending to back herself onto a guy's schwantz, while he was sort of cantilevered below and behind her. If he does get it up, one false move and she breaks it clean off. I laughed my ass off. Okay, then. Right as I aimed the remote at my Sony HD flat screen, I stopped and studied the close-up on the woman's working orgasmic face. I looked again. They shot away, back to the churning hips and air-fucking. Back to her face. They switched it up. She was going down on him now, her hair strategically covering any potential contact between her lips and his flaccidness. He was almost there now. Then, it hit me. I waited for him to finish the mime, hoping to get another good look. There is was, her licking her lips, smiling up at him. My God, *it was Sara,* my brother Rondell's wife! It was Sara "Lovelace" Cabot, sure as I was sitting there.

I left the channel were it was, mesmerized, hit the TIVO record button and sunk back into my recliner. Next the "info" button. "Cancun Capers" would run another twenty minutes. "Exotic exploits of three women on their Caribbean vacation". I was glued to it. In the next scene, the same woman and her two female roommates did an acrobatic three-way on each other, a much easier feat to pull off realistically and cinematically. Between the quasi-munching, I got a few more glimpses of her face, albeit within an inch of perfectly trimmed blonde landing strip. It was definitely Sara. And she definitely had a *long* tongue.

By the time "Cancun Capers" had come to its conclusion, a scene in which Sara and her two friends are shown sitting on the plane going back home, looking exhausted and very smiley and happy, until the male passenger sitting next to Sara whispers something in her ear and off they go to the bathroom. Role the credits. My brother Rondell had married a professional long tongue.

I decided to stay with the beer, and some leftover Chinese and sat there wondering what to do next. Call Rondell? Call Sara? And say what? My gut feeling was the whole thing would play out on its own. It had seemed Rondell was even encouraging her to let me in on it when he talked about her middle name in the bar that night. So, instead, I worked on the Chinese and prepared for "Chains of Passion", coming on next. A women's prison air-fuck flick. Why I was witlessly amused by these things, I had no idea. An enlightened guy like me should no longer be aroused my anything less than the real thing.

Just then my cell phone rang. It was Connie.

"What in hell are you doing, hon?" She purred.

Guilty, I looked around to see if she was in the room. "Just home. Bored. Eating left over Chinese."

"Pass. How is she?"

Same Connie. I really missed her, to tell the truth. I missed the chaos. I missed the screwing. "How are you doing, Connie?"

"Well, let's see, Thomas. Now that you've gotten to know me a bit, you know I don't color it much. This sucks. I'm lonely, depressed, horny, and feel like I'm walking on coals barefoot. I… I don't know what the hell to do with myself. It is so quiet now, which used to be wonderful this time of year… but not *this* year. I even miss the asshole."

That was probably the first *nice* reference to Rudy I had heard since the funeral. The Hari Krishnas that showed up at the cemetery set Connie off so bad it was everything she could do to keep from asking Wahoo to execute them all. She had no real problem with them, or with Rudy being with them, but it was just that they were *there*. It pissed her off she would have to explain to everybody else *why* they were there.

She continued on. "Rudy just got tired of empty tube Viagra hard-ons, demanding young broads and me. He could only take so much of the backwoods farting brigade with Babe and the boys. Fish are just fish after awhile. So, there you go. He traded it all in for a gown and a shaved head."

"So next question. How's the weather?" I asked, squirming. This was the first time I had talked to Connie over the phone. I imagined her sitting there naked eating a beef jerky while watching "Dancing With The Stars". She had me at a BIG disadvantage. I really missed the sex.

"Oh fuck you, Thomas. Question is, are we really going to fall back into our caves for the winter? When am I going to wrap my legs around you again? Questions like that."

The phone seemed warmer in my hand. "Good points. All of them," I said. "I thought about you today, actually." This was really a lie. A pink panty shot, assorted juggling boobs walking around, a protruding nipple here and there, all, in all, most of my day mentally, but close enough to a thought about Connie Mulroney.

"And?"

"And what?"

"Don't make me beg, Thomas. Give me something to sleep with tonight."

I laughed a little. "What about… like Wahoo and…."

"They're all married. They're all back in their caves, too."

"Okay. Let's see…," I was such a shmuck. An ill-equipped moron dealing with an expert in the field. "How about this? This is… Monday. I don't have a class on Friday afternoon. I can take off at noon and drive up for the weekend."

"Seriously?"

"Sure. Why not?"

"I'm sliding off the couch just thinking about it."

If this is what it felt like-phone sex- I wondered if she was going to ask me for my MasterCard number. "Then it's a date."

"A date. Jesus. Thomas." I heard her laugh away from the phone. "You know what? You're right. Let's make it a date. Let's go to dinner, dancing, the whole thing. I know just the place." She paused to scold Twinkles for something. "You're a genius. That's just what I needed."

My good bye was just as awkward as the rest of it.

Sara wasn't in the "Chains of Passion". I was maxed on being amused and entertained anyway, so I switched over to the Weather Channel. I cracked another beer, ate the rest of my Chinese and waited for a look at the forecast for Minnesota over the weekend.

# CHAPTER 16

Tuesday. Second day back teaching. Same girl, same seat, front row. Different short dress. Same result. Powder blue panties this time. I handed out a revised synopsis for the semester. The one I handed out the first day had a typo. I had somehow managed to give Thomas Jefferson a new first name.

"Mr. Cabot, uh, dude..., Wahoo Jefferson?" some smart-assed punk had asked loud and clearer than I make it sound.

I looked in disbelief. "Ah! ... My apologies. Can you imagine? ... Just to make sure you were paying attention. And you were."

Rather than having to look at the name *Wahoo* with an "X" through it for the whole semester, and the thoughts that would boil up with it, I was happy to make new copies and destroy the old ones.

I mumbled through the morning, mailing it in, angry at myself for my inability to pull it together and rekindle that *thing,* or whatever it was that made teaching enjoyable for me. Where did it go? I asked myself. Where did I go? What happened to the little old blend-in-with-the-wall me? Powder blue panties as a world view? I wondered if I was walking around dragging one leg, a crippled hand and arm held up against my chest, a gob of drool down a corner of my mouth, eyes glazed, zipper half open. Just a thought. I was likely the easiest going, non-threatening, unassuming person you knew until very recently. Comparatively, I might have been on the edge of becoming a madman

113

unlike any known in the free world. Powder blue panties. Pink. I was thinking in all pastels.

I sat down at Starbucks for a caffeine lunch and pulled out my lap top. I figured, if the girl in the front row did that one more time, it would be on purpose. Maybe, she was in love with me. Or maybe she just wanted to fuck me. That seemed to be a popular notion over the summer. I had been with more women in three months that I had been in the sum total of my life prior to that. Residual effects, though. Something set free. An amoeba that may have been stuck to the side in my head managed to free itself and travel to its predetermined location somewhere in my groin. *That* completed the connection between my brain's ability to conceive of insatiable lust and my physical ability to erect at will.

Just as I smiled at the thought of how Maria had unwittingly started me on this journey, I stared down at the screen and spotted an entry in my email amidst the spam offers for Xanax, Viagra, Russian Grandmothers and Fun in the Farmyard. *Largemouth, what's up?* I almost deleted it with the rest, but only one person had ever referred to me as *Largemouth*, and that happened only once.

> Hey Largemouth-
> Remember me?
> Just taking a chance- I'm in Chicago tomorrow for a one-day seminar.
> Fly in tomorrow morning, back out Thursday morning. Looking for a fishing coach for Wednesday night.
> Know anybody?
> Mattie

My groin launched, sending a volcanic message up through my stomach and its hot lava continued on to the front of my brain where it fried what was left of my lobal sensors, then settled back down into familiar territory. I emailed back-

> Mattie-
> Remember you?

Just tell me the place, time. The coach has
cleared his schedule.
Largemouth

I can't say something kicked in because I was already in gear and looking
for a race. I inhaled the dark, wonderfully bitter Sumatra blend coffee
and anxiously walked back to campus to teach my next class. My step
was a bit quicker, my mind suddenly singular and resolved, the endless
string of odd moments at bay. Maybe this is how love felt. What else
could make you laugh out loud, alone.

I was on the train going back to the city when I spotted the
billboard- THE SYBARIS- *Where enough is never enough.* I had heard
about the place before, sort of a classy hot sex theme park hotel in the
west suburbs with a price tag that kept it all respectable and acceptable.
Unless you got caught being there. My first thought was this might
be a bit contrived, but then again, so was email and easy references to
*coaching.* I don't know. That Sybaris sign featured a limousine arriving
at its door. Why not?

The Four Seasons. Out front- eight o'clock. In her email Mattie
said she had a client dinner she could politely escape by then. I had
the stretch limo pull up front and I opened the side door and just sort
of hung there, hoping I wasn't going to look like I left my masculinity
checked in my closet in this Tommy Bahama beige silk shirt thing the
guy at Macy's insisted I buy. If it was me coming out that door, looking
for me, I would go with me, just on the basis of how good I smelled.
I was hoping she wasn't really in to the Minnesota lake bay duckweed
smell.

As I tapped the tinted glass window of the first limousine I had ever
rented, and waited, I wondered if I had reached too far reserving the
*Endless Tahiti* room. Each of the rooms at the Sybaris had a theme. I
could choose from the *Star Wars* room, complete with silver blue space
suits with lots of zippers; the *Geisha Guest House* room, renown for its
assortment of infamous swinging wicker basket chairs made for the
imagination; the *57 Chevy* room, featuring a real 1957 lilac colored
Chevy convertible with a plushed-up oversized back seat and all the
music to go with it. And many others. *Endless Tahiti* seemed the right

choice. It boasted of a king-sized hammock that sat in a virtual grass hut set in front of a wall-sized projection of endless surf, sunrises and sunsets, even dolphin and whale sightings. The floor was heated sand and simulations of beach, surf and bird sounds promised to take you to another world from which you would never want to return.

This from a guy who could now look back at the past ten years of his life and describe them best as ordinary. A guy who grew up with strange, uncomfortable thoughts about the parenting around him, baffled by home spun prejudices and mixed messages. Living in the shadows of bigger things and bigger lives I could not begin to understand was not a bad way to go, I figured, but now this… this adventure I was on, this new sexual tension that seemed to grip me and push me around… this could be fun. It was okay to just go with it, I reasoned. No need to understand it, figure it, break it down into basic elements and try to fit it into an Excel or Word program.

Eight-fifteen. I'm getting a little nervous. These were all *firsts* for me. This is really fucked up if she doesn't show.

On the other hand, I'm heady with the thought we don't need to slow anything down for dinner and small talk. Right to the chase. I considered small talk an enemy, lurking, forever trying to outflank me and make me say things so insignificant I regret being awake.

Eight-twenty-three. I check my cell phone for missed calls or messages. Nothing.

My observer reads my mind and suggests I deal with my expectations. Why?

Then, there she was, bouncing through the brass doors held open by a black man in a red uniform. She was looking. I was waving. I expected a two-piece ladies' business suit or a long, flowing dress, something in black or dark tweeds. It was a black dress alright, but short, high-necked and tight to her body with black high heels to match.

We stood up about two inches apart, smiling. "Could you do that again?" I asked.

"Do what?"

"Walk over here like you just did. I could watch you do that all night."

"That doesn't sound like much fun for me."

"In that case...," I kissed her, lingered just a moment, and waved my hand towards the awaiting back seat. I had told the limo driver earlier I would handle the door duties for the evening.

"Well, let's see," I said as we settled in, "what... ." My words flattened against the tip of her tongue in my mouth. I was pretty sure there was no reason to figure things out right away. I did not think it was possible or probable that a tongue could be long enough to actually make contact with my tonsils, but, sure enough. Another first. Seemed like the nerve endings there connected to the base of both of my heels. It was extraordinary. And if she could, I could. I waited until I had the opening and went for it.

"Agggghhhh! Aaccckk!" she hacked and spit up a little, once I retreated. "Jesus, God, Thomas. Easy, boy."

I would need work on the technique. I wanted to ask her how she managed to snake her tongue down my throat without choking me, but it seemed a mood killer of an idea.

"Sir? Where to?" came a voice with a heavy middle European accent through the narrow opening down the long stretch of space between us. Mattie's hand was already on me through my best pair of silky dress pants and I responded accordingly.

"Uh. Do you... ."

"Just drive," she whispered in passing against my ear.

"Uh. Maybe just up and down Lake Shore Drive. We'll look at the skyline. Uh. She's from out of town." A stupid thing to say, but I couldn't take it back.

Before I could say anything else to make things worse, Mattie had swung up and over me and her short black dress got as short as it gets. My hand moved down and deftly under and up. "No panties! You go to a business meeting with no panties on?" I was a complete moron.

"Shut up," she laughed. No sooner did I hear my zipper going than she was lowering herself onto me. Hot? I thought I might smell burning flesh, but instead my head filled with the peach smell of her hair and the return of her amazing tongue in my mouth. Though completely into the moment, I wondered again how she got that thing so deep into my throat opening. Then stayed there. Without choking me. It was a little creepy, though. As if I was being forced to eat one of her body parts.

We struggled with pace, as though we both were trying to dictate it, slumping to the side, then angling up and back until her head hit the bank of amber glowing rope lights on either side of a long, tinted glass sun roof.

"Ouch!" She gritted her teeth. "Fuck!"

I took it as a command and changed the whole direction, pushing her up and back down on the expanse of floor in front of us, withdrawing, getting her repositioned while striking a little pose of my own. I gently manuevered her legs out and up over my shoulders and looked down at her from above. I imagined myself with an undeniably sexy and menacing look on my face. More likely, it probably looked liked I was getting a cramp.

"Go for it, tiger…," she said, returning the look with a dare glowing in her eyes.

Affirmative. We found a rhythm and locked in. The jack hammering had begun just as staccato, tuba dominant music began pumping from the ceiling speakers. It was even harder to ignore the Polish lyrical accompaniment, let alone give a thought to the perfect view our driver must have been enjoying in his rear view mirror.

We were rocking on turns, gathering speed on straight-aways and we began speaking in tongues, making noises that brought out the beast in both of us. It must have sounded like we had invented a new language to our audience of one. Moans of pleasure were one thing. This was like some sort of ritualistic chant that required response and refrain. If it was me listening, I would have called either the paramedics or an exorcist.

I remember having a hand gripping each cheek of her ass when we went airborne, defying a moment of gravity, then beginning to tumble. I heard an oddly loud groan that came from neither of us, then suspended silence followed by a halting jolt and a splash. *A splash?*

The car had stilled, engine off, then I began seeing water seep into the car from the bottom edges of the side windows. I could see the Chicago skyline in the distance through the darkened glass, but my head cocked to one side in the realization there was a darker horizontal line moving up the windows. It was a *waterline! The car was sitting in water. And we were sinking!*

I could here the driver screaming and cursing in something that could have been Polish as I tried the doors. Mattie suddenly realized what was going on and began screaming as well. I threw my shoulder into one door, then the other. Nothing doing. I fell back awkwardly to the floor because my shoes and pants were still around my ankles, but there was no time to find it funny. As I laid back and pulled my pants back up I was looking at the upholstered roof, and the skylight that ran the length of the back seat area between the amber rope lights which were still on. "Get in the back seat!" I yelled to Mattie. She moved quickly while I repositioned myself, pants up now, and made several attempts to kick out the sun roof with my heals. I cussed it, swore at it, but it wasn't moving. Then, just as I braced up for one more try, the glass panel quietly retracted smooth as silk. I looked up at Mattie. She had found a button on the control panel above the back seat that opened it very nicely.

I quickly helped her up and out. It was little tighter squeeze for me, but I made it in time for us to stand up on the roof and assess our surroundings. The car was sitting about thirty feet off shore in a small boat harbor just off the edge of Lake Shore Drive. Several people had assembled hoping to witness our death, and we could see our driver swimming very badly for shore, obviously leaving us for dead as well. We looked at each other, two deer in the head lights, and jumped into the water just ahead of the sinking of the Polski Titanic.

The cold water was the least of our concerns as we swam side-by-side. When we got to shore, some people that got beyond their hunger for witnessing death helped us up the rocky rip rap. We had a story to tell, but no one to tell it to. I bent down with my hand on my thighs to get my breath and turned to watch the limo bob slightly, hood pointing upward before it disappeared beneath the surface of the water. I stood back up and moved along side a very rigid Mattie.

"Your zipper's open," Mattie said.

I straightened her dress where it drooped off one shoulder. "Lost your shoes."

We hugged like any two people who had cheated death. Our driver was huddled in a blanket someone had given him while police cars and sirens were closing in and more people gathered for an impromptu change of pace from their normally uneventful evening walk along the lake.

My heart pounded at a bad ending avoided. "I gotta ask," I mumbled, watching as a kind hearted older man put his jacket over Mattie's shoulders. It was a warm September evening, but chilly if you were soaked to the bone. "I'll be right back." I made my way over to the driver huddled in the blanket on the incline of the shore. We looked each other over as he carried on a conversation in Polish with a bystander who obviously understood what he was saying.

"What happened?" I asked.

He spit out a flurry of words out that made no sense to me. "He says, it was you're fault," the bystander said, translating in English. "He says, you were having sex with your girlfriend in the back of the car and made it difficult for him to concentrate on driving." The bystander, a gray-haired man in his fifties, seemed an unfazed messenger. He shrugged. Then a crooked smile snuck up one corner of his mouth as his eyes turned to get a better look at Mattie. There wasn't anything I could do to improve on his fantasy. Even as a drown rat, Mattie looked vulnerably attractive.

An hour or so later, The Chicago Police had finished interviewing the driver, Mattie and me, and were having a little conference while their rescue boat began pulling the car from the bottom of the harbor. Mattie and I had declined medical treatment from the paramedics and we were discussing our next move to get out of there when one of the officers walked over to me and pulled me aside. I wasn't sure what I should be preparing for, but I didn't feel very good about it.

"Okay," he began, "so this is what happens. This is the third time for this guy. Do you want to press charges?"

"Charges? For?"

"Lewd, lascivious conduct in public, endangerment, and a few others we can include. The guy's a menace." He looked around to make sure he wasn't being overheard. "Okay? He whacks off while he drives. This is his third accident in about fourteen months. But this was one is a beaut. Into the harbor. Beeee...utiful."

I could see the driver was still huddled under the blanket, head down. I didn't want to know any more.

"Actually, if you could just get us a cab, that would be great."

The officer shrugged and talked into his shoulder radio.

As I walked back to put my arms around Mattie, *Limo Ride From Hell* came to mind as another theme room for the Sybaris.

She hadn't said very much since the accident.

"The thing is...," I said, following the officer up some steps to a parking lot. "We've been together twice. I've been in the water twice."

She looked up at me with a weak smile. Her body still seemed to tremble beneath my hand at her shoulder.

"You okay?" I asked.

"I just need a hot shower and a nice, dry bed." That strong, assured voice was tame and resigned.

"I can understand that. I want to say the night is young, but...."

"You, Thomas, are my hero," she said, and curled her arm around my waist.

"Actually, you're right. I saved a dog from a fire once."

"Screw the dog."

"Almost as bad."

"What?"

"Never mind.... You were the one who pushed the damn button that opened the window."

"I know.... It's all just kind of a blur. I just remember you kept moving... and I just also remembered you tripping because your pants were down around your ankles." She began to laugh and covered her mouth, as though it wasn't allowed under the circumstances. "And I remember how you kept asking me if I was alright, that we were going to be alright...not to worry.... I'm just going to take a wild guess and say most of the guys I know would have panicked. You didn't so much as raise your voice as I remember ... other than to make sure I was alright." She squeezed my waist with her arm.

"I'll panic later when I realize what really happened. I'll be the guy running through the street stark naked screaming his head off."

"I doubt that." She stopped walking and leaned up to kiss me full on the lips. "Plan B- my room at the Four Seasons, room service, and we finish what we started. Then start again."

# CHAPTER 17

One long-ass drive. The yard light cast some shadows across the newly placed roofing trusses on the house being rebuilt at Sunny Blue as I pulled my Subaru into the turn around. I was expecting the Winnebago, I guess, but it was gone. Connie's black Cadillac Fleetwood was parked in its usual place. Scanning about, the only interior lights I could see on were glowing through the windows and sheer curtains of what I knew to be the Bluegill Cabin. I took a Connie chance.

"My sweetie's on time, " Connie said, giving me Connie-eye as I walked the Cabin. She was sitting naked on a creaking stool by the big kitchen window at a slightly taller pedestal table. She was lopping gobs of gray clay onto what appeared to be the beginnings of a statue of some sort.

"Ok. I give up." I shoved my hands in my front pockets. I assumed she might be unclad to some degree, but naked is not exactly what I expected. She looked good, though. Her dark hair was tied back, gold hoop earrings bobbing, eyes afire, now moving back to her clay. There was an underlying solvent or chemical smell in the air but in moments it gave way to the essence of Connie. Being around her anymore gave me this mesmerizing sense of warm, melting sweetness and arousal. And nothing in my world smelled like Connie and lingered on me like Connie. A welcome respite long, long after the touching was over.

I moved over to her and kissed the top of her head. Heaven. Walloping heaven.

"Go into the bedroom over there. You'll find a robe on the bed. Take your clothes off and put on the robe and come back to me. Okay?" Connie-wink.

A simple pleasure doing as I was told, a minute later I emerged in a navy blue robe.

"Not exactly the look I was thinking about for the past couple of weeks. But close." She gazed down at my black Nikes. I kicked them off. "Better. Socks. Please."

I tried a casual *been there* pose.

"The one over there on the table by the couch is done." She motioned. I walked over to get a better look. It was a clay bust of a man not familiar to me. Though I thought the work on its own merits was pretty amazing, I didn't want to take a chance of guessing- particularly since I didn't have a guess. I mean, guessing *Rudy* would have been a big stretch. During the long ride up, I had decided I wouldn't even bring up his name unless she did. I understood people mourned differently, and Connie was not the easiest person to understand.

"Nobody you know. He was my experimental model."

"Whoever it is, it's really good. How long have you been sculpting?"

"Just started. That's the first. I wanted to see what I could do with the clay. I like the way in feels in my hands. Almost electric. Like it's alive and connected with my soul."

"Did you take a class or something?"

"No. Just stopped at this little art store in Gull Lake that was going out of business. They had all this stuff lying around.... I started... and it just kind of went like that."

"God, Connie, you've got a gift for it."

"Well, that one was from memory. Some guy I balled a long time ago. *Huge* dick. Never forgot him. Actually," she paused, thinking, "I was going to do the busts with a cock in place of the Adam's apple, but I figured that had been done to death."

"Imagine that." I glanced down to make sure my robe was closed and shifted my feet.

"So anyway, I wanted to see what I could do with a live model. You."
She shot me those eyes and the big smile she could have patented. "How
'bout you sit over there... right under the light."

I moved to a wooden straight-back chair next to an old, goose-
necked floor lamp that had been turned upward. I sat down. "You want
me to pose or something?"

"No. I don't think so. I think you just kind of sit there."

We didn't say much for the next hour or so. I could hear the wind
picking up a hustle through the trees and the water lapping at the shore.
The peace and quiet of a September night that promised to be cold and
cuddly was delicious, and gave me plenty of time to kick it back a few
notches and contemplate my degrees of insanity, and that pierced left
nipple and the tiny gold dog bone earring she had threaded through
it.

I saw her glance up at the clock above the kitchen sink. "German
Corner serves until midnight on Friday's. You up for it?"

I nodded. "Sure."

"This whole thing is making me crazy horny, though. You?"

"Absolutely."

Connie immediately set down a narrow metal awl and wiped her
hands on a towel. She turned on her stool, got up and walked over to
me and dropped to her knees. She had me up in moments, took me
to the edge with that wicked tongue of hers; hands-free, brushing and
squeezing my earlobes with her floating fingers. "That looks about
right," she said, looking at my dick like she just finished decorating
the tree. "You, Thomas..., I have to tell you, are the king of the four-
minute fuck. We'll have all night to make sweet love, but let's fuck and
eat dinner first." With that pronounced and cleared up, she got up and
bent over the drop-leaf square kitchen table and arched her back. I was
going to call her out on that "make sweet love" comment, but decided
there was nothing to be gained that wasn't already gaining.

Being led or following or leading made no difference to me when
the view I had commanded immediate action. I got up, eased into the
hot suction of her pussy and hit the timer button on my hips as they
began to churn away.

I was lost in freeze frames. She was pushing so tight back up against
me I thought I could levitate. I *was,* ...I think, when she belted out,

"Fuuuuuuck!" She moaned loudly and her torso shot up at me and shuddered back down. Then again. And again. I felt her insides collapse as my hands gripped her hip joints on my final thrust.

Time. Three minutes, forty-seven seconds, including my add-on at the end. I tweaked the gold dog bone through her nipple and eased back.

"You like that?" She asked. She had her hands spread out to the corners of the table and her head hung still while she shuddered out. I could feel the last of the small twitches on my dick.

"The twitches?"

"The Nipple pierced thingy, idiot."

"I like both. Minneapolis?"

"The guy doing it was amazing. I didn't fuck him though. He smelled like old chicken soup and tuna." She eased herself up and I disengaged. We both heard the *quiiiissssh...shaaa* as I slowly withdrew and fell out. "My God, Thomas. What is it with you? I could fuck you four minutes at a time all day long."

No time to be sheepish, I thought. Sex Gods cannot be sheepish about their gift. I stood there naked, drooped, and shrugged. Then I caught a glimpse of the finished bust over by the couch and remembered his place in history and mine. I grabbed the robe.

"How 'bout a quick shower and off for dinner? I'm in the mood for Weiner schnitzel. Yah?"

"Yah." I said. "Heil Hitler."

German, Swedish and other European restaurants were common to the central Minnesota lakes area, but the German Corner had been a family run institution since before Hitler took a liking to young, blonde Arian men. Of course, the host was none other than Adolph Heimsluth, the third; the great-grandson of Adolph Heimsluth, the original owner. And, of course, he knew Connie, and made big hungry eyes at her like the rest of the men I ever saw around her. He sat us at a nice little table in the semi-dark where you could smell the sweet-sour of spicy meat frying in the kitchen. He gave her another kiss, but I could see his eyes fixing on her breasts. Her broad nipples were still finding a way through her bra and the thin satin blouse. At first, I wasn't sure he would leave, but fortunately other customers gathered at the reception stand and he left reluctantly.

I thought it smelled kind of heavy and greasy, but then the smell of Connie came my way over the table and I was fine. "What is it with you and men, again? How does it go?" I asked.

Our waitress, a young, cute blonde girl with short clipped hair took our drink order. Connie seemed amused. "Men are all very easy to figure out, as long as they still want sex. I simply imagine having my own dick, and thinking all that matters in life is getting it off. *That* gives me insight on 99.9% of the men on the planet. I figure the remaining tenth of one percent are or should be castrated for crimes against nature.

"And what about you? Connie, you're the sexiest, horniest damn woman on the planet for Godsakes."

"I think like a man, Thomas. Like a man wants a woman to think. But, ironically, it gives me the control. Nothing happens without the pussy. Unless, of course, if you become what Rudy became... asexual, unaccountable, a vague distortion of the man he used to be.... Sad. Very sad. Also, very unsatisfactory. You just can't deal with a man like that. He's no longer a man. He's... something else."

We sipped drinks and looked over the late night crowd. The band was coming back on stage for their last set of the night. There was Garland Luhrsen and his accordion. As he got seated and comfortable, his grim face peered around and spotted Connie and I. Connie waved. Garland looked down tight to his neck and adjusted the straps where they hooked up with the accordion.

"What a fucking asshole, " Connie lamented. "Just a big blob of shit that Rudy took a kind heart to. Never seen the guy smile, never a gesture of kindness. But he worked for Rudy like he was his slave."

"I know."

"Interesting, though, to watch him play that damn accordion. You watch. He'll look at the others playing and he picks up on what he sees and the vibrations. Some people think he's pretty good. I think he stinks. He doesn't like me much either."

The music was Bavarian , Polish, and horrible. Connie was right. Garland's long bony fingers on his right hand sometimes jittered around on the keys trying to find the right notes. From the glares he was getting from the other three band members they were, at best, tolerating his presence. By the third song of the set, I would have bet the look on the drummer's face would have turned to a bright smile if he could just jam one of his sticks right up Garland's ass.

I continued to watch the comedy on stage when a thin, middle-aged woman walked up to the table and gave Connie a hug. I couldn't hear what they were saying, but when the music mercifully stopped to the applause of three obviously very drunk people, I still couldn't hear what they were saying. Then I realized they were talking with their hands, signing, and only mouthing words. The woman leaned down and gave Connie another hug and walked off after giving me a nod and a quick smile.

"Garland's wife, Leona," Connie said. "I would have introduced you, but it gets complicated. She's deaf and dumb as well."

I shrugged it off. "You know, Connie, is it me, or why does everybody stare at you? Even the women." It was like some automatic reaction that made me jealous in one way, puzzled me in another. It wasn't so much that I thought she should belong to me, but why was it *everybody* seemed to look at Connie like she was naked.

"Well, let's see. Half the women in town think I'm fucking their old man. The other half think I killed my husband. The men? Half of them want to fuck me, and the other half want to fuck me- again." She smiled.

It was impossible to tell when Connie was kidding, and it was infinitely more fun to guess.

We got the hell out of the German Corner none too soon. Just being in the same building with Garland Luhrsen made me check to see if my skin was peeling off the bone. Nothing felt right when he was around.

Back at Sunny Blue, we settled back into the tiny, warm Blue Gill cabin. We sat on the old couch and talked for awhile. Just when I thought it was on the verge of going intellectual, I would find myself counting her nipples. One. Two. One, two. Every time I saw Connie I wanted her more. She brought out a primal urge in me that would creep up inside until I felt like I was seeking prey. I could have leaped up and landed on all fours, growling and seeking my next meal. I was taken by everything about her. Her age was sexy, her broad ass was sexy. Nothing was unsexy about Connie Mulroney.

I was laying naked in bed waiting for her to come out of the bathroom when I thought I heard a little knock on the door. I couldn't be sure.

Connie walked into the bedroom, her full figured body naked, big breasts jutting out in front of her, and attached to her left hand, the right hand of the woman she described as Garland Luhrsen's wife, Leona, equally as naked, tiny breasted, other hand to her lips, seemingly very tentative about this.

# CHAPTER 18

"Cracker Barrel for breakfast?" I thought I heard through my left ear, the one not buried in the pillow. Then a whisper and the unmistakable smell of Connie hovering above my other ear. "Just kidding." She gave me a kiss on the cheek. "Come on. We have to be there before sunrise."

I opened an eye and shot up. "What time is it?" I could see it was still dark.

"Almost five. Come *on!*"

I rubbed at my face and sat up. "Where the hell are we going?"

We jumped into Connie's Cadillac and she sped off with that all-knowing smile on her face. She took most of the curves of the narrow road leading out to the highway under fifty, but she pushed it to the floor otherwise. Why was I not surprised she would have a heavy foot?

"I think we finally wore you out, sweetie. You fell asleep about three. Leona kissed you good night. On your cock." Connie laughed and shook her hair back. I lacked the words. Connie looked gorgeous to me in the bluish light coming off the dashboard. "She doesn't say much, does she?" Connie deadpanned.

I put up a hand, letting her know I got it.

"Girl *knows* how to eat pussy," Connie said, clicking the turn signal.

I just looked over at her in the bluish light, wondering what she was going to say next.

"I'll teach you. It will be fun."

Within about twenty minutes we were pulling into a gravel drive with a weathered stained plywood sign that said "Andy's Aerial Adventures". As we bounced across a few pot holes I could see we were approaching a small wooden building, and just to the other side of it, I spotted an orange, white and blue hot air balloon plumping and rising up. There was a weak amber edge to the skyline over the lake behind it, promising a fitting sunrise.

Connie pulled the car to a stop. "Breakfast and sunrise over Blue Heron Lake. I've wanted to do it for over ten years. We're doing it."

I followed out of the car, but as I eased along side of her, my stomach began torqueing up. "I do not do well with heights," I announced clearly. My acrophobia was possibly a well kept secret but it was the right time to get it all out there in hopes of rerouting this date to the Cracker Barrel out by the interstate. All I heard was the gravel crunching under our sneakers.

"Did you hear me, Connie? I am afraid of heights. I can't explain it. I freeze up." As we got closer, the wicker basket beneath the inflated balloon looked liked it held unspeakable evil inside.

"Well, then it's about time to get you over it, don't you think?"

"No. I think not. I can live with it. Right here on the ground."

"Nonsense." She stopped us and hugged me, then reached down and grabbed my balls, which, by the way, were a little achy. "Big boy like you?"

I was torn between the moment I was choosing to live in and the reality I had known. When I was a small child my mother had taken Rondell and I to the John Hancock Building observatory in Chicago. It was a hundred stories up. When I got close enough to peer over the edge, everything inside of me went haywire, a thousand kinds of fears consumed me, and I think I feinted. Ever since, even a trip up a six-foot step ladder was a challenge for me. The years since had only crystallized and defined it for me.

"I will wait here for you if you really want to go," I said.

"I *really* want to go. With *you.*" It might have appeared like she was dragging me at this point. ""You're going. That's final. You'll be fine. I'll blow you the entire trip if you need me to."

I can honestly say the thought of sex repulsed me for the first time since before the summer, when any thought of sex was an unfortunate waste of time.

We were standing within ten feet of my worst nightmare. "Can't do this," I mumbled. I could hear the blood my heart was pumping in my ears.

"Good morning!" Came a way too cheerful, high-pitched voice. "Andy." The short man reached out to shake my hand. "Connie, welcome!" He gave her a big hug. "Finally, I get you in my balloon, hey." He dropped his high pitched voice to a menacing baritone for effect, and twitched his very thick, reddish eyebrows a few times. Andy looked like a freckled leprechaun, maybe all of five feet tall. When he stood next to the platform for the basket, it made the balloon look even taller. Maybe even taller than the John Hancock Building. Maybe. And here I was, being held against my will, by a woman, maybe old enough to be my mother. Maybe. The whole thought process came quickly out of necessity. The subject matter was nothing less than horrific. I was not to think of Connie and my mother in the same lifetime, let alone a sentence. It was almost as if I could feel my brain swelling with the need to sort out one thing from the other and deal with the fear factor than had settled in. Possibly I was not yet awake and I was in the midst of one of those pre-dawn power dreams that are full of everything from subterranean dragons to three-eyed men chasing me with guns to controlling women who laughed at my requests to get up to pee.

And what was that whole thing with Garland's wife again? Leona. Garland Luhrsen, perhaps the scariest man I had met on the planet thus far. Even Wahoo didn't scare me as much as Garland. With Wahoo, you could see what you might get and it was pretty easy to picture how he would go about tearing you apart. But with Garland, I would look at him, see the baby seal guttural anti-christ; someone who shut the door behind him when he got home at night and boiled someone for dinner. So while I am standing there in near anxiety induced cardiac arrest, it occurs to me I have been to bed with both Garland's wife and what I perceived as Wahoo's secret squeeze- at the same time. I was a dead man with a waiting list. What difference would it have made to die falling out of a big Easter basket from a couple thousand feet in the air?

Andy made a couple of trips back and forth to the balloon. "Ready, sports fans? Sunrise in about fifteen minutes, hey. Let's hop to it."

I followed Connie up the steps haltingly, like I was walking up to the gallows. I looked back to see if the preacher was there behind me, but really just to see how far I was off the ground. Four steps. Not a lot? Three too many.

"Your coffee, sir," Andy said with a wide smile. He handed me a lidded Styrofoam cup.

The basket shook and wobbled when I got in and I cuddled in next to Connie out of instinct. I put my arm around her and gave her a kiss on her cheek. "If we die, I'll kill you," I said.

"Oh, relax, Thomas. Good Lord, I can feel your body trembling. You're going to give me the shakes."

"This is insane," I whispered as I watched Andy toss away some long ropes and hop into the basket behind us. Easter basket done. "Whatever you are punishing me for, it's working."

*"Punishing you?"*

I just looked at her, then held my breath as Andy tossed the last rope down and we began to drift free and upward. "Shit!"

I could feel Connie's eyes on me, then her short laughter and a grin she was too proud of. "This is going to be fabulous. Not a cloud in the sky."

I tugged at my jacket. September mornings were getting pretty chilly, let alone being fifty thousand feet off the ground in the midst of death wielding wind sheers and unexpected thunderous lightning and horizontal rain. Where the *fuck* was my parachute? Just what the *fuck* would we do if something happened? Like this. Like getting higher off the ground. That no-turn-back point, like being half-way across the ocean on a jet liner. I was sure I could no longer safely jump to the ground, though every muscle in my torso was poised and contracted, waiting for the command from my brain to *go*.

"*Relax,* nut job," Connie said. Comforting me in her own way, I suppose, she snuck a hand down in front of me and grabbed my aching nuts for a double squeeze. I was sure Andy could see that. I wasn't about to turn around for confirmation. My one hand was woven into the wicker on the top rim of the basket and the other had permanently bonded to Connie's collarbone. My neck was thick and fused under my chin to keep my eyes from drifting down. I should have pissed before we left. For sure.

I was so frozen in my fear that, at first, I didn't react to the sound of the flame shooting out and up from the burner. Then my brain found space to let the sound creep in. "Shit!" We were all going to burn to death in mid-air. I had seen the video.

"Look at that!" Connie marveled, pointing to the lengthening orange glow that gained intensity as we got (gulp!) higher.

Having to piss was just an afterthought. I was trying to focus on something that would keep me from crapping in my pants. My dick felt like someone was humming a tune through it. So I focused on that. Like coming down the front side of the Ferris wheel when I was a kid. One of those things that a man just can't adequately explain to a woman without getting the *eye*.

Connie shook out of my death grip and reached inside her jacket pocket for a camera. She snapped off several pictures as the intense orange glow gave way to an orange ball of fire easing its way up on the horizon. Then she turned the camera on me. "This is nearly as interesting," she snickered.

Consumed by fear as I was, I could not help but think we were really in a movie studio. There was no sense of movement, and other than the incessant, jarring hot blasts of the propane heater, there was no sound. We were just *there*, evidently just floating along as perfectly as possible on a perfect morning for the perfect sunrise. So, I did the unthinkable. I unlocked my neck just enough to let me eyes look down for a moment. Mistake. Big mistake! This was no *fucking* movie studio.

"*You* are worth the trip," Connie laughed. I had no idea what I must have looked like, but I was ecstatic she had the thought to take some pictures of me they could lie across my chest in the casket. Scratch that. There wouldn't be enough of me left together to scrape into a casket. She could pick the best picture and send it to my mother.

I wanted to spout about my recent flirtation with death in the limosine debacle, but decided the whole explanation too complicated to chance opening the door on that one. I was, in fact, still reeling from the night before with Connie *and* Leona, tossing around the notion that

Connie was at least part lesbian, Leona was at least part lesbian, and I was…, what? Part lesbian, too?

If that meant anything at all, it was an ongoing fascination that I suppose at another time would have made me ill to think about. Not now. Picturing and figuring the picture was one thing, participating was another. There was a whole different set of endorphins and buzz buttons involved with getting into the act. So now, in the case the question would ever arise… have you ever been with two? I could and would answer… *why yes, I have.* In my case, I could not compare it to the fantasy because I hadn't had that yet.

I floated with the wind on the short term memory accuracy of those hours for a few more moments, then it was back to the precious moments I had left before I would fall to my death.

"I'm hoping for your sake that empty look on your face is because you are as amazed as I am," Connie said.

"She is a beaut, this morning for sure, hey," the little leprechaun added unnecessarily.

I felt obligated to nod.

Connie moved behind me and put her arms around me. When I did not respond much, she used her thumbs and index fingers to twist my nipples through my windbreaker.

"Owwwweeee," I think I said.

"Just wanted to make sure you were still with us…. I didn't bring a mirror to hold up to your mouth to see if you were still breathing."

I moved my hands over hers. "This is… *really* something."

"That's all you have for me?"

If I were to tell her the truth, it would be that I could not wait until it was over, one way or another. I was consumed by fear and likely scarred for life. But I didn't want to ruin her time with this. I could only hope the unpredictable Connie part would not possess her and make her do something weird- like rock the basket. God knows what else she might have in mind. Whatever. And it better not include the leprechaun. It occurred to me right then that Connie Mulroney was *always* up to something. She got out of bed in the morning up to something. This is what happened when you came to know Connie and her ways. Perhaps nothing was better than being around Connie when you knew her, but you never knew what she was going to do or say next.

*It some crazy, insane way,* maybe this is what it felt like to want to just be around somebody and love them that way.

"Just curious," I was saying back to Andy, "How do you get his thing back?"

"You don't," Andy laughed, knowing he had me.

"That's funny." I tried to nonchalant it. Easy mark that I was. There was such an eerie quiet to everything. The only noise cracking the barrier was the occasional bird calling to another or a feint wisp of breeze. If I wasn't told otherwise, I would have sworn we were just hovering, not going anywhere.

"Actually, I've got a pair of munchkins that by now should be trying to start an old Ford pick up truck and giving chase to us. Assuming they aren't still drunk or dead. I forgot to check."

I leaned over to Connie. "Guy's a real comedian."

"But, hey, not to worry, hey." He reached out and patted Connie's shoulder, clearly annoying me. "She comes down where she wants, but I give her a hint."

"We going to do that water thing?" Connie turned and asked him.

"Oh, ya. You bet, hey."

My stomach amazed me by dropping even further. "*What water thing?*"

Beginning with the throaty chuckle, this guy had me reeling. "What we do, see, is drop right down over Connie's place on Blue Heron Lake and just bounce the water a little bit. Wind's just about right, the way I figure. Look down to your left; you can see the lake coming up."

Did that. Did the figuring. Came up with *why?*

"Sounds like fun," Connie added to my misery, playfully poking me in the ribs.

I began to think this might be a good time to tell Connie I had already had my *water* experience for this week, and that I was still dealing with the visuals of another woman's face nestled between her legs. *That* unsettled anything that might have been left of the real world I left behind earlier in the summer of this year.

"Sounds more like a death march to me."

"Thomas. Where is that fun loving, curious-for-life guy that miraculously stepped into my life this summer?"

"He's still in the front seat of your Cadillac, captivated with how beautiful you look in the morning." I swear that is what came out.

I thought she was going to cry. She put her hands to either side of my face and just looked at me as her eyes got big and glossy, breathing a little sigh and pushing my hair around like she was fixing it somehow.

The next thing I knew, we were dropping down over Blue Heron Lake and I was looking down, in spite of myself. I got this comforting thought the largemouth bass in the lake I had gently released after catching would school up and protect me from any harm should this go awry, which I was sure would happen. Andy had a shit-eating grin on his face if there ever was one, and I was dead-on sure that if he thought he could dump me into the water at a hundred miles an hour and manage to keep Connie for himself, he would do it. Maybe shortly.

Nonetheless, my fear was giving way to the fascination of the gentle descent to the quiet waters below, and just as he said, we dipped down and the basket slashed at the water just in front of the Sunny Blue Resort- the Blue Gill cabin, for good measure. He cranked the burner just as we touched the water and the basket swayed and rocked to the side, and away we went; back up towards the sky, like a bird that had just been rewarded with a fish for its diving efforts.

"Awesome," I grinned, leaning and holding on, putting on a good show in my throw-away underwear.

# CHAPTER 19

I figured asking Rondell about women was risky, but I was not somebody who embraced or felt very comfortable with talky friendships, so I didn't have many choices. My brother Rondell was my best friend. Though a short, rather skewered current analysis might give the nod to the merry widow, Connie Mulroney.

"So the thing is," I said, biting into a corn beef and rye from Schluman's Deli, "this woman hits me like a Mack truck. All the buttons, all the levers all being pushed and turned at the same time."

"She know that?" Rondell asked. He had the pastrami, just to be different.

"What do you mean?"

"Does she know she's doing that to you?"

"Oh yeah. She talks about it even. She talks about everything coming down to the fact she's *got the pussy.*"

Rondell spit up a bit of dark rye crust. "Damn fucking right about that, my man." He shook his head and we both watched a new flock of birds landing around the bench next to ours. The fools were setting out scraps before they were done eating their lunch. They would pay for it. Better them than us. "How old is she again?"

"I guess, fifty or so. I don't know. It is the last thing that matters, I guess. If she was eighteen or eighty, she would still fascinate me. What she says… what she does… I never know what she is going to say or do next. It's a trip I never thought I would be on."

"Hot, man."

"It is."

"Did she kill Rudy, you think?"

I looked at Rondell to see if he was serious. He might have been. "Hell, no. I was there… ."

"You were *there?*"

"We were… uh… banging away in my little box of a room when he apparently stopped breathing in his bed."

"*Their* bed."

Anyway, the coroner or whomever said he died from acute apnea, or whatever."

"Right. In our neighborhood, brother, their would have been a bit more of an investigation into that, don't you think?"

"Why?"

"I know this might seem shocking to you, Tommy, but husbands and wives kill each other every day and most probably try their best to get away with it."

"Oh, great. Condescending lawyer crap from my little whoopty-shit lawyer brother."

"Easeeeee. You might need me someday."

"Need you? I needed you to stand up for me when our Dadeo whipped my ass with that fucking belt. That's when I needed you."

"You probably deserved it. I have to admit, though, it was hard to listen to from another room."

"Fuck you. He never touched *your* black ass."

"He knew better."

Going there was unexpected and I sure as hell didn't want to stay there. "Anyway, Connie was a mess. It was just bad. Tragic."

"Yeah. I'll bet Connie is still sitting around in a black shroud."

"You know, I'm not all that sure I like Rondell the lawyer. He's kind of a know-it-all asshole."

"They pay me for that. Quite well, it turns out."

I was going to go on about how well Connie knew everybody up in the Lakes area, that she had a good support system, and how every man that came around her seemed to be attracted to her is some way.

Visions of Wahoo Doyle Fortnight wafted up from my corned beef. I shrugged it off. "How is your lovely Sara these days?"

"Outstanding. She's in L.A. right now." Rondell pulled a Heineken beer from a paper bag and sucked about half of it down. He seemed to want to think it over for a moment. "One part wife, one part crazy bitch, and one hundred percent pure cunt. Hell, though, they're all cunts at the end of the day." Satisfied with that, he smiled and filled his large mouth with pastrami.

I nodded, not necessarily agreeing, but thinking that was the biggest gem of an observation I was going to get.

"Did she ever tell you about her *career* that night in Mulroney's?" He eyed me to see if he got a direct hit.

"Well, actually, no. *But...* I happened to be channel surfing I think it was last week one night and... ."

"Let me guess... *Cancun Capers?* That was her. I married celebrity." He waited to get the satisfaction of my amazement. He put up his hands and gave a halleluiah. "She says the art of making it look real is more difficult than it looks. I tell her I would have to agree because it doesn't even come close to looking real to me."

"You knew she did this before you married her?" I asked.

"Of course I did. Well, sort of. Anyway, I figured, what's the big deal? It pays a lot of money. She's a frickin' movie star, man."

I waited for more. Eating. Drinking my Diet Coke.

"Okay. So she's a slut. But, no complaints."

"I can hear that."

He slugged the rest of the beer down. "Connie's got it right. Keep fucking her."

Surprise, Two gems.

"Anyway, we'll be lucky to make a year, so who gives a shit. Ask me about work. Work is much easier. I am the rising non-*Heeb* star."

"You're kidding, right?"

"I told you, let's talk about work. Talking about women over lunch should be a felony."

"Okayyyyy.... . I'm losing my interest in teaching."

"Why?"

"Girl in the front row... Best as I can tell, wears different color panties every day. This morning, I was sure she didn't have *any* on."

"Commando's cool. Best color of all."

"Point is, my mind is just adrift in sex. All of a sudden."

"Making up for lost time, Tommy?" Rondell laughed with appreciation. "My older geek brother, the man whore."

"Yeah. Maybe that's it. Maybe it's my time…." I don't know if I ever said anything more mindless and meaningless.

"Don't fight it, man. Sound like you are trying to fight it off like it was something bad. Follow it for awhile and see where it goes. Hell, look at me, I *fall in love* with psycho women and *marry* them. Drunk! Twice already. What an idiot! I'm telling you, you got to wear it loose. The minute it tightens up with the bitch, move on." Rondell seemed glad to get that out, finished his beer, and cracked the other one he had in the bag.

As I sat in gridlock traffic on the Kennedy Expressway trying to get back to Harper College for a three-thirty class, I considered the conversation I had with Rondell and decided it was a do-over.

It wasn't that traffic was crawling; it was that is wasn't moving at all. Horns were bleating in pain and suffering while I suspected Webster's was taking a severe beating inside hundreds of cars. I opened my window, as though that was going to help, then shut it and opened the car door instead. That would really help. I got out and went around to the back, got up on the bumper and tried to see what might be ahead causing the problem. As far as I could tell, the problem was there were bumper-to-bumper cars as far ahead as the eye could see and whatever was causing that problem was beyond the horizon. Translation- I was screwed.

Amidst the mish-mash of white noise and real noise I could hear a woman's frantic voice screaming. It was coming from the mini-van behind me and the female driver of that car was going to war with whomever she had at the other end of her cell phone. I tried to ignore it at first, but there was such a strange panic-stricken tone to her voice it could not be ignored. I had to look again. Her head was down, buried into the steering wheel and the cell phone had been thrown to the passenger side top of the dashboard. I hesitated, but seeing no movement except across the way going east bound, I walked back to the mini van and tapped on the driver's side window.

Her head jerked up and back and she looked at me with big teary eyes and misplaced anger. Nonetheless, she rolled the window down and gave me another look. This was clearly that of desperation. It was only a moment before I heard a collaboration of noise that I could only define as screeching animals and wailing birds. My head was turned to the source coming from inside the back of the car. I shot a glance past her head and saw three identical infant car seats each holding a screeching, wailing child no more than a year old.

"Earaches, I don't know. All three!" she burst out. "I can't get them to stop crying. Molly has a fever of 103 degrees, Mindy almost 103. Marcy sounds like she is swallowing all of her bodily fluids." She took a deep breath. Her voice shook. "We are on our way to our doctor's office on Pulaski... Then this!"

Not equipped. Not equipped, a little voice inside my head offered. Run like hell.

Where? I asked. Just where the hell would I go? My observer laughed and pointed at me from atop the sound barrier along the freeway.

"God, I'm sorry, lady." Her whole face seemed to be gathering and tightening in the space above her nose between her eyes. She was actually quite attractive and wore a tan under platinum blonde hair that suggested she just returned from some place warm, the tanning salon or used a great tan-in-the-tube. Her hot pink nylon jacket was spotted with what I assumed was baby food, or baby something. "Triplets?" What did I know? I had only seen them on television.

"I don't know what the fuck to do," she said as she threw her seat belt back and crawled back over into the back to console the babies.

Any piece or part of thinking what I could do to help seemed to stop as abruptly as the traffic. Nothing was moving. Not an inch. It was a parking lot. Her radio was on the news channel and I think I heard something about an overturned semi near the Western Avenue exit ramp that was blocking all lanes. Mostly what I heard was the vibrating racket of the babies and the woman trying to console them.

"Mommy will make it better, sweetness. Don't cry, sweetheart," she softly repeated to each to no avail. If anything, the crying of at least one of them had taken on a throaty, gurgling dimension which ripped at both your eardrums and your heartstrings.

"Triplets." I said, again to the uncaring hoards surrounding us.

As I considered whether or not I had seen this in a movie, cars stalled in an endless line as either a tsunami or an alien spaceship swooped in, I came up with an idea. I ran up to the car ahead of me and explained the situation to the driver, a young, Spanish looking guy I actually called "dude". He smiled, and pulled his car ahead as far as possible. I jumped into my car and did the same, then ran back out to the car behind the minivan. A middle-aged black man on a cell phone bought my story as well and backed his car up as far as possible. I was pretty sure we had enough room. I got into the minivan and with a seven-point maneuver managed to turn it off onto the right shoulder. I hadn't ever considered being in the far right lane a stroke of luck, but it was on this day for the pretty lady with the baby whatever on her jacket.

"Okay, you can drive up the shoulder to the exit ramp just ahead and take Diversey over to Pulaski. "Go!"

She jumped back into the driver seat and looked up at me. Her eyes and face relaxed a bit, even though the noise level continued to rise.

"I don't know how to thank you," she said, putting it into gear. She had full lips and a wide smile.

"Just go," I said. "You're welcome." I watched as she sped past the line of cars in the right hand lane and off onto the exit ramp. A few more followed her, getting the idea.

Marriage? Babies? Never. Triplets? Suicidal. Very nice lips though. A blow job would have been nice. I managed to spin it back into my world.

I was twenty minutes late by the time I got to class. I condensed my lecture on the Declaration of Independence; anyway, a boring litany of garbage not worthy of the grand men who signed it. It hit me that not a single girl in the front row of seats was wearing a skirt. I resented that. I thought of Connie. A killer? Mattie. I should have called her instead of the email asking her if she made it back okay. She never answered back. Veronica? Oh my Lord, Veronica. How could she not be on my mind every moment? Getting her brains fucked out in Iowa City. And what about Maria? What about Maria? I think she got stoned a lot.

More that I thought. Then there was Leona. Did I need to include her? She blew me, I think.

A hand went up.

"Yes?" Praise God and give the kid an *A* for interrupting this drek of a lecture.

"Who is Wahoo Jefferson, dude?"

# CHAPTER 20

October was a series of weekend trips to see Connie with some pretty shitty teaching efforts in between. The drive would get seemingly old, but with the autumn colors changing with each weekend, it was more like a tour than a long drive. The first weekend in November we decided to meet in Minneapolis for a big city diversion, saving me a couple of hours driving as well. She picked the Grand Hotel. I thought it was a little pricy for what we would do in it, but she insisted on making all the arrangements and paying for it as well. The weekend would include a twist, she said. We would meet in the lobby bar, *but,* we were to pretend we were two totally different people than we were.

"What are you talking about?" I asked during our phone conversation earlier in the week.

"You pick out somebody else to be, I'll do the same. Then we'll see if those two people make a connection. We'll go from there."

"What if they don't connect?"

"It'll be a short weekend for those two people."

I strummed my fingers on the coffee table in front of the television. I was watching *Space Station Erotica* and looking for Sara. "You sound like you've done this before."

"One time," Connie said.

"And?"

"He was a reincarnated Viking who had been at sea for four years."

"And you?"

"I was… a sex researcher. I interviewed guys about their sex lives. Measured their cocks. Things like that."

"Swell. How did it end?"

"How do you think?"

"Well, since you were already *that*, you can't be *that* again, right?"

"That's fair."

"Okay. I'll see you at eight o'clock, in the lobby bar."

"You'll see *somebody*."

*Wild guess.* I'm thinking the Viking was Wahoo, big, burly, and unusually hairy for a Native American Indian. No matter. And Connie- the sex researcher- was Connie.

The leaves were gone and the grays and lifeless browns had set into anything above curb level. Oddly, I was thinking about Harry's bar. Buying it. Running it. I could run the bar at night. Maybe start writing during the days. I wasn't cut out to be a history teacher, for Godsakes. There was a world around me I knew nothing about and more women were apparently attracted to me that I could have thought possible. And, the thing was, they *wanted to have sex with me!* I came to the conclusion I was not maxing my opportunities at anything by teaching, which had largely turned into a daily routine of formula outlined lectures moving out over my lips while I scanned the front row for beaver shots. I was feeling wildly irresponsible and unaccountable. Childish, maybe, but I was thinking very adultish and sprouting semi-erections with only the slightest effort of imagination involving women I knew, and many women I didn't know.

Call it a sexual awakening of sorts, for lack of a better term. Perhaps the reason I was apparently becoming more attractive to women was they were becoming a more attractive option to me. It used to be the thought of *being* with a woman was such an overwhelming process it just scared me shitless. A date to me should have come with that sign you see in a gift shop – *You break it, You buy it.* I don't remember ever disliking women as a result, but ultimately I could talk myself out of any potential involvement and settle for a date here and there, an occasional bedroom romp or a disinterested hand job. Most women I knew on a casual basis reacted to me in the same way, keeping a comfortable distance as if they knew something wasn't quite right. There was Susan O'Reilly, who lived in a crumbling house two blocks down. Susan and I shared some curious and light experimental moments in her basement after school my senior year in high school. She was the first, and only woman in my life to whisper that she loved me. She did it twice; both times we were fighting for territory on that filthy maroon corduroy couch in the basement. Both times I had my hand down the front of her jeans. I figured she had no choice. I was going to college. I was her ticket out of the neighborhood.

I had lost track of Susan, but thought of her at times. Somebody told me she was a very successful hooker in Tampa, Florida. I doubted that.

When in doubt, just wait for Connie to take the lead. That is what I decided to do as I walked into the lobby bar at the Grand Hotel in downtown Minneapolis and adjusted my tie. I was wearing the one and only suit I owned. It was black with muted pin stripes, made by an Italian tailor in the neighborhood who dropped dead in his little shop not long after. I thought I might need it for interviews after college. It was still stylish, I suppose, but I felt like a walking corpse and had to consciously keep from striking a pose. I thought the solid purple tie made me look rich. I got the idea from watching Regis Philbin or Donald Trump probably.

The place was high class, smelled of polished mahogany and fresh oriental lilies. Big money and old money. I took a chair at the bar and ordered … a martini. This should be good, I thought. Two or three martinis and there would be no doubt I would be somebody else. I couldn't handle hard liquor. Leave it to Connie. I already felt some lift and buzz at the idea of living dangerously.

I figured she was watching from somewhere in one of those dark booths along the wall, so I ate the olive like I was making love to it. I hated olives. Green bitter turds with a red, regrettable bonus inside.

I never understood what people saw in gin. To me, the smell of the polish on the mahogany and the gin was the same. I hadn't drank the polish, but imagined the taste likely the same. I could feel my kidneys beginning to rot. But I got one down and ordered another. The bartender was the silent, pompous type, having you believe he came to work in a Mercedes and went home to a castle in the country with a circular drive.

Little fucker must have seen me gag on the olive the first time around and doubled up on this one. He had that unmistakable snob sneer that made you want to jump right over the bar and slap him so hard his toupe flew off. Then choke him to death with his little fake bow tie.

"How we doing tonight? I asked.

He nodded. "Just fine, sir." His lips and teeth didn't move. Little prick. And I was doing okay, too. Just for the record. I ate both the olives in one gulp and only felt myself twitch once. I'd show the little bastard.

I was, in fact, becoming giddy and warming to the guy in the suit with the purple tie. He could have been many things; but for sure, he was filthy rich. That was it. I would be a filthy rich male nymphomaniac pervert. I began to think about really filthy things to say for the part. Maybe this could be fun after all.

There were more than a dozen people in the bar, most of which looked like they belonged with rich, classy nymphomaniac perverts like me. But no Connie. I never knew her to be late. I was working into the second martini when a dark-haired, very tall woman sat down on the chair next to mine. She ordered a Merlot and set her tiny gold-sequined purse up on the bar between us. I tried not to be too obvious, but she had an eeriness to her that didn't quite complete itself in the low light.

"Hello," she said to me. All I could think of at the time was the line from the Jerry McGuire movie- *You had me at hello.* The voice was husky, the eyes flirtatious and heavy. But even in the low light, I could see this wench had a five o'clock shadow for the ages.

Not on my menu.

I nodded politely, felt constriction in my groin area, and heard a very loud, clear voice in my head telling me to finish the martini and take a walk. Just as I began to get up, a polite little version of dolled-up loveliness sat down on the other side of me. Looking a bit closer to make sure this one didn't also have a beard, none other than Leona Luhrsen threw a big, gracious smile my way. I smiled back at her, probably suspiciously, and looked just beyond her, expecting Connie to show up in maybe a leopard-skin cave girl outfit with six-inch spiked high heels.

"Hi Leona," I said, making my mouth exaggerate the words she could not hear.

Unlike her (gulp!) husband, Leona didn't make any sounds at all. Not even when she was cumming, which was otherwise, quite exaggerated, as I recalled. She signed the smart-ass bartender for a drink and the son of a bitch signed her back. Then she handed me a note.

Your Teacher Has Arrived.
See you at graduation, later.
Love,
Connie

I ordered another martini. Three olives this time, the little cocksucker.

To say it was odd to have a drink and conversation with a deaf mute was an understatement in my life to that point. We motioned and gestured back and forth and I mouthed words, much to the amusement of the girl/guy on the other side of me, I was sure.

"Where... *is*... Connie?" I mouthed.

She shrugged and smiled widely. She actually looked quite gorgeous. Her hair was done "up" and pulled back to reveal a satin white face with high cheekbones and dark, flickering eyes. The make up and lipstick and the sheik black satin outfit did not say she lived in a ramshackle cabin back in the woods somewhere near Blue Heron Lake.

I looked around for guidance and an infusion of logic, but instead, Leona finished her drink and put her hand on mind, pointing to the exit with the other.

I paid the bill, left the bartender a few dollars and followed Leona out the door. Her hand pulling mine.

Up an elevator we went. She lit up the number nine and we got off on the ninth floor. She pulled out a card and we walked up to room 9006 and went inside. Another big smile from Leona as she quietly made her way to the king-size bed, pulled down the cover and began unbuttoning her blouse.

Once we were naked and gathered together at the middle of the bed, she gave my earlobes a twist, winked at me and gently pushed me down and over her stomach. My nose began to tickle with tiny hairs that smelled like musky long-stemmed roses. Then she was all hands and long, slender fingers, pushing, pulling, positioning my jaw, encouraging and directly the tip of my tongue, occasionally tweaking the tip of my nose, which I came to realize quickly meant *"no"*. The slight twist of the earlobes meant *"yes, that"*, and then, when I really started to get it, she could direct traffic by pulling and twisting on one earlobe or the other. I don't know how much time passed, but when she began to buck at me with a vengeance, I knew we were making progress.

I spent the night in Room 9006- of that I was certain. After an exhausting classroom session and the near dislocation of my jaw, Leona and I had ordered some drinks through room service. I ordered a pitcher of martinis, *hold the olives,* and can't remember what Leona ordered. I am pretty sure we screwed until I passed out. Nonetheless, I woke up on my back with a pair of legs straddling my neck and the smell of a familiar French perfume and a sweet dusting powder in my nose. The hands were poised at my earlobes. I took a deep breath, swooning in an overheated hangover, and dove in. Waking up might have been an option, but just getting beyond the fogginess of the hangover under the *circumstances,* was remarkable to me. Click. Click. The silent teachings of my Zen master began to kick in. Do *not* dive in. Shorter, lighter, well placed strokes of the tongue, then establish a rhythm, vary it a bit, sense her uniqueness, respond to it. How could I forget? I would *never, ever* forget.

I was feeling the fatigue in the jaw again, hoping I could outlast it. Then, subtly at first, then gathering the storm, the hips were in a light grind over me and my earlobes were being massaged like deep muscle tissue. Suddenly my face became one with the enemy and all stood still. It would not let go. I heard what sounded like a Linda Blair snarl and a scream that bounced and vibrated off the high ceiling. Less I die from affixiation; I was given a small space for air before the wet heat was back down on me, then moving slightly back and forth. Another scream, followed by four or five lesser, yet still formidable screams. My earlobes had been squeezed down to the thickness of band aids.

"Ohhhh mmmyyy gaaawdddddd!" I heard. "Fuuuuuck!" she yelled at the world. Then, warning me by the rapid change in earlobe flicking, she came again and collapsed next to me on the bed.

"Good morning, Connie," I yawned. My face must have looked like somebody cracked an egg over it.

"Jesus. You learned well," she spoke into the pillow. She took a deep breath and turned over on her side. "You are now the perfect man, Thomas Cabot."

"Perfect! She says." Only God could save me from a martini hangover.

"It was the only thing missing from your arsenal. You learned the best from the best."

I struggled to get the upside. "Sounds more like a competition to me. Whatever," I laughed, not believing any of this. Who would? Connie, of course.

Connie laughed and threw herself back into the pillows. "Leona would love that."

I scratched my head and rubbed my eyes and got up to get a towel from the bathroom. By the third wobbly step, I swore off anything with gin again.

"Who says I was done?" I heard Connie saying.

"Just… retooling," I said. I walked back and sat on the edge of that bed and looked at possibly the most beautiful full-figured woman I had ever known. A woman, in the sense of one who looks the way she would want to be remembered in her life. She may or may not have been a teen beauty or a curvaceous thirty-something, but no doubt she would be the envy of any woman wanting to look this good at fifty. It became more pronounced and obvious each time I saw her. She had that soft sexiness in the morning that made you want to jump her bones and put on your footy jams at the same time.

"Now, you." She reached over and grabbed my wrist. There was a little more husk to her voice in the morning.

Room service was on its way to room 9006 for the second time. Connie, dressed in a Grand Hotel fluffy white terrycloth robe directed the young Spanish looking girl to set up the table in front of a large sliding door leading out to a sky that was throwing around noisy sheets of cold November rain.

"So just curious…," I began, over Eggs Benedict and much needed coffee, "what happened to Leona?"

Connie was sorting through the basket of muffins and breads. "She had to get back for her daughter Caroline's soccer game this morning." She shuddered. "I imagine it would be a little wet and chilly out there." She smiled up at me.

# CHAPTER 21

Sunday night. Somebody was driving my car back to Chicago. I was behind the wheel, best as I could tell, but it wasn't me. My head was still following up on the events of the weekend, still doubting what happened, happened. I was thinking about imaginary lines; how somebody like me draws them up so carefully and how easily somebody like Connie Mulroney steps over them. I was deliriously baffled by this woman and her presence in my life to the point I could hardly remember her being married to Rudy. I could hardly remember Rudy. There was unsettling to it all, a sense it was a fit between other things for us, a nonsensical romp that would end at some point and return us to our personal demons. But for now, I was having a blast.

As I pulled around the last corners in the neighborhood, I had decided this was like wishing there was more to the movie when it was over. But then, I would feel that way because the ending was good. I was a mess, my thoughts slamming into each other like twenty kids in a moon walk built for ten. My whole life was now based on what would happen *next*.

The *next* appeared to be waiting for me to come back to my apartment. As I drove closer I could see the yellow police tape everywhere, a half dozen City of Chicago squad cars, an ambulance, two six-wheel fire trucks, and news vans from Channels Five and Seven. A small crowd of people were huddled under spot lights just outside the tape by the front entrance of the building next to mine. I had difficulty finding a place to park, finally finding a spot four blocks away and walked back carrying my duffel bag, which contained my one and only suit and a great Regis Philbin purple tie. And three pairs of clean, folded underwear. Never used.

I didn't see or smell smoke, but recognized one of my fellow tenants from down the hall standing with the others while cops and others went in and out of the building. "Hey, Sanji. What's up?"

Sanji Harossefji turned to me. "You just get here, man?"

"Yeah."

"Wow, man. Some dude had his step-mom held hostage in the building next to ours. I guess Tiandra knew him. It was like her ex-boyfriend, or some weird shit."

"Tiandra? Tiandra who?"

"Tiandra Jackson. You know, lives in the apartment next to yours? She's over there talking to the cops."

"I didn't know her name until now. Sorry."

"Sometimes you're a pretty weird dude, Cabot."

"I am well aware of that, Sanji." Then I took another look at Sanji and reconsidered. The new normal.

I had seen Tiandra Jackson, exchanged hallway greetings, even opened the outer security door for her once or twice when she had a bag of groceries, but I didn't know her name. I knew that face. And that was indeed the young black girl that lived in the apartment next to mine.

"So what happened?"

"Check this out." Sanji sounded like a caricature of himself sentenced to live in American culture. I wasn't sure where he was from, but I was certain it was full of terrorists and bad guys. "I could hear the dude screaming out the window at the cops to back off. Then I heard shots, crazy shit going on and next thing I know they bring him out in a body bag. They took the old lady off to the hospital but I guess she was just in shock or some shit. You missed all the action, man."

"I guess." It was hard for me to work up the frenzy Sanji was enjoying. "Looks like it's over now."

"Freaky shit, man."

I left Sanji to whatever fantasy he was working on and went inside. When I got to my door on the second floor, there was Tiandra, sitting on the floor in front of her door, head down on her knees, arms wrapped around her head.

"Tiandra?" I asked, as if she should be impressed I knew her name all along. "You okay?"

She looked up at me. Brown eyes in the middle of big white circles with a face still wet with tears. She wiped away. "I locked my keys inside. I was so upset with what was going on... I just ran out."

"Violin?" I saw the leather case on the floor next to her. "Or... ."

"Violin"

"You play?"

"Chicago Symphony. Alternate."

"Actually, that explains the music I hear through my walls from time to time. I always thought it was a CD. Can I help?"

"If you have a cell phone I could borrow to call a locksmith, that would be great."

"Sure. Here, come on inside and sit down." I opened my door and she followed me inside. I handed her my phone and dumped my bag on the floor.

"You want a beer?" I asked.

She nodded with a cracked smile.

"Two beers then."

She made her call. "I got an answering service. They said they would page them."

We settled into opposite ends of the couch and I tuned to the second half of Sunday Night Football. "You know, I think I'll order a pizza. Interested?"

"I guess I'm not going anywhere. Thanks for asking. I'm sure we'll get this resolved shortly."

"Not a problem."

They weren't delivering anymore so I phoned in a pick-up order to Louie B's down on the corner. My Chicago Bears were getting it handed to them by the Minnesota Vikings anyway. I told her to make herself at home. When I got back, the screen was on mute and Tiandra was playing her violin to the silent slaughter. She stopped when I set the pizza box down on the coffee table in front of the couch.

"Thanks." Her voice was soft and her expression blank, but a crinkle of a smile tugged at one corner over her mouth. "Sausage. Perfect. It was very nice of you to offer." She set the violin down and grabbed a piece.

This was one of the moments when everything froze for me. I was recalling watching Tiandra ascending the stairs in front of me several months before. Plump sway back booty shifting and lifting. Not for me, but definitely for somebody. The smell of pizza in the air, and Connie on my clothes, I was completely focused on the size and movement of Tiandra's lips. It was like some addiction had come over me, some panting insistence I go to the inference of something sexual at the mere thought, vision, or smell of female.

"The guy was an ex-boyfriend," she began, as though this was a conversation we had already started. "A terrible drunk. I mean, the funny thing is I was thinking of moving away. I have a sister in Nashville. They are putting together a new symphony orchestra down there. Here I'm just an alternate. Down there it might be different."

Her calm was almost uncomfortable. But I could go along. "I have to tell you how much I enjoy you playing. Even though it's just through the walls."

"Do you ever go to the symphony?"

"Like as in the Chicago Symphony? No. I never considered myself eligible for that kind of an evening."

She nodded at me and scarfed the pizza down, wiping her chin on her sleeve. Then she picked up the violin again and started playing. 36-6 Vikings. A final. I left the post game on mute as I sat back in a bean bag chair across from the couch and allowed myself to be carried into the gentle, soothing melody she was playing. Pizza in one hand, beer in the other. I watched Tiandra begin to bring her body language into her music, swaying just slightly as she pulled the bow through. The music, the pizza, the moment. It was exquisite. Unexpected and exquisite. She would need to tell me when she was done. I wasn't going anywhere.

I don't know how long I had been asleep, but I awoke disoriented and floating like satellite debris in space.

"Sleepy head," Tiandra called out to me from the couch.

"Sorry. It was like a beautiful lullaby."

"A compliment then."

"Oh yes."

"Still don't believe this...," she began again, as I sucked down some warm beer. "Violent, unpredictable, out-of-his-mind stuff. But I just can't imagine after two years of not hearing a word from him he would be capable of this. I mean, really, I thought I heard he was dead. Killed in a car wreck down in Champaign almost a year ago," She said, as though she had been talking to me for awhile. Again, her calm way of just simply laying it out left me with a little more head work than I cared to do.

We talked for awhile about crazy people and I grabbed a couple more beers.

She used my cell phone to call the locksmith again. Answering service. Another message. "Well, I can't stay here, for sure," she said. "I'm going to take a cab over to my friend's place on Halsted."

"Can I give you a lift?" I asked.

"I can cab it. No problem."

"Really. I don't mind."

"Okay then. Thanks." She had a great smile of white, perfect teeth and the large, wide dark vermillion lips up close that gave me a bit of a shiver. *Shut up!* I told myself.

"You can stay if you want." I could not believe that came out of my mouth. No lines anymore. Who was I kidding?

I waited for the laughter or the slapping rejection. Got neither. "You are a *funnnny* white boy," she said with a wistful shake of her head and just a hint of a smile. "But I like you. Too bad we didn't meet a while ago."

"We did. We met quite a while ago, walking down the stairs one day last summer."

"Right you are."

I was regretting this. She just looked at my face and seemed to study me for warts. "Right you are."

I got up and traded the flat screen for the CD player and put on some Cold Play. When I moved over to the couch I noticed Tiandra chasing a few pills down with her beer. We seemed to move to the middle cushion at the same time and went right to work on each other. She unzipped me and worked her hand into my jeans while my middle finger sunk into a wetness that already had sopped her thong. We both quickly found some urgency and in no time at all we had heaped our clothes and I was positioned above her on the couch. She move one of her legs up onto the seat back and pulled me into her with a single accurate jerk.

She moaned and sucked her breath in as I began moving in and out. But something just wasn't quite right. I could not seem to get the right angle to go with the rhythm we were attempting to find. I fell out once. Then I seemed to catch more hair than wet. Back in I went, and out. Back in. Twenty more strokes or so and I got this weird thought my dick was a baby carrot swimming solo in a simmering crock pot. I was slamming around like a rookie. I think I was still hard, but I couldn't be sure. It was like there was a loose rubber band at the bottom of my cock and the rest of it was free to shop for a place to go.

"Deeper!" She urged, pulling on me with unexpected arm strength. She was scaring me now. I got one foot on the carpet, hooked my other foot underneath a seat cushion and grabbed on to the armrest above her head with both hands. She had one leg around my neck, the other pressing the wall above the back rest and we were as leveraged as two people can be. A misguided move at this point could hurt somebody. I still couldn't feel anything except a sensation there was pooling buckets of hot fluid coming out of her beneath me. I'm guessing she could have used three of me. Finally, just before I thought my back might snap, she initiated a readjustment. She took my hand in one of hers and we sort of wedged in as a team along side my overheating piston. She came before I did, and fortunately for me it was loud enough and animated enough to make me follow soon after.

Tiandra got up without a word and went into the bathroom. I got up to get a towel from a kitchen drawer to wipe myself off, then started blotting at the mess on the couch. The middle cushion of my couch felt and smelled like it had taken a dip in the ocean. For the time being, I just turned it over.

My cell phone summoned me from the coffee table. It was the locksmith. Tiandra had left my number. Of course. She came back out of the bathroom and I handed her the phone. She was quite the picture leaning into the doorframe, naked from the waist down. I got a pretty good look at that thing, mostly a curly edged triangular mat of black hair that had a fuzz rod to the belly button and tufts spreading onto the fronts of her thighs. I had a right to be scared.

I gulped.

"He's finally here," she said.

To her rescue. And mine.

# CHAPTER 22

I didn't sleep much that night and couldn't wait for another shower the next morning. Another long one. I was tired as hell but I was going to decontaminate after the Tiandra sliming if it was the last thing I did. Afterward, I went down the street to Starbucks and said hello to the new girl behind the counter. I didn't have the energy to tell her I thought she was the most beautiful woman in the world this Monday morning. I settled for a low-fat blueberry muffin and a Venti, bold and black.

Whenever I was driving to my mother's house, it would conjure up some memory, good or bad, and by the time I got there, it had usually come and gone. On this day in November, cold and raw, I recalled sticking my ten-year-old head out my bedroom window to fill my nose with the wonderful smells coming from the open windows of Mrs. Sebastiani's kitchen next door. In contrast, our house had this blending fragrance of cod liver oil, Senekote and a K-Y Jelly tube left open somewhere.

"Hi Mom." I leaned around and kissed her on the cheek. The kitchen smelled about the same, adding the essence of burning toast.

"Hello dear." My mom was at the kitchen sink, dressed in a black, floor length, patterned Oriental silk dress/robe thing. "I'm having an English Muffin. Care for one?"

"No thanks." I sat down at the kitchen table and set the package down. "Just wanted to bring his power drill back. I've got a class at eleven."

My mother kept watch over the toaster. "I don't like the way this thing toasts. It burns everything."

I looked to be sure and leaned over her shoulder to turn the adjustment down from *MAX* to something in the middle. "Try that. That *thing*, Mom, is over twenty years old. Maybe you could ask him for one for Christmas. Better yet. Now I know what to get you."

"A toaster? " She turned to me for a moment. "How sweet, dear."

"So...," I said, readying a jump into the deep end.

"Things are okay," she said. "I haven't had a *BM* for almost two weeks, but I've got a suppository working right now."

The cod liver oil smell seemed pretty heavy. Maybe that is what is was all along. Suppositories.

"I had lunch with Rondell," I said.

"I think Rondell will run for President." She scraped the black char off the English muffin and started buttering. "I hope I'll vote for him."

I began tapping the table to an imaginary song. About six bars. Refrain. Six bars. Refrain.

"You could call him *Dad*, Thomas."

"We've been through all of that, Mom."

"It would please him so."

"Right. I know."

"They're having a poor season. Only won two games, I think. He has been out of sorts. But you know your father. He's already planning on a new set of plays and things for next year."

I started to say he *wasn't* my father and, no, I didn't know him- didn't want to know him- but the self-serving caught in my throat and I backed off. Mostly. "Maybe they need a new coach?"

She gave me a puzzled look and got back to working the muffin.

"Anyway, gotta go, Mom." I got up and watched her ladle on another huge glob of butter. "I love you."

"Dear?" She turned as I opened the back door. "You *are* coming for Thanksgiving, aren't you?"

"I think so," is the best I could come up with. I gave her a hug, a kiss on the cheek, just barely avoiding the smear of grape jelly near her nose. "When is that again?"

"On Thanksgiving, dear."

I wasn't sure what or how things got processed in my mother's head. I was just glad to get out of the house before *he* showed up. No need to update the memories of seeing him walking around *his house* farting, and toying with his shwantz through his pants like it was some ritual we all enjoyed.

In the days right after that I started spending a lot more time in Harry's. I had a stool I started to call my own. I wasn't quite sure what it was, but I somehow saw myself in this place, owning this place, changing the name to, maybe, *Cabot's Corner.* Something that had a small, comfortable feel to it. What about bras? What about bras on the high ceiling? Add some lower rafters the ladies could reach. I mean, why not? Chicago, The Sunny Blue Resort; what difference did it make, really? And if you are going to spend a lot of time in a bar, why not run the place? I knew how to do that. You can drink and run the place at the same time. It can be done.

It was a quiet night, maybe a Thursday. Harry was flipping the bird at Jay Leno on the television. He said he hated the guy. He would change the channels with the remote until he got to ESPN, but he would always pause at the NBC channel, wait for a clear head shot of Leno, then flip him off. "Fuck you, you bastard," he would yell, flip him the finger and then move on.

"Harry? You still thinking about selling the place?"

He leaned over like we had secrets. "Every fuckin' day, these days. I tell ya, Tommy, I got to get South. Warm weather. I can feel the winter coming in my shoulders, my arms, my hands, my ass. Everything fuckin' hurts. I got to get the hell out of here once and for all."

"Thinking Florida?"

"Yep. Brother-in-law's got a double-wide down there about two blocks off the ocean in Vero Beach. I can get it for a song. He's got lung cancer and heading for the hospice any day now."

"Too bad. Sorry about that."

"Yeah. For him."

Harry set me up another beer and pushed my money back at me. Then he did a double take and a big smile broke out across his broad face. "Holy cripes, here comes trouble."

He was looking past me at two young women walking in, both with jet black, short spiked hair, matching tight black leather jackets and, unless I was seeing double, identical cuteness.

"Hi Daddy," one cooed as she walked up to the bar and leaned over to kiss Harry. The other pursed her lips and blew with a big smile attached. Harry looked pretty happy about it.

"What brings you two hooligans to the slums tonight?" he asked.

"Just missed you is all," one said.

Harry leaned forward and set his chin on his hands. "Uh huh." There was no doubt these were identical twins. Whatever perfume they were wearing was oozing and squeaking out with the smell of chilled leather. Both voices were a bit on the husky side, but didn't give up their feminine side. They were tall, slender, to be looked at with patience and consideration, it seemed. Looking at twins- *really* looking at them was far more than just interesting. There was so much to think about. What about moles? Were they in the same places? Okay. So it only took me about thirty seconds to wonder if they looked as identical naked as they did with clothes on. Once I was there, it took a life of its own. In duplicate..

They slid down toward the end of the bar as Harry did the same. I couldn't hear much of the conversation, but from what I saw, Harry was no longer thinking about the brother-in-law, or Jay Leno. He face was lit up and every white hair on his head seemed aglow.

They stayed twenty minutes or so and left without having a drink.

"Hell's afire," Harry said, shaking his head as he walked past me. He served up some drinks to other customers and made his way back. "So what did you think of that?" He twitched his bushy eyebrows.

"These days, what goes through my mind... I might be arrested. Doesn't it make you wonder how they actually get into jeans that tight? Nothing else under... ." I shuddered.

"When they were a lot smaller, I used to put them on. Now...."

I shot him a suspicious look.

"They're my daughters, Tommy," he laughed.

I pointed to his happy face. "That's just not right, Harry."

"Gotcha!" he laughed.

I had a few more than I would normally. We went in and out on the idea of selling and buying, and suddenly, when I realized there was nobody but Harry buying drinks- for me- the idea seemed to lose its steam. I hadn't heard the cash register flip a number in over an hour. That is what I liked about Harry's- it's easy, quiet comfort zone- but with the vision of an ownership upon me, *Cabot's Corner* looked pretty broke.

"You believe it's going to be the frickin' holidays in a couple of weeks. What the hell," Harry said as he poured himself a shot of Wild Turkey. "That's what the kids were in here about. They want me to close the place down over the Thanksgiving weekend and take them and the old lady down to Vero Beach."

"Sounds like a great plan."

"Sounds okay. But we get a lot of business in over the holidays. Lots of people want to just sit and drink in a place like this."

"I can see that. Just look at them fighting for a stool."

"Thursday nights are shit. You know that, you horse's ass."

"Well, gee, if memory serves me right, Thanksgiving falls on a Thursday almost every year."

"Okay, smartass. *You* want to work here that weekend? I'll split my take with you."

"How about I'll just take my share as I go. Then you won't have to bother counting it out so even."

"When did you get so damn cocky? Who lit your ass up?"

I took another drink. "It was a little fucking dog."

"What?"

"Never mind. Long story."

"Anyway. Like I said, I'm looking to get out of this nut house and there will be plenty of time for Florida beaches and so on. Let the guy die in peace first."

"Decent of you, Harry. Fucking heart the size of Kansas."

"Well, I'll tell you what, hot shot. You don't seem to be carrying any freight around on your arm these days. Why don't you come to the house on Thanksgiving. I know you liked my girls. They'd bury you."

"Holy shit! I don't believe you said that."

Harry and I jousted for maybe another hour before I left. When I got back to the apartment, I could hear violin music coming from next door. A now unwelcome remembrance of perhaps the worst sexual experience of my life. The can of Oust was still on the counter where I left it. I sprayed there. Sprayed everywhere. Then to the couch. I got out the upholstery cleaner and brush I had purchased earlier that day and gave the middle cushion another once over. Then I aimed the can of Oust at the cushion and nailed it for thirty seconds, or until the can went empty. I decided if the smell wasn't gone in another day, I would have to trash the couch or just go with two cushions.

The violin strings were not nearly as soothing as before. Just as I was getting out of another shower, my cell phone rang.

"Thanksgiving. I am inviting the whole summer staff and their families over. That would include you." Connie sounded coy and boozy.

"And...."

"You're with me, sweet. If I'm only going to get you on some weekends, you're all mine while you're here."

I was trying to picture the seating arrangements. The gathering around, the turkey being carved- by Connie. Who else? Garland, Leona? ...The shudder curled my tailbone.

"You *have* to say yes," she said, as if to remind me.

"Yes," I said, returning to Connie-matic.

"Okay, Mr. Excitement, I suppose I could have asked somebody else..."

"But they're all married."

"*That* was a cheap shot."

"Sorry."

Drying off, phone tucked between my ear and shoulder, walking through the apartment, sniffing around like a blood hound, I believed I was finally getting the upper hand. I would get another can of Oust the next day just to be sure.

"It's better when you're here," she said, ice cubes jiggling, a rasp developing in her voice. My affected world view was projecting close ups of Leona's face between her legs. I was sure Connie was more than capable of multi-tasking, but just as I was about to ask, she ended the call with a quick "Good night sweet prince."

Out of droning habit, I sat down at my computer to check emails before I fell into bed. Amongst the offers for Xanax, Viagra, edible herbal roaches, everlasting salvation- cheap- and women who craved big cock, was an email from somebody tagged VME.

Hey, Genius
College is a drag. Nothing but little boys without a clue. I'm bored. The banker starting to look good to me. I need you. Want you.
Come to Iowa for Thanksgiving. We'll fuck until the cows come home. I mean that.
Missing you,
Veronica

I read it again. ... I don't remember how many times.

# CHAPTER 23

I told my mother I probably should take Connie up on her invitation to be with her and the Sunny Blue Resort staff. They had all had a rough year. I told Connie it would probably be better if I was to stay in Chicago with family. Rondell would be off with his wife somewhere else, he had said. I thanked Harry, but told him I knew he was playing me with the twins thing.

Those weren't lies, I told myself, again, as I felt the frozen gravel crunching under my tires. Like most things new to me, as I turned into the driveway leading up to a white two-story farm house with a wide covered porch and the weathered, crimson red barn and buildings scattered just beyond, I warmed to the apparent history all around me. Two or three dogs were barking and escorting my Subaru along, giving me their slant on things. The low gray skies were starting to produce the predicted snow. Everywhere I could see rolling bands of brown land sliced with draws of trees and fence lines. It looked like Middle America forever. On mute.

"Oh my God, look at you!" came the words from the girl who came running up to my car as I got out. She jumped up, threw her arms around my neck and wrapped her legs around me. A hugged her back and stood there like a cat's scratching tower until she finally let loose. "I have *missed you,* Genius."

"I missed you, too. Maybe I didn't realize how much until this very moment." I felt myself stirring against the pressing crotch of her jeans but fought it off.

"Whoa," she said, flicking her tongue at my ear. "I'd say Happy Thanksgiving but Mr. Happy is already with us."

She un-mounted me and I eased her back to earth. I took a full look at her. Gorgeous. Almost perfect. No new piercings that I could see. Hair same, short, cute cut to give her face the lift it deserved. Eyes looking up at me the same way, begging me one moment, taking no prisoners the next. Just the warmth of her was matching up to my anticipation of being with her. Still, I thought it unlikely such a thing that lived inside of her when we met in the summer could still survive into the winter.

She led me across the drive up the walk to the house with her arm curled inside mine. "You brought snow. Thank you. If we get a lot, it will be the most beautiful thing you have ever seen." She sounded almost philosophical. That was new.

I smiled at her. I could feel the awkward parts of me trying to surface everywhere. What the hell was I doing here with this perfect young girl and her perfect little family in this perfect little place? Interesting choice. Risky. Even a year ago it was something I would have never done. I would have chosen *anything* else.

We went in a side door that led through into the kitchen, and the moment Veronica swung it open I could smell the turkey cooking. Something else as well. Undeniably, a warming apple cinnamon pie. It was a large, bright room with lots of blues and whites, with a smiling, aproned mom, standing, stirring something at a cast iron stove.

Veronica walked me over to her like a stray cat she found outside and wanted to keep.

"Mrs. Creighton. Happy Thanksgiving." I smiled and reached out for her hand. She bypassed the hand and reached up to kiss me on the cheek and give me a hug.

"Welcome, Thomas. And please, call me Eileen. I'm still young enough to have a first name. Honest!" She gave me a flick of her eyes of twenty years before and put me at ease. Sort of. "Don't let Gram's apron fool you."

"Daddy and the brat are picking up Gram," Veronica said. "Come on. I'll show you around the homestead."

Eileen winked an okay to me and went back to her stirring.

"I have to tell you it smells terrific in here. Apple Pie?" I sniffed for her.

"Cinnamon Apple pie, cooling on the sill over there," she nodded towards the window over by the kitchen table. It was cracked open a few inches. Lace curtains bounced in a light breeze around the perfect apple pie.

Veronica took me by the hand and pulled me away. I didn't really want to go until Norman Rockwell signed the painting.

"The dining room, of course," she offered. I counted six perfect, place settings of blue and white china and shiny silverware around a centerpiece of small pumpkins, gourds and fragrant flowers spilling gracefully from a wicker horn of plenty. A look in any direction found Early American originals, not a speck of dust, not a chair to be moved, not a picture to be straightened. Not even a little.

"Can I blink now? This is something out of a magazine."

"Not yet," she said, quickening our pace a bit and pulling me through the living room.

I had more observations to be made but I was being pulled into a small bathroom at the moment. With a quiet, quick flourish, our jeans were at our ankles and her hands were flattened against the wall over the toilet tank. She pushed her back side up and high on me and I was buried with a single, long stroke. We both gasped in amazement at the sudden hot and wet and got to it with a hushed flurry and buzz. Her hips urged and pumped and moved on my stomach like the latest model with added horsepower. I caressed the back of her head and moved one hand around to touch her beautiful face. Her mouth found my index finger and bit hard as she increased her speed. I looked up at the high ceiling and marveled at the wisdom of my choice.

"Shit!" she blurted, catching a glimpse out the window. "Here they come. Fucking blink!"

We finished blinking and buckling just in time, and for all appearances we were just hanging around in the living room quietly observing still life. Mr. Creighton walked in steadying an old woman with a jowly face and a cane. "Hello, Tom," he called.

168

"Not here, moron!" the old woman crowed. "Over there. If I sit on that Goddam rocker I'll never get up the rest of the day without filling my Depends." Her teeth seemed to roll around her words. Surly came to mind.

"This is my mother, Tom. We just call her Gram," Mr. Creighton said with a nervous wink. Gram looked up at me while she eased into a high back wing chair. From the look on her face, it seemed like she knew what I had been up to and did *not* approve. I made a move to help when it looked like she might keel over the side, but Mr. Creighton assured me he was in control. There was something odd about Mr. Creighton. Underneath the opened coat, he had a black and white collar on.

When he stood up, straightened Gram into balance and wiped something off his hand, he extended it. It was too awkward to question it. I would wash up later. Anyway, it wasn't like he didn't catch me staring at the collar.

"Missed you at Church this morning, Tom," he remarked with a smile. "I'm a farmer, but I'm also a Presbyterian minister. Just a little church we have down the way. Been there a lot longer than any of us."

"And you thought you knew all about us Creightons, " Veronica mocked lightly.

"Tom, make yourself at home in every way possible. Have a seat here in the parlor if you like. We are delighted you are here," Reverend Creighton offered and ran back into the kitchen like he forgot something.

"The *parlor,*" I repeated. Softly.

Veronica leaned over to me as we both watched over Gram. "I can feel you bubbling out of me."

I had nothing. I just smiled at Gram. "Turn the damn TV on, "she said.

Gram had settled on a Matlock rerun when Veronica's little brother shot into the room. We shook hands weakly. The look on his face said I was *not* a usable electronic; therefore, useless in his grand scheme. He finally spoke. "Who farted?"

Veronica glared at him. "Do you have any idea how annoying you are?"

He smiled and pointed at his grandmother. "Her brand." He gave me a long accusing look as well and scooted up a long oak staircase.

"That Andy Griffith," Gram was saying, "I'll bet he's got a boner as long as a grazing bull." Her teeth rattled.

"I take after Gram," Veronica said.

I had somehow commandeered the Lazy Boy and became quite comfortable watching the TV with Gram while the others scurried about. I asked if I could help, but my offer was declined and I was politely reminded I was a guest. Gram didn't make the exciting end of Matlock, and a quite handsome shot of Andy Griffith with his shirt sleeves rolled up, but from the way she was snoring, the moment had come and gone for her.

In a sequential passing, Veronica pulled me out of my chair and back into the powder room off the parlor. "Just exactly like the last one," she whispered, dropping her jeans and bending over into position. There was something about her way. *Something?* I ripped into her with a bit of violence that surprised both of us. She reached back with approval and ground into me with everything she had. I don't think it took us more than a minute before we were on our tips toes, muffling ourselves and nearly collapsing over onto the vanity.

Gram was still sawing them off. Veronica was half way back to the kitchen when she turned and passed me going back towards the stairs. "Have to change my jeans. Leaking through." She kissed me on the cheek and scampered away. I found a football game and settled back.

Gram stirred and shuddered a bit towards the end of the first quarter. I could feel my eyes darting back and forth between the old Magnavox color console and Gram's breathing patterns. Then all of a sudden, she stopped all the ceremonials and she was still. She was dead still, chin nestled down tight on the collar of her gray knit cardigan sweater. My fingers tapped, my instincts came alive and began scanning away, wondering if I should shake her or just yell for somebody or... God forbid, what else. Her whole body jerked suddenly and her eyes shot open, blinking rapidly, her gums moving her teeth around. She cleared her throat with a rather rattling glob of something coming free and she turned to stare right at me.

"Turn it back to Matlock!" she blurted, launching some saliva my way.

"It's... over, Gram."

She wasn't sure if she should believe me, but she eyed the remote in my hand. She knew I had control. "Find somethun' else then."

I pushed the buttons and off we went.

"Back! Go back to Gunsmoke."

"I think that was Bonanza, Gram."

"Who cares. Big guys with big boners. Go back!"

It was Bonanza. Hoss Cartwright. Pa. Little Joe. All guys with big boners.

"Turn it up!"

I wasn't all that interested in the fuzzy picture football game anyway. If anything made me understand the spoiling of having flat panel television, this was it. It hardly mattered on a Bonanza rerun. Or guys with big boners. Gram was far more interesting.

Veronica walked back in wiping her hands on a towel. "How are thing going in here?" she asked. Knowing.

"Well, I think you're right. You take after your Gram."

Gram either couldn't hear very well or pretended not to hear very well. I couldn't tell for sure. Her eyes bounced around when they were open.

As Veronica approached, I could see her head tilting and eyes moving in the direction of the bathroom. When she began to reach for my finger tapping hand I could hear somebody shuffling down the oak stairs and the bathroom door shut.

"Fucking brat!" Veronica shot from a tight mouth.

Gram's eyes swirled. She smiled strangely.

Veronica kissed me on top of the head. "We should get your things and get you settled in upstairs," she said to the top of my head. "I just need to finish helping my mother with something."

She walked back into the kitchen making sure I could train my eyes to the little cleft that waggled between her legs in those tight blue jeans.

Gram was groaning a bit. I wasn't seeing it, I would never admit I was seeing it, but it appeared she had dropped her left hand into her lap and had pushed down the folds of her dress in her lap enough to get a good grip on whatever she had going on there.

Shawn was singing in the john.

If you're sitting in the john
And the toilet paper's gone
Be a man
Use your hand.


Over and over again. Louder, until I was sure it would take a reaction to get him to shut up.

"Got it!" I yelled.

Shortly after, the toilet flushed and Shawn emerged victorious. He shot me a quick smile and retreated back up the stairs, humming away. Happy child.

I really tried to avoid looking at Gram, but when she began to tilt her head up and waggle her tongue between her rattling teeth while making sounds like she was gargling marbles, I got up and walked into the kitchen.

"Man oh man, it smells great out here," I said.

Mom was singing along to a Ricky Nelson CD she had playing from a small boom box on the kitchen counter. I don't have any idea why I knew that except he was the only one that sounded like that. All dreamy-eyed and carmel corn.

Veronica looked at me and pursed her lips as she dried off a large pan with a towel.

"I thought I would get my bag."

"You do that," she said, while her Mom kept singing and toying with something in a casserole dish.

I couldn't believe there was already at least a couple of inches of powdery snow on the ground. The sky looked like it had been painted an iridescent gray. Glowing gray, if that was possible, shooting down streams of white fluff against a back drop of endless flat lands and rolling hills. She was right. It was extraordinary. I had never seen snow dropping out in the open like this, unperturbed by anything around it, just falling and settling without a sound or something stepping on it, flattening it or bringing it back up as it rushed by. I stood as still as I could and put my hands out. Closed my eyes. There it was. I could *hear* snow hitting the tip of my nose. Oddly enough, my thoughts eased to a halt, my heart beat seemed to slow, and the thought of world peace struck at my core.

I stayed just like that for as long as I could, not moving a muscle, riveted to the ground.

"Genius? What the hell are you doing?" Veronica ran into me so hard she knocked me off both feet and we flew back onto the snow covered ground. I wasn't sure if that was her intent, but nonetheless she was lying on top of me and I wasn't sure what might come next. A kiss. On the lips. Gently. I reached back to support myself as I kissed her gently back. Our lips would let go, then touch again. Again. Toss in some snows flakes melting and running down our faces, and it was like we were caught up in some dream sequence. I looked into her eyes and saw something different. A softness maybe. A deepness, maybe. We just looked at each other for I don't know how long, then kissed a few more times. The lips. The cheeks. The eyebrows. We got up without a word and stood there in the snow, holding hands, our arms outstretched, two people asking nothing of the snow except to fall in silence and melt on us.

Getting my bag was an afterthought, but getting back inside seemed a better reality as we hustled into the kitchen, soaking wet. Veronica's Mom looked at us like we were covered in bee stings and ran into the laundry room off the kitchen to fetch towels. We took the towels and she joined in our laughter for a few moments before getting back to it with Ricky.

Veronica motioned for me to pick up the bag and follow her. Up the stairs and down to the end of a hallway with a few doors on either side was the guest bedroom. It was greens and blues and fluffy pillows and a double bed heaped with thick, billowy spreads. We were on it within moments and fighting each other's clothes until we both won. We bit and nibbled and chewed on each other until I could sink into her as deeply as I thought possible. Then, just when I thought it could never feel any better than this, some place inside of her that was grabbing me grabbed more, pulling me deeper yet and surrounding my cock with a flush of searing wet heat that I would never survive or adequately describe. I came so deep inside her and with such force I could not breathe or move anything else. She held me right there, as tightly outside as inside, gasping in my ear with short bursts that were probably too loud, then bit my earlobe. She let out a loud groan, and as I my senses slowly returned, I was sure I heard little feet padding quickly back down the hallway.

"Oh my God..., Thomas...," Veronica said, throwing her arms around my neck. I held her tightly and kissed her ears and cheeks and lips. Right then, at that moment, looking into her eyes, again, I wasn't sure what was happening inside of me but something had a new, unfamiliar raw edge of pleasure and peacefulness I had never known. I never wanted to stop kissing her, holding her, and yes, making love to her. Not ever.

"You... I... I don't have the words, Veronica. I just know I have never felt what I feel right now. Never. I don't know what it is.... But I like it."

She reached up and stroked the side of my face. The sweet fresh bread dough smell in the room mixed well. "The firewood!"

"What?"

Veronica shot up and grabbed her jeans. "My Dad. I told him you would help with the firewood. I can hear him throwing it down by the front steps. I'm sorry. I forgot to ask you. Hurry."

I fumbled, pulled and stumbled as best I could.

"Damn, Genius!" Veronica pulled her jeans up but left them undone as she grabbed the doorknob. "How much more do you have in that thing? I'm going to have to change these, too. Gee, do you think my mother will notice I've changed my jeans twice already and you've only been here a couple of hours?"

I smiled. No words for that one either.

# CHAPTER 24

Norman Rockwell had long since taken the pictures, but he was staying for dinner as well. There might have been some question as to the proper Rockwellian credits for some of us at the table, but the preacher and his wife were above it, right down to the Blessing.

"Father, we thank you for things far beyond the bounty at this wondrous table you have provided us...." Reverend Creighton's gentle voice carried across tall tapered candles burning in the soft light of dusk as snowflakes the size of Host wafers fell outside at the frosted windows. Thankful, indeed. I didn't know where to start, and it was likely I would not be able to stop if I did. I felt right then like the luckiest man on the planet.

This was the first time I had seen a turkey carved by a live person at a dinner table with utensils not plugged in to the wall. There was quiet, very comfortable silence while we all admired a lost art. My mind sorted through its keepsakes and quickly decided a look forward was the best thing it had to offer. How could life get any better than this? Compare it to ... what? My mother forgetting burning rolls, baking a canned ham, sweet potatoes and black-eyed peas for Thanksgiving to the pronouncement that "there won't be any damned turkey in *my* house. *His* house. The one he moved into less than a year after my father died. "Just get the damn dinner out *between the football games*," he would order her. Then, if we were lucky, later on, he would fall asleep in his recliner and we could all breathe again.

Then Veronica sneezed twice.

"Allergic to sex, maybe?" asked Shawn.

"Shut up, creep," she replied through her teeth. Then she added, "vicious little twerp," for emphasis.

Mrs. Creighton took a big sip of wine and put on a frown of confusion for all, and began passing food, saving a measured glare for Shawn.

Reverend Creighton was humming something light and biblical, smiling broadly at the serving bowl of mashed potatoes he moved along to Gram. Gram cleared her throat of the marbles and seemed to approve as well. She walloped a big spoonful down on her plate, then another.

"Your father has picked out a special reading for after dinner," Mrs. Creighton announced as she took another swig of wine.

I felt Veronica kick me under the table.

"So, Thomas, Veronica tells me you are a professor of American History," said Reverend Creighton.

Mrs. Creighton beamed and drank some more wine. I wondered what Ozzie would say if Harriett pounded the wine down like that in front of the Beaver. "Teacher. I'm technically just a history teacher, sir."

"At the college level."

"Junior College."

"I see." He glanced over at Veronica as if to thank her for the glorious spin she must have put on my status. "Are you then… working on a Master's or…."

"I gave it some thought," I said, aiming a fork over a plate that could not hold another thing. "I guess I'm still giving it some thought." I sipped my wine. "I'm not really sure teaching is for me. I sort of lucked into the position while I was subbing for a sick professor. He died. They offered me the job. So I became a teacher sort of by default."

"So what is it you would really like to do," Mrs. Creighton asked.

Shawn spit up some green beans in a forced laugh. His silent exchange of f-bombs with Veronica wasn't lost on me.

No one had really asked me that question in quite some time. I hadn't asked that question in a long time. "I'm still giving that some thought as well. In the mean time, teaching pays the bills."

I expect they thought there would be more to come out of their polite inquiry than that, but the uncomfort zone passed quickly as everyone seemed to be settling into stuffing faces with food from clicking forks.

"I wanted to teach once," Mrs. Creighton said softly.

"You teach, dear," the Reverend interjected. "Sunday School every Sunday for how many years?"

"That's *not* what I meant, Floyd. Don't make it worse..."

The vicious crinkle on Gram's face let all know she did not approve of anyone taking issue with her Reverend son.

"I wanted to teach first-grade. I wanted to light up little lives to the world around them. Teach them how to write, spell, add, subtract. Little children remember somebody like that forever, don't you think?" Her little smile found some more wine.

"Mrs. Barkman," I said.

"Sorry?"

"It was Mrs. Barkman for me. My first grade teacher. And you're right. To this day I remember her for exactly those things. Being the first person to get through to my little mind."

"I remember Mrs. Danley," Shawn added. "She smelled like cow plop and had tits that sagged to her waist." He shot a look at Gram for effect.

"That will be quite enough, young man," The Reverend said with a warning finger.

Something told me there was nothing Shawn would like better than to get sent to his room where he could lock into a video electronic world in which he could vaporize us all ten times over.

Veronica didn't say much, but she sighed a lot. Like right then.

"Are you going to stay with us the weekend?" Mrs. Creighton asked me. She hadn't eaten very much, had settled her chin forward onto one hand, wagging her wine glass in the other.

"That is very gracious of you, Mrs. Creighton, but I will need to leave on Saturday morning."

Veronica shot me a frowny face.

"Eileen. Please. Call me Eileen. And the Rev over here, just call him Floyd. Where's just *old* family folk here." She smiled broadly and refilled her glass from the carafe on the table.

Floyd even raised his eyebrows at this refill. I think it was number three. I wasn't keeping count, but Veronica poured one for herself with a look on her face like she might be doing it to keep one away from her mother.

"When did you turn twenty-one, young woman?" Eileen asked playfully.

"You don't know the half of it," Shawn laughed. I noticed he had shaped his mashed potatoes into four letters on his plate, poured some gravy around to get them to stand out, then slid it over just enough for his grandmother to see.

"You think I don't get it? CUNT!" she rattled that one off the ceiling.

Floyd exploded and pointed. Shawn was gone. That left the five of us, but Gram soon pushed away from the table and eased up out of her chair with a thunderous flatuation that had us all hoping that was all it was.

"Next time, help her up, Floyd," Eileen said with a little edge in her voice.

Gram waddled off into the parlor, flipping us the bird over her shoulder and eased back down into her chair. "Somebody work this damn remote for me! And I'm not watching no Goddam football."

When Floyd and Eileen decided to huddle up in the kitchen for a chat, Veronica put her head on my shoulder. "Welcome to my world, Genius."

"The *Genius thing.* What did you tell them about what I do?"

"You mean the part about going to Harvard, Dr. Cabot?"

"Great."

"It sounded good to me at the time. Actually, at the time, I was thinking about how great it would be to ride you within an inch of your life but I didn't think they were ready for that."

"What's with the *Genius* tag, anyway?" I asked.

"Remember? That day you said you would find a place to fuck me by high noon. And you didn't, of course. I had to track you down in your own shower later. I just remember the look of sincerity on your

178

face. Here was this 18-year-old hard body dripping for you and you couldn't figure out which leg to put your weight on, dude. It was pretty funny. So."

"I would have thought I made up for it after that."

"You're getting there." She looked around and kissed me on the cheek. "Turned nineteen two weeks ago. Just so you know you're further from the scary edge." She got up and started to clear the table. I rose to help and she pointed me towards the parlor.

"No, please, not *that!*"

"Gram's harmless."

"I took another look. It looked like Floyd had her set up with *Wheel of Fortune*. Don't you have some cows for me to feed or something?"

"Cows are all fed by this time of day. Sit down and just relax. We'll take a walk after I finish up. I've got something special to show you."

"I'll bet you do."

A smile. That smile. A little waggle of her tongue. I guess I could put up with whatever Gram had in store for me for a little while anyway.

Actually, Gram was in and out by the time I pulled up in the chair in the parlor. I got back up and threw a couple of logs on the fire Floyd had built. The least I could do. I sat back and even closed my eyes a little. I could hear dishes clanking around from the kitchen. Yeah. Well, I guess the third year of a temporary teaching job at a Junior College couldn't quite be called a career just yet. A progress report began to roll across the screen in my head. The Degree from University of Illinois. Nice. Great on the resume. Bunch of nonsense before that. Bunch of nonsense after that. Geeky computer guy eating alone and channel surfing and teaching history. Pretty good teacher, evidently. Temporary tag allowed them to keep rehiring me for a fraction of what a full professor would make. The kids liked me. I didn't know exactly why. One student had called me "quirky, but fun." I knew as much about being quirky as I knew about being cool. Good or bad thing?

But now, unleashed, and exposed for all the world to see, I matured into a full grown man walking around with fresh fingerprints on his zipper. If asked, I suppose it would go something like this- "Yes, I was once just a confused, overwhelmed menace to myself that hid from real life behind a computer screen or a television remote. But *now? Now,* I REALLY like women; young ones, old ones, black, white, any color at all, any size at all, sex, all sex, all the time. When will it end? Never *is* the right answer. Never… never… never…."

"Connie!!" I woke myself up and Gram as well. In my dream, Connie Mulroney was preparing to slice off my Johnson with a rusty Official Boy Scout pocket knife being handed her by Garland Luhrsen. I rubbed that one out of my eyes and shook it out of both ears. My heart settled back into my chest. I looked over at Gram. She looked normal for her.

"Where do they find these stupid people," I think she mumbled. "Pat Sajeck. Damn dick the size of my little finger couldn't nail a dead squirrel."

Bathroom break, I was thinking.

"What about you?" Gram turned slightly towards me. "You got a big dong? You look like the type."

There was no escape at this point, I figured. "Oh yeah. *Big* dong." I held up my hands and framed a space at least a foot wide.

"Good. That's good." She curled her lips in a bit to get the rotation on her dentures going just right. "My husband, Orville… ." She looked at me a little harder. "Did you know him?"

"No, ma'm."

"Oh. Well, Orville had a big one, too. Even when it was soft it ran down the side of his leg a good ways. But when he got that thing up and going," Gram laughed and coughed up a bit. "That was really something. I'll tell you."

I think she was waiting for me to marvel at her good fortune. "I'll bet you miss him."

"Been gone, let's see now… maybe almost twenty years. Woman never forgets her first love, son. Never."

It got quiet after that. Thank God.

"How you two getting along in here?" Floyd asked with a flourish.

"Just fine," I offered.

Gram had nodded off again. "She been sleeping the whole time or…," Floyd asked.

"Actually, she was quite the conversationalist for awhile," I said.

"She tell you Pat Sajeck had an infantile penis?"

"Among other things."

"Sorry about that. You want to give me a hand with some more firewood? Nobody gives a shit about the reading except Eileen, anyway, and she's in the bag."

# CHAPTER 25

She said she knew where we were going, and she had the flashlight. The snow had diminished to swirls mostly coming off the fence lines and tall pine trees. A bright moon cast down shadows lengthened on the snow that could have been drawn by an artist and the quiet hush was disturbed only by an occasional *moo* or *eerooo* from a shifting beast inside the barn.

"Those are Black Angus," Veronica advised me. "Beef cattle. Most of them will be murdered in the spring."

"Am I allowed to guess where we are going or am I limited to knowing what's going to happen when we get there?"

"Ohhhh. I am becoming that predictable?" Veronica asked.

"Never mind."

A short distance later we were standing underneath the darkness of a towering wide oak tree with a trunk that must have been three feet across. She shined the light up a bit higher on the trunk. Short wooden boards, two-by-fours, attached to the tree, one after the other going up. They were steps that led to a rectangle of weathered plywood and wood supports that suggested we were looking at the bottom side of a tree house.

"Veronica's Veranda. Daddy named it when he built it for me. I was eight."

"After you?" I grabbed the flashlight and lit her path. She banged the snow off her boots and up she went like a cute little monkey in a hooded parka. I focused the light just above her hands as she pushed a plywood door open and climbed up inside. Next I had her head in the spot light looking down at me with a goofy smile.

"Well, what are you waiting for? Scared of heights?"

Shit. If she only knew. But it was too dark for the real fear to set in, and really, how high could it be anyway? Up I went, nearly missing a step. They were made for feet a lot smaller than mine. I reached the top and crawled inside. She was lighting a candle with a propane fire starter, then another. The aura of the light reflected against little white lace curtains on narrow rectangular windows all the way around a space that looked to be about shoulder high. It was maybe the size of a small merry-go-round, or octagon, too dark to tell for sure. I rose up on my knees to get a better look. You could see the second story lights on in the house, the two big mercury yard lights on high poles and that big moon. Shaggy high-looped carpet covered the floor up to walls of natural knotty pine wood. Not exactly like a doll house. The candles had the place smelling like warming vanilla syrup in a matter of minutes.

"I'd love the little pine table and chairs if I was a dwarf," I said.

"You were a dwarf once. Exactly the point. This is my favorite place to be in the whole world, where I go back to being … a dwarf. A little person with just tiny little friends and tiny little things to worry about. And now I'm with my favorite person in the world, in my favorite place to be. So that only leaves my favorite thing to do."

"You taking a philosophy course or something?"

"Dude…" Veronica opened an old cabinet door and pulled out a big fluffy down quilt and we were quickly huddled underneath of it, using the flashlight to play you-show-me-yours-I'll-show-you-mine in defiance of the cold night air.

Afterwards, we lay there looking out at the stars through the long windows. My head was propped up against a wall, I was stroking her short hair and the nape of her neck as she lay across me with the blanket pulled up tight. I still wanted to take some credit for this, for anything that seemed to happen to me, or for me, but I was becoming resigned to the facts. And the facts suggested someone who lived and died before me had been reincarnated and just recently discovered he occupied my body, and set up shop. This also explained that feeling of a presence, looking at myself as though I was a third party, the random commentary, and more recently, the disappearance of the third party and the commentary. It was the only thing that made sense to me and I was growing quite comfortable with it. Whoever it was, in his last go around, had some sex life. Or, suppose it was a woman? Why not? Part sensuous, part slut. I could be grateful for either one. Certainly being both would be a gift.

"Do you believe in reincarnation?" I threw it out. Why not.

"Hmmm," You say something?" Her face was nuzzled into me and the down comforter.

"I was saying… do you think this is your first time around on earth or do you think you've been here before?"

"Odd question."

"Not really. If you're me. Or If I was somebody else who is now me."

"Dude. Fuck me."

So much for the philosophy. Then again, maybe that was Veronica's philosophy.

She somehow worked me into operational again and swung up over my middle, sinking down on me as wet and hot as ever. The comforter was a tent over her head anchored at the blue jeans down around my ankles. I figured my cock would have the dry heaves this time around, but then she did that thing again where she got the end of it and drew it higher into her secret place and held on until it coaxed me into another trembling surrender while she nearly broke it off at the base.

"What *is that?*" I had to ask.

"What is what?" She was laughing!

God dammit! She knew! "Okay, then. I guess it wouldn't be news."

"I read Cosmo now, dude. Interesting stuff. Some of these tips are like from women who must be professional vaginas or something."

"Do I dare ask how you try something like that out?"

"I just did. And it worked." She had collapsed over me and pulled the blanket up.

"Is this not the perfect place?"

"It is right now."

"I spent the weekend in here about three weeks into the school term."

"Why?"

"Why? I hate it, that's why. School's boring. Easy, but boring easy."

"Come on. Bundles of guys," I said

"Lots of gay guys. Tons of gay guys. Or, let's see… the idea of a good time is some beers and reefer and a blow job before they stick it up your ass. What do you suppose they learned at home?"

"Hmm. What do any of us really learn at home? Where do you think you picked up that voracious sexual appetite of yours?"

"I told you. Gram. She was a shiftless whore when she was young. She told me so. And she has no regrets. Her advice to me was don't miss any if you can help it. But, I don't think she was plagued by all these ass fuckers like I am."

"Plagued."

"Let's change the subject."

"To what?"

"Who have you been fucking since I last saw you?"

An honest answer I thought not possible.

"He who hestitates is a terrible liar," she said. "Okay, let's see. How about we just see how many times we can do it in twenty-four hours. Let's set the record. What do you say?"

"What is the record, anyway? Do we get an asterisk for your family being around?"

"According to *Cosmo,* it is likely that of a tribe in Africa where the men take four or five wives and bang away at them each and every night. Interesting enough, apparently there isn't much information about white people on the subject."

"So what else have you learned in college?"

"Shush. This is more important. So what we do is submit the record to Guinness. Let them try to figure it out."

"They will come out to verify. Then what? We perform some magic tricks or start fucking in your mom's kitchen while they hold a stopwatch by your ass?"

"The visuals are turning me on."

"You're kidding. Again? Now? Already?"

"Genius… I have a confession. I really think I'm a nymphomaniac by definition."

"*Cosmo?*"

" Logic. Mine." She rolled to her side and started to massage my groin. "When I was twelve, I discovered my mother had five different kinds of *headache* vibrators in her night stand. One even had a gizmo at the end that twirled and had all these little nubs on it. *Oh. My. God.*"

"Sharing vibrators with your Mom? What a perfect end to a day with Rockwell."

"I got so good at it by the time I was in eighth grade I could cum at my desk if I could get my hairbrush into my panties."

"Please don't think I'm less than fascinated. Go slow if there's more, okay? You are rubbing where the skin is pretty thin right now."

"So then you can imagine how hard it was for me to stay a virgin, what with boys and their gritty little fingers and dry humpers and perv bankers…. The high school years weren't easy. I pretty much took care of myself. Until I let Billy do it. Graduation night. It was like he was sticking a little hunk of warm clay up in me. I had this sudden whack of pain, then it gave way. I mean, he's having a seizure and I'm feeling *nothing! I mean nothing at all!*"

I readjusted and slowed her wrist with mine. She moved down on me, licked, sucked and held, her tongue moving inside her mouth. I was there.

"Then there was you, Genius," she said, rolling underneath of me and locking her legs around my calves as I cautiously eased inside of her. There was nothing the least bit cautious on her agenda. "I'm starting to cum already. Hit me home, baby."

I guessed what was making this all possible was we both went off with great efficiency. Not once had we needed to either wait for the other or struggle to get to the finish line. Two squirrels with nut bags full. We groaned heavily and I could feel her clench inside. I was sure all I gave her back was a vapor, but it still felt impossibly fabulous.

It was like a casino in Las Vegas. No clocks anywhere. But the dropping temperatures of the Iowa winter air told us it was time to get back inside. I think we were done. My balls ached as we walked through a pristine kitchen into the parlor. The Reverend had returned Gram to the rest home in Altoona and he was out cold in a rocker by the fire, newspapers across his lap and spilling to the oak floor. The soft mixing of burning hardwoods and apples hung in the air like a longing that never really goes away. We tiptoed up the stairs, which seemed to make the creaking boards louder.

"Mom's in bed reading either Stephen King or Ralph Jones."

"Who's Ralph Jones?"

"He's a local manager of the Hy-Vee grocery store. He wrote a novel about a butcher who... butchers." Some publisher dude from New York bought it."

When we got to the top of the stairs, I waited for her lead.

"No, we aren't going to sleep together, Genius. Not that I wouldn't like to do that more than anything. I just think they might find that awkward, particularly if we made the racket we usually do."

I didn't have to tell her after all. That I was going to need a break to let it scab over or something. If anything, she just got tighter as the process went along. She knew it. "I understand. I think I would feel the same way." I did feel the same way.

We kissed sweetly, and hugged like people in love and said goodnight with smiles and sparkling eyes. I closed the door behind me. What the hell was that?

# CHAPTER 26

The little clock on the night stand said four-twenty-nine. I heard a sound like a cabinet closing on an uncertain set of hinges. There was darkness at the windows and the smell of coffee brewing. I had a down quilt up around my neck shielding me from the thin chilly air in the room. I felt so at ease you would think *I* was born and raised here. This was *my* room, my place in the great wide bad ass world. No forboding fears allowed in Altoona, Iowa. No haste, no overbearing conversations, no threat of terrorists for miles. Just a down comforter in room of crisp clean air.

I pictured Floyd on his way out to tend to the cattle and farm chores, pulled the blanket up a little tighter and rolled back over into a deep warm sleep.

It seemed like only moments had passed when I felt something touching the bottom of my left foot. I blinked a few times, then shot up to find Veronica at the end of my bed standing there in a turquoise satin shorty robe, twirling the dangling end of the sash below a devious familiar smile. "Tickle, tickle," she whispered.

It was almost nine. "That might have been the most incredible sleep of my life," I said. Her hair was still damp and clinging to her head, fresh out of the shower. "A shower sounds great about now." I sat up and she flopped down beside me. She smelled like fresh apricots and sweet powders. Her hands began to wander and as they did, I became keenly aware I might have still been sporting some lightly bruised tissue along my manhood. She leaned over me and bit each of my nipples, then stopped and looked up at me and shot a breath mint in my mouth she had pulled out of her robe pocket.

"Mom went to the store. Dad's in the barn. The brat's where else. Time for a good morning fuck."

At some moment during our mint freshened exchange of tongues, it dawned on me. The perfect time. I maneuvered into position and started trailing down across that taught skin of her stomach that still screamed *illegal*.

"*Genius...,*" she cooed. "This ought to be interesting."

I went to work. A thing learned like that would be difficult to unlearn, I figured. Not that every woman was the same, in any regard, but if I were to believe what Connie had told me and Leona taught me, most women respond to the same things. If they are good things.

As was my custom in this current reincarnation, I lost track of the sense of time and I was down on Veronica for what seemed like quite awhile. Her hands moved around and over my head, pulling me in a little, moaning, calling my name a few times. Then she seemed to slink her hips down a bit and caught a rhythm against my tongue. I was barely moving it, short flicks working *the spot,* as Connie would call it. As Leona so deftly demonstrated. It was as if Leona was watching, grading the performance and I was not about to disappoint her. Veronica cranked into full grind. I could feel and smell the heat coming out of her as she got both her hands on the back of my head and tried to force my head inside of her. I held my ground though, doing what I was told, and when her inner thighs began to tremble out of control, I knew what should be next.

"Ohhhhhhh gaaaaawwwwdd!!!" Veronica screamed, bucking me off with a jolt for a moment, but I latched right back on. She was still creaming and grabbed a pillow and put it over her face just before she yelled a nonsensical flurry of obscenities into the center of it. Her hips thrust and quivered, then again. She fought for a better grip on the back of my head, got it, and pulled my hair and pounded my scalp as another round wracked her entire body. Finally, her hips went slack and she collapsed away from my face.

"*What... the... hell ... was ... THAT...,* " she gasped.

I looked over to see if Leona approved. "Maybe you're not the only one who reads *Cosmo.*"

She laughed breathlessly. "Yeah. Like you could learn to do that in a magazine. God. Multiples, Genius. You have to promise me you will never *not* do that to me." She pushed at her heart. "Dude."

I could have done without the last reference, but figured the *dude* thing would eventually die its own death. "How 'bout if you relax a bit and I run through the shower?"

"Only if you promise to hurry back. I'm in love, Genius." She looked at me with those dark, watery eyes over the flush on her cheeks. She was one sexy kitten.

"Hold that thought." I got up and threw on a pair of gym shorts and a t-shirt and grabbed my shaving kit. I could hear the doorknob turning. What good fortune she remembered to lock the door. Then I heard a light knock.

"Gotta match?" came Shawn's voice through the door. I waited a few moments, took a deep breath and opened the door. He was gone, but he left me a few wads of Kleenex on the floor.

I had a choice there, but decided better me than Veronica dealing with it. I picked up the Kleenex with severely pinched fingers but found nothing horrific added. No foreign or alien substances, no evidence of scarring for life. My face let loose its scrunch, and judging by the peeking eyes from the doorway down the hall and the shrill laughter as he slammed his door, I had been great entertainment for the Brat.

I floated down the stairs after my shower to find Veronica in the kitchen busy making us a breakfast of eggs over easy, hash browns, biscuits and gravy and sausage. She greeted me with a wink and a smile and nodded towards the table where a hot cup of coffee awaited. On the second sip, Shawn zipped through the kitchen and flew out the door with I-POD earphones jammed in his ears under a stocking cap. He winked at me, too.

I glanced out the window as a car picked him up in the drive and sat back with a grand stretch and took in the return of Rockwell. I did the quick math and figured this might be the first time we were in the house together alone. It could only be a matter of minutes until we had desecrated Rockwell's kitchen. She wore a loose fitting white gauze top hanging over tight blue jeans and knee-high black leather boots. I would swear, it was right at that moment, watching her wield the spatula, flipping and stirring with easy determination over her cuteness, I wondered if I was warming inside for a different reason. It was that same indefinable sense that came over me a few times when I was with Connie. How do you explain it? A sense of ease and comfort, lifting, spreading and sustaining. A slowing of the world and necessity. Agenda free. All these thoughts rattled around in my head as though they were cushioned from any fall and could settle in any order they wished. Simply, life was so good, so easy. Just to be. To be with her. Beyond adorable, beyond the sexual appetite of a predator, was perhaps, something else I was gathering around. I didn't want to go so far as to use the *L word,* as that would put me undeniably in love with at least two women, maybe three, if you include the electro-shocked Mattie, likely still mumbling to herself somewhere out East. And what about unfinished business with Maria? Not a view on earth better than watching her walk away from you in a short skirt. But what if she walked back in? Even, in a rather perverse, oddly sensual way, Leona, the silent lover? Could I go so far as to wonder what it might be like to be with a woman who never spoke? Extraordinary expectations that could not possibly exist, really. I would not know how to be a chauvinist or a feminist.

"Penny for your thoughts," she said as she put it all down in front of me. It took up two blue and white porcelain plates side-by-side.

"It would cost you a lot more than that." I waited for her to sit down opposite me. "Wow, look at all of this. My God, she can cook, too?"

"Dude."

There it was, the little piece that didn't fit. I needed to remind myself she was only nineteen. I needed to remind myself I was only twenty-eight, coming back from going on fifty. I hadn't had biscuits and gravy in forever and could not wait to dig in. I did. And as good as it looked; it was possibly the vilest thing I had ever put in my mouth I had to swallow. Swallow I did, and when I did, away went the comfort zone I was in. I hurriedly got a mouthful of eggs and hash browns to follow, a heavy gulp of coffee to rush it down my throat, hopefully killing the taste. I somehow managed a smile. "Terrific," I lied, while wondering if the biscuits and gravy recently ran out of the anus of a pig. I noticed she didn't have any on her plate. "No biscuits and gravy for you?"

"No way."

"Why's that?"

"Gram's old family recipe, but none of us seem to get it right, including me, I'm afraid. To me, it tastes like ass. You don't have to eat it if you don't like it. You won't hurt my feelings or anything."

"My thoughts. Exactly." I used my fork to give the whitish beige glob a push to the side of my plate. The comfort zone had returned. "Everything else is great, though. Thanks." Then it hit me, again. "And by the way, you look absolutely beautiful this morning."

Veronica paused chewing and searched my face. I think she was blushing. Or glowing. Maybe both. "You didn't need to say that. What would you have to gain you are not already getting?" She was impish, maybe looking for more.

"Just the truth is all," I said. "Sometimes I look at you... and I remember you when you were... little. That goes away pretty quick when I realize how beautiful a woman you have become."

"A *woman,* no less."

"Trust me. No less."

She sipped coffee and ate tiny bites. "I think I like this side of you, Thomas Cabot."

"And that's another thing. This is all new to me. I'm no pro at all of this stuff. I mean, I've never been in love before...."

She look startled and just stared at me. "You tell me when you're done talking," she said softly.

"Well," I nearly choked on too big a bite of sausage. "See, I mean I've been with some women...."

"Obviously."

"But nothing came of it except, well, the usual stuff, you know."

"The usual stuff. Sure. I get it."

"But with you... Jesus, it's like *wild!* AND! It's like there is more there than just that. That's the part I know nothing about, tell you the truth. But it's right there."

"So... you think you are in love with me, Thomas Cabot?"

"I... I'm crazy, right?"

"Okay. I mean, you already know I've been in love with you since you ripped open your shorts on that nail on the dock. You had me when you showed me your hairy ass."

"It's not so hairy. Is it?"

I helped her with the dishes. Afterwards, she threw her arms around my neck and we kissed with a luscious effort that had me stirring in my jeans. I was pretty sure I was ready to go again.

"Believe it or not," she backed off and looked up at me. "I'm actually still shaking inside a little from your little gift this morning. How 'bout you take a ride to town with me. I need to make a deposit at the bank. Then when we get back, you can help me vaccinate the new piglets."

Had I stoked the fire or put it out? Had I actually taken the grind out of her hips for awhile? Damn! There was a moment.

"Did you say *vaccinate pigs?*"

"I did."

"Geez, can't we just get right to that?" I laughed, shaking my head.

"We could, but we'll be such a mess after." She leaned into me as we walked out to the car. "My little banker has stopped making his payments. I figured I owe him a visit."

A creepy feeling came over me like I was about to become an accomplice in a crime. Sort of like the feeling I got when I answered questions for the coroner after Rudy Mulroney's death.

When we got to the bank, there was a sign on the locked front glass door:

Closed due to death of Robert Sneerd, our President

Will Reopen Monday at 8 a.m.

Veronica never said a word as we got back in the car. She rolled down the window when she spotted a middle-aged woman she evidently knew walking across the street. I don't recall how she asked the question, but I'll never forget the answer she got from the woman.

"They found him Thanksgiving night out behind his garden shed. They aren't saying, of course, but word is out he blew his damn head off. Tell the truth… I always thought he was kind of weird anyway, always gawking at everybody, especially the *really* young girls."

The rest of what they talked about went the way of the wind, but I couldn't help but think about how they must cut the pieces of a puzzle when it is still together, then throw all the pieces in a box, then some patient soul with nothing else to do puts all the pieces back together again. Was the puzzle meant to stay together then? Or was it meant to go back into a box in pieces to sit on some closet shelf? The hell with teaching history. There were other things to think about.

"Imagine Thanksgiving next year for that family," the woman was saying as she began to walk on.

There was an uncertain look on Veronica's face. I wasn't equipped to figure it out, or know if I was even supposed to figure it out.

"I love you, Genius," she said. A tear made its way down her cheek as she put her hand on top of mine.

# CHAPTER 27

That night, huddled beneath the blankets in Veronica's Veranda, her usual passion had an underlying sadness that was sucking the air out of our balloon. So when I left Saturday morning as planned, the woman that had pummeled me into love was a little girl waving to me in the driveway, then walking away with her hands shoved into the front pockets of her jeans. I could only imagine how she was processing the whole thing with the banker. Only imagine. But it seemed like she needed to do that without any help from me. *Ill-equipped* came to mind, quite clearly.

As I headed north on Highway 35, little waves of guilt began to creep up on me for feeling I had *escaped*. I thought of turning around a few times, going back to Altoona, and even just heading back home to Chicago, where I could hide in my apartment behind a computer screen, or a flat screen television while flat out motionless on a couch with recently cleaned upholstery. But, something just kept my foot nailed to the pedal and the car pointed north.

It took nearly to the outskirts of Gull Lake before my thoughts shot out from between Veronica's legs and hopped up between Connie's. Connie was certainly right about being the one *having the pussy*, but she didn't have the only one, as it turns out. My head was spinning from trying to fit my little world around a Veronica Creighton, the chit-chat about being in love, of all things. With the radio on, punching around from soft rock to country to oldies, recounting the two days at the farm in some detail brought up a shudder more than once.

But moving past the pastures of Iowa to the tree lines of Minnesota lake country brought on a larger reality to me, one more familiar to me, one that scared me less and eased me back into the headrest for the first time since I left the farm.

I had never seen Sunny Blue covered with snow. Against the backdrop of pines and the ice covered lake it looked forgotten and silent, but content with things as they were. There were still a few piles of new lumber covered with blue tarps and snow. The cedar siding on the house was nearly completed and newly set windows still had labels on the glass. Connie's Cadillac sat in an open garage with the panels for the new door sitting along side of it on the concrete floor.

I knew where she would be.

I walked over to the cabin and gave a knock.

"You're knocking now?"

I walked inside and found her naked, sitting at the table by the window, my partially sculpted bust being manipulated by her talented fingers. She leaned up to receive my kiss and looked me over quickly. "Sit," she said. "We need to finish."

"Why?"

"Because we do."

We sat in silence, not that unusual for us, when generally I toyed with thoughts about what Connie might say or do next. You could never really tell if she had something on her mind or if she was engaging you in one of her many head games. An hour or so later it did occur to me that she hadn't as much as grabbed me, urged me or beckoned me, let alone flirt with me. Her hands were constantly moving. I watched her flattening clay around eyes sockets, digging and smoothing and then reworking it all. It was eerie, as though she was carving an interactive headstone for my grave site.

"I gotta go," I said.

She seemed a bit put out. "Number one or two?"

"Number one, mom."

"Good. Just go outside. Plumbing's turned off in here for winter. You'll have to walk up the house for number two."

I stood outside peeing along the back side of the cabin thinking I was going to have to write something a hundred times on the black board next. I walked back inside and resumed my seat in the straight back chair. "You pissed at me for not being here Thanksgiving?"

"You're here, now." She said without much of a feel.

"Pissed or not?"

"Not pissed. Just a lot on my mind." She kept working. "Just because I'm sitting here concentrating on this doesn't mean I don't want to fuck you, Thomas. A little spoiled, aren't we?"

"You did the spoiling."

"So I did." She shook her head with a quiet laugh. "So I did."

I smiled. Vindicated.

"How is Veronica doing?" Connie asked, not missing a beat.

My stomach fell to the old linoleum on the crooked floor and rolled off to the baseboard like a stub of a pencil.

"Eileen Creighton called me on Thanksgiving to see how I was doing. Wasn't that sweet?"

"Very."

"At first I thought I would see how deep I could get you in, but then I got a bit of news myself that changed the fun in all of that. So who am I to blame you for wanting a piece of that, anyway, right?"

I tried a little laugh of agreement. It sounded pretty contrived to me. "Uhhh …."

"Uh. No shit, Thomas. Uh." She imitated me better than I thought she might. "Men are so predictable, Thomas. When you have the pussy, it is so easy to see."

"I was thinking that, actually. I mean, I understand what you mean when you say that."

"You might. But that wouldn't change anything. The pussy still rules."

About a dozen more pussy analogies came to me right then, all of which I swallowed back down. Either way, a self-serving effort. I decided on simple agreement. Hadn't that always been best around Connie, anyway? I could only imagine what trouble I could be asking for to challenge her to any sort of dual. I would settle for an attempt at clearing the record. "I didn't bullshit you about that, really," I said.

"Really?" She seemed more than amused. "As I recall, didn't it go something like you were expected at Mommy's house?"

"And that's true, actually. I was *expected,* but I negotiated out of it."

"You negotiate with your Mother? At your age?"

"Not exactly. She's changed a lot over the past ten years, Connie. You wouldn't know her. She's just not all there. I don't know exactly why, or where she is at, but in an odd sort of way I think she's actually happier now that she really doesn't know what goes on around her."

"Wouldn't we all be?"

"I told her I would take her out for dinner during the next week. She was thrilled."

"And so, you go to Iowa to stick your wiener in the tight little teenager for couple of days then throw your boxers back on and head north to fuck the old lady before heading back to Mom. Getting pretty clever for a complete novice, Thomas."

"Well, I don't know. I just got here...."

"And playful about it." She stopped to cuss her work for a moment. "I like you when you are playful. Sit still!"

I did. And I caught the first gleam of those exotica eyes when she yelled at me.

"I should be flattered. Right?" She hissed.

"Yes. I drove what, almost four hundred miles, again, just to hear you tell me why I shouldn't have?"

"That was pretty lame. But, I am glad you are here." She stopped to offer me the smile of a thousand melt downs. "I need to finish you up."

I wasn't biting on that line quite yet. "Veronica is a sweet girl. I could not turn down her invitation."

"But you could turn down mine." Her voice was whimsical. "Sweet, yes. Eileen says she hates college because the boys are all gay."

I laughed.

"So how sweet of you to help get her life in balance, Thomas."

"I did my best. Everything you taught me."

"Everything...." The silence returned. Connie started humming something to herself and continued her work. She was a master at letting conversations dangle out there at some point where you wondered if they were over, or if you should sharpen your spear and prepare for another round.

"Listen," she began, waking me. "I have a proposition for you. How would you like to buy the Sunny Blue and the tavern?"

"*What* are you saying? You're not serious."

"You would probably never know for sure, but let's suppose I am. Would you be interested?"

"Yes. The crazy answer would be... *yes*." I saw myself tumbling out from behind the bar at Harry's and running up Clark Street, heading North.

"Wahoo's divorcing. We are going to move to Maui. Actually, I'm going to go there first, as soon as possible, and he'll come when things are finalized."

I was pretty sure I heard that right, but I must have looked like a deer in the head lights to Connie. "Wahoo Jefferson," I mumbled

"Wahoo what?"

"And you. Makes sense, really." The stuff that was wrapping around me seemed a mix of elation, sadness, hurt and finality. Confusion, really. Things, feelings mixing in a way I had never processed together in my young life.

"Of course, it does. I need to move on from this. It is as if Sunny Blue and I have given each other all we can. Rudy's gone, the fire... all the bras...." She looked out the window and paused for moment, then returned to her work in earnest. "Maybe as it should be." She gave me Conniesmile. "See how easy I can make this for you? God, to be young again."

There were cob webs still shaking out of my head on this one. All the details I wanted to know weren't going to show up here. I was sure of that. I would get the story that fit Connie's agenda.

"So I would sell the place to you on a ten-year contract. You send me a monthly payment, I turn over on my beach blanket and all is well. Nothing fancy. No big attorneys, all the bullshit. We can have somebody in town and the bank set it up. Or your brother, Rondell can do it. It doesn't matter to me. I might stop back to check on things once in awhile. And, if you take care of that gorgeous body of yours, fuck your brains out and then go back to my beach blanket. How does that sound to you, Thomas?"

"Sort of like a dream sequence. This a game, Connie?"

"It is always a game, Thomas."

"Jesus."

"Is that a yes?"

"That would be a yes. I'm playing." Hell, yes, and the hell with the history of Thomas Jefferson, Wahoo Jefferson, and the whole lot of them.

# CHAPTER 28

Eight months of upheaval and resettling, more movement and reaction than planning and disposition. It wasn't all a big deal because I was already at least somewhere else in so many ways. Nonetheless, it still had an awkward feel to it standing there in the bright July sun at the top of the Sunny Blue Resort turnaround. Straight and tall, freshly showered, dressed in my tight, single-pocket blue t-shirt over blue jeans and boots, Veronica under my arm, awaiting the arrivals. She wore a little orange Flintstone's Band Aid on a finger she cut when the shower rod she was gripping gave way. I got most of the credit. She said it was a small price to pay for our short, but very spirited communal morning shower.

"Here they come!" she squealed.

It was the Creighton's Volvo, alright. As it eased to a stop, I counted four in the car. Make that, Floyd, Eileen, Shawn and *Gram!* The car doors popped open one-by-one and they flushed out and stretched in the sunshine while Veronica ran up to give hugs around. Even Shawn got a short hug. I can only imagine what he was mumbling at the time. Gram exchanged a quick hug with her as well before uncomfortably bending into a good fart that killed whatever mood had begun for me. Veronica and her family just ignored it. It was Gram. If Veronica really did take after her grandmother, which she assured me she did in almost every way, I would begin offering up special prayers this feature was left out of the package. A farting sex kitten was an oxymoron in my book.

Rondell was due any time as well. He and the air fucker had separated, so to speak, and he was not taking it too well. Evidently, she was fucking a lot more than air. I suggested he come up and stay in one of the brand new rooms off the back of the house and stay as long as he wanted. They weren't really finished inside yet, but then maybe he could get into that, maybe pick up a paint brush and do something mindless, but useful.

After all, there was only so much a former history teacher could do. Thus far, beyond my useful bartending and money counting skills, I was adding a skill on a daily basis out of necessity. Little did I know all the things I helped Rudy and Garland do around the place would come into play like this. A little carpentry, a Godsend, a little electrical, a blessing over and over, and knowing how a septic system works? *Priceless.* Of course, there was almost always too much to do, given my learning curve at the time. I could get it right. Eventually. I needed to use a lot of common sense and some things likely requiring an hour of anybody else's time might take me five hours. So, introducing my new, *bestest* friend in the whole world- Garland Luhrsen.

It came down to the immovable, strange, unsmiling object versus the new guy that would keep him gainfully employed for as far as he could tell. Garland wasn't just a brain-knarled, noisy breather. In fact, my guess is he was just about as smart as he wanted to be. And not a wasted brain cell more. I had yet to find a thing broken he couldn't somehow fix. The tougher the problem the longer he might spend inside the tool shed or in that fenced area that hid all the hideous miscellaneous stuff guests weren't supposed to see, but ultimately he would emerge with a gadget or a cobbled together do-hicky that did the job. And that day, my third as the official new owner, when we discovered the junction box for the septic system needed to be dug up and replaced? *That* was a beauty. Garland and I, up to our knees in other people's poop and a foaming sea of pee, just digging away, side-by-side. It was me on all fours, puking. Not Garland.

We were quickly becoming buds. Of course, he still didn't smile, he still made these haunting baby seal noises for no apparent reason, and most of the time he stared at me as if to say when all was said and done, he would still like to slice off my head while I was sleeping and shit down my neck. And he would do it, too, if he thought he could get away with it. My thought of this alone would define our relationship and continue to fuel my desire to find our common ground. At first, I had this idea of carrying around a little pocket spiral bound notebook and writing down my necessary part of the conversation. He would gesture and scoff at me and refused to write anything down himself, which infuriated me, yet I was astonished how quickly we became able to carry on our communications without the notes. He taught me a series of gestures and self-taught signing that worked incredibly well. What it boiled down to was whatever we were doing, whatever needed to be done, had a way of speaking to us without words. Simple nods and gestures in the quiet of an early summer morning were enough to get most days moving along.

So I speak of my Veronica, my sweet little Veronica who, above all others, captured my heart, my urges and my imagination. I didn't even know I had these things until they came together in one thought around her name. Sure that I was trying to connect the amazing sex with every other thought or emotion I might have been trying to explain to myself, I invited her to come and spend the summer with me after she was finished at school. Officially, as far as her parents were concerned, she helped clean the cabins and take care of guests. Unofficially, she was my constant companion, my nymphomaniac roommate, and the best underage bar maid on the planet.

"Thomas."

"Reverend Creighton. Good to see you again."

He looked at me no different than any other father who knew you were bonking his daughter unmercilessly. It wouldn't have mattered if she was thirty. "Just Floyd up here, Thomas. Just another guy trying to wet a line down and catch the big one. That's all."

"Yes sir. And they've been hitting pretty good this past week."

He glanced over at Veronica and her mother laughing over something. "She looks radiant. All lit up, Thomas." He smiled, patted me on the shoulder, closed his eyes and took a deep breath.

"Cabin number four. The usual," I said, handing him the keys.

A bull-legged Gram dressed in a mid-calf length navy blue polka dot dress over black Red Cross shoes ambled around slowly, picking at the curling white birch bark on the trees and swatting at some flying insects that may or may not have been there.

Shawn Creighton looked taller and gawky; all shoulder blades and knee caps as he slowly approached me. "Whassup, dude," he wisecracked, bobbing his head. His voice screeched high and low at the same time. A little acne just underneath the jaw line. He hated me more than ever.

"Hey, Shawn." Anything more was an invitation for trouble. I fended off some weird variation of a handshake that didn't work very well.

We had barely packaged the Creighton's into their cabin when a black Hummer with gold custom trim rumbled by to a ceremonial stop. A hand thrust an open Budweiser into the air to make sure the coast was clear before the big body of my brother Rondell oozed out of the high seat. I walked over.

"Little brother, don't worry about a thing. I have arrived." The more he drank, the harder he hugged. Why was that? I heard something give in my ribcage.

"Rondell, my main man. "Six-pack or twelve-pack?" I asked. He reaked.

"Long-ass trip, man."

I could see the fatigue and a twelve-pack in his eyes. "Let's get you settled in, bro."

"Nap would be good," he yawned. "Shitty buzz, anyway."

I took Rondell around the back of the house to the new version of the room I used to stay in. Seemed strange enough. He got a bead on the bed waiting for him and went straight for it like a Spanish bull on a death charge, arms flopping out to the side as he bounced down and lay still. That was one less thing for me to worry about for the moment.

By the time we opened Mulroney's Island Tap at four-thirty, there were people actually lined up to get in. A first. This was going to be some Fourth of July Weekend. I was hanging a bra before five o'clock, a new record. I suspected the plump, now braless red head had been a few other places with her following of friends before they got there, or, it might just have been she wanted to get those unfazed gel bag puppies on display for the rest of us to see.

*Note to self-* special section of ceiling to denote fake boobs. *Another note to self-* Doesn't matter. Splitting hairs.

"Are you ready for this?" I asked Veronica, as she finished refilling the bar fruit containers. She looked amazing in a canary yellow tube top and big hoop gold earrings. With each day her little girl side got cuter and her young woman side got more pronounced and stated her sexy as well as it could be done. At times I was delirious with the cocktail I was mixing. Love, sex, lust, male pig, naïve fool and hopelessly lost around a brain amuck, albeit, ill-equipped to handle nearly anything I was doing. I think I was starting to figure out that I might spend most of my life trying to figure out why certain things were the way there were and why I was involved, like writing some history book, or I could be the black part on the page, the stuff that moved right along with it. Better to be part of the surreal than sit back and just take notes.

"Are you, Mr. Sunny Blue?"

"I will never be ready for anything. Not even you. Never you. You look amazing… but…."

"But what?" She profiled for me.

"Turn around again." She did. "Okay. It must have been a reflection of the light. I thought I could see your ass crack."

"Genius, if I wanted my crack to show, believe me, it would show." Her eyes gleamed over a big smile, she winked at me and went off to wait on a table. There was some Maria in that sway, even the denim blue jean skirt looked the same, but my carnal knowledge of the landscape beneath and its explosive nature gave me a chill. There was only one Veronica. And maybe that was it. She was part Maria, part Connie, part Mattie, before they all grew up, and before I grew up. Though ten years older than Veronica, I could easily have been ten years younger.

I watched her smile the smile as she took the order from a middle-age guy sitting at a small table in the corner. Not that is would be a big deal, but I thought I recognized the guy from somewhere. Didn't look like a fisherman or somebody who would just happen by. He wore an old fashioned wing-collared off-white shirt that could have been a good bowling shirt if it had some writing on the back of it. Just didn't seem to fit with this early raucous crowd.

"Brandy seven," Veronica said.

Natch. Zip. Done. I was the fastest bartender I knew. I could do some of the stuff ala Tom Cruise in the movie *Cocktail,* but I usually

205

didn't do it unless I was giddy from serving myself. Doing it sober made me feel like a complete moron.

"The guy over there?" Veronica didn't point. "Could be a serial killer dude. He's got one of those floating eye things. *Very* creepy."

"I noticed. But with his good eye, he likes your ass nearly as much as I do."

She put a swizzle stick in the drink and turned, then stopped and looked back at me. "Let's just talk dirty to each other all night."

"How dirty?" I dared ask.

"Filth. Eat me. Eat all of me until I scream out for mercy."

She smiled, playfully licked her lips and off she went. It was good for me. Just watching her being watched was great fun for me. The first week she was here she learned after midnight the groping hour began; pent up customer fantasy began to play out. It could be like dodge ball out on that floor as the horny toads came out of the wood work.

"Two Leinie's, brandy-sour, vodka tonic, fuck me until I feel it in the back of my throat." She was still smiling.

That was my girl. This was not a good plan, however. After about an hour, we were both so worked up we needed air. What we really needed was somebody to cover for just ten minutes.

The screen door swung open and Rondell shuffled in. Every head in the room moved his way, forced to consider a large, black man with scowling eyes crushing the life from a barstool.

"Bro," I said as softly as I could.

"Big bro. Give me a Chivas rocks,"

A bit of a dusty bottle on the top shelf in these parts. Probably last touched when I poured his last drink in August the summer before.

"Just keep 'em comin' and put it on my tab." He smiled weakly.

"Yes sir."

He was rubbing some awake into his face when I turned to a familiar voice. "Two Buds. I want to suck your cock. *Now.*"

Rondell straightened up suddenly and looked around for the source.

I dipped into the cooler for the Bottles and Veronica counted out some change.

"What the...." Rondell gave us a tired lawyer look.

"If you're going to sit this close, you might want to cover your ears," I whispered to him, then moved over and set the bottles up on a tray for Veronica. "I'm going to eat you until you cry for mercy."

She was back quickly for another order. "Leinie's. Vodka stone sour."

I hesitated. Waited.

"I'm so lubed I can hear myself walk," she added.

"Truce!" I yelled out, a bit too loud. "This is working too well," I said, calming down slightly.

"Suit yourself. Bite my nipples harder."

I leaned over and kissed her across the bar. "I can't handle it."

"I know. You are so easy."

The place was jammed to the rafters by nine o'clock. I overheard enough conversation to find out not one, but two of the bars within drinking distance of the Sunny Blue had evidently closed up for good. Business was booming at Mulroney's. I tacked up my fourth bra of the night and started thinking I was going to have to recycle some of the older bras to make room. Box them up? Salvation Army? I looked up at the ceremonial bra I had hung up above the register before we opened for the season. Connie's. Just to keep her close by. I ran the keys to check the take and thought of Rudy, Connie, Wahoo, and my extraordinary luck.

When Veronica approached the bar this time she had a red swizzle stick twirling in her mouth. The end of it sported a tight little knot. "Whuuuut?" She had not totally lost the innocence.

"Nothing," I laughed.

"Two Leinie's, Brandy-seven. Pronto."

Did I tell you I love you?" I yelled.

"What?"

The noise was rattling the chrome bar grips. I reached across and turned her shoulders and got my hands gently under her chin. "I will love you until the day I die."

She looked into my eyes, took the straw from her mouth and replaced it with two more fresh ones, then proceeded to entwine one to the other with her tongue, letting the perfect square knot hang out just below her lower lip for my examination. "It only gets better, Genius."

That's when I decided I better start writing some of this stuff down.